COUGAR CHRISTMAS CALAMITY

HEART OF THE COUGAR, BOOK 8

TERRY SPEAR

COUGAR CHRISTMAS CALAMITY

Heart of the Cougar, Book 8

PUBLISHED BY:
Terry Spear

Cougar Christmas Calamity
Copyright © 2020 by Terry Spear
Cover by Terry Spear

Discover more about Terry Spear at:
http://www.terryspear.com
ISBN Print: 978-1-63311-065-6
ISBN E-Book: 978-1-63311-064-9

To Stephanie Plumb, another Christmas book to put you in just the right mood for this Christmas season. Thanks for loving my books!

FOREWORD

Synopsis

Cougar shifter Jessie Whittington plans to work on her psychic romance book before Christmas at the Whispering Pines Resort on the North Shore of Lake Superior, but peace and quiet aren't exactly what she's going to get right before Christmas.

Former army ranger Emerson Merriweather has returned home after being ambushed on a Black Ops mission, and now learns his uncle has died. When he meets his only guest at the cabin resort, he's surprised she's a cougar too. Before long, a blizzard hits, bear shifters wreak havoc, and he's helping Jessie decorate for Christmas. Something he never thought he would be doing.

Jessie's definitely the light in his life but he still has to take care of the man who set him and his team up during the mission. He knows he will be looking for Emerson to finish the job. Mystery and intrigue are the name of the game and things aren't always as they seem.

PROLOGUE

hree former army rangers and two navy SEALs made up the Black Ops team that had the mission of rescuing a group of kids from insurgents in South America. The insurgents were waiting for a payoff that wasn't coming—at least not the kind of payoff they were expecting.

The men were all eager to save the kids. Ex-army ranger and cougar shifter Girard Smith had given the men the mission. He'd worked with them before and Emerson Merriweather—though he went by the alias of Thor—and his team had no reason to believe that this would be different from any other deadly mission they were being highly paid to handle.

"Hey, Condor," Kline, a former navy SEAL, said, as they were being helicoptered to the secret location, "I hear you're up to number seven on potential wife choices." He was the joker of the bunch, fun to have around, whether they were planning a mission, in the middle of a fight, or at the end of the mission.

Emerson smiled. Condor was a wolf shifter like Emerson was a cougar shifter, but the other three men on the team were strictly human. They wouldn't know just how important it was for a wolf to find the right mate.

"Six," Condor corrected Kline. They'd trained together in the navy and were the only two who actually knew each other's real identities. "That other woman didn't count."

The guys all smiled.

"Hey, Gardiner, I heard you were in a club brawl last night. Kind of cutting it close to mission time, aren't you?" Condor said to the former army ranger, getting the heat off him and his love life, and putting it on the team member who should have known better.

Gardiner shook his head. "I had to let off some steam."

He was always letting off steam. He was a real asset on the mission, focused, dedicated, but when he was Stateside, he was a drinker, been through three wives already, but thankfully hadn't had any kids. He was currently divorced and always eager for a mission.

Emerson didn't like that Gardiner would start a fight at a club right before a mission though. Not when he could have ended up in jail and put the rest of the team in a bind. He was always the instigator of the brawls, so Emerson didn't have to ask what led up to the fight.

Next mission, Emerson might have to bring on a different guy to replace him. The kind of jobs they went on were too dangerous to allow one person to jeopardize the whole team.

Robertson was quiet as usual. He only went with them on this trip to be able to afford Christmas presents for his children, otherwise he wanted to be home for them. His wife was a gambler and all the decent money Robertson made on these risky missions went to feed her addiction. Robertson was intending to sock this money away this time, divorce his wife, and take care of his kids, no more Black Ops. He didn't trust that his wife was looking out for the kids while he was away.

But on the mission when Emerson and his men arrived at the school where they were to rescue the kids, they discovered the building was in ruins, rubble everywhere, partially standing brick walls, partially standing classrooms and roofs. It didn't look at all like the reconnaissance photos Smith had shown them. The coordinates were correct, so that wasn't the issue. Emerson had a twitchy feeling crawling around his skin. There were no kids here.

No one was here—they thought. Until the shooting began.

They'd been misled, misinformed, or sold out. Right now, all that mattered was that Emerson—as team leader—got his team out before they all were killed.

When the gunfire began, Emerson and his team ducked for cover among the ruins, trying to learn where the two snipers were and where the others who were shooting at them were situated.

Condor took out one of the snipers. Emerson maneuvered behind partial brick walls and finally reached the other. He shot the shooter in the head and the man dropped to the ground, dead. The rest of the team were shooting at the other gunmen, the firepower way too much for Emerson and his team to handle, he was afraid. Emerson and the team were outnumbered and didn't know the terrain like the insurgents did.

It was a bad situation, but Emerson was determined to get his team out alive.

Gardiner tried to reach another wall, fire rang out, and he went down. Emerson fired at the man who had shot him, just as the gunman made a move to turn and hightail it to another location. The man dropped his weapon and did a face plant in the rubble and didn't move.

Emerson made a low dash to Gardiner to see to his injuries and hurried to field dress the bullet wound on his leg. Condor raced to reach them and dropped in beside them. The SEAL shook his head. "I told you I had a bad feeling about this."

Yeah, Condor had and once they got here, Emerson had too. Sure, Emerson had smelled Smith's stress when he had signed them up for the job. It was a stressful mission, but now Emerson was thinking Smith wasn't as stressed out about the case of them rescuing the children as he was of the members of the team returning to hunt him down if any should survive.

The insurgents were still shooting in their direction and Emerson and Condor were hunkered down, saving their rounds until they could take shots that counted.

"Smith sold us out," Condor said.

"Yeah," Gardiner ground out. "I'll kill him."

Emerson nodded. He hated to think that of another cougar, but it did happen. Anything for money—or revenge. He couldn't think of a reason for Smith to go after them for revenge though. Emerson had no idea what Smith's finances looked like.

The last mission they'd worked with Smith on was to rescue American college students in South America, and they pulled that off without a hitch. This time, Condor swore Smith had looked shifty-eyed when he told them about the mission.

"I'll kill that SOB," Condor said.

"Agreed." Emerson felt the same way and would do something about it as soon as he could. "We need to get out of here and reach the pick-up zone—a new one though. We're not going to beat this firepower, I don't think."

"Gardiner's wounded," Condor said, as if that was a reason to kill everyone who was out to get them.

"He'll live," Emerson said, hoping he was right. But they needed to regroup. If Smith was behind the ambush, he needed to be the one they took out—permanently.

"Robertson got hit when I took out the one sniper." Condor motioned to a broken section of wall. "I checked on him and bandaged him up. It's a shoulder wound." Condor let out his breath. "I got to get back to potential wife number six," he said as if that decided it.

The women Condor dated were always potential wives. Emerson swore Condor would never settle down. He was too easily bored. This is what he lived for. Fighting, killing, freeing hostages, the adventure, the grittiness. Settling down with a she-wolf wasn't really in the plans for now.

After this for Emerson? He wanted something else out of life. He didn't want to give up his life so that someone could get rich by it. This was his last mission.

Another burst of gunfire from the other ranger and from the ones shooting at them stole Emerson and Condor's attention.

Kline wasn't too far away, but they couldn't see him now. Most of the heat was on him though. Emerson couldn't give up, trying to get his men out of this situation no matter what. "I'm going behind these suckers and you draw their fire."

"Go for it." Condor got ready to shoot the insurgent who was trying to hit him.

Emerson moved low around the piled-up rubble and finally reached a vantage point where he could see a nest of three shooters. He lobbed a grenade into their hiding place, and it went off, killing all three men.

Emerson continued around to the other side of the building and saw a man raise up to take aim at Kline down below. Emerson fired a shot and killed the man, but another shot Kline, who was concentrating on two other men who were shooting at him.

Emerson raced through the rubble to get to the other men and killed two, Condor taking out a third, but then Condor went to Kline's aid.

Two more shooters were climbing through the rubble, trying to get a better vantage point to shoot at Kline and Condor. Emerson couldn't get a good shot at the gunmen. Damn it. But as soon as one raised up to shoot Condor, Emerson took the man out. The second one targeted Emerson and hit him in the arm. Emerson ducked back behind some pilings.

He'd seen at least three more shooters, could hear them coming for him, and he was ready to shift into a cougar and just take them out. He could maneuver a hell of a lot better on all this rubble as a cougar, for one thing. Leaping into the fray and tearing them to pieces suited him just fine.

He moved out of the shooters' view, afraid that his friends were wounded or dead since he hadn't heard any gunfire from any of them.

He came out from behind one of the partial walls and saw a man trying to sneak his way around him. Emerson shot him, then ducked back and headed in the direction of Condor and Kline. When he was a few hundred yards from their location, he saw the two shooters making their way to where he was going. He shot one of them, and the other hid.

Emerson listened. He didn't hear any other movement, no gunfire. He prayed there were no others than the one he needed to eliminate and that he could reach his friends and get them out of here. But he knew if he tried to go for his friends, the lone gunman would shoot him down. Instead, Emerson went way around through the rubble, using the piles of bricks and cement and partially standing walls to hide himself. He moved like a cat, careful not to expose his position.

And then he was upon the guy, shooting him before he could get off a shot. Being shot once was bad enough, Emerson thought, as he considered his own wound. The pain hadn't set in yet, but he was bleeding, and he knew he needed to take care of the injury. He hurried to Condor and Kline's location. Kline had been hit in the shoulder. Condor had a head wound and was holding on.

"Smith," Condor rasped under his breath and motioned to a section of building still standing.

"He's here?" Emerson couldn't believe the bastard would send them to their deaths and watch to see that it was done. He figured he would have waited like a coward to get word somewhere far from here.

"There." Condor motioned to the building. "Get me out of here."

"Yeah, buddy." Emerson bandaged Condor's head wound. "I'm going after him. I don't want to move you or the others and have him shoot us while I'm doing so."

"Yeah, just hurry," Condor said.

At least the wolf had faster healing genetics like the cougar shifters. "You got it." Emerson headed for the area that Condor had pointed to and he even smelled Smith's scent, but then he came across tire tracks and heard a vehicle start up somewhere beyond the building.

Smith had to be fleeing, figuring Emerson would kill him! No one was left to deter Emerson from eliminating Smith.

Emerson took off running, trying not to sprain an ankle or break a leg in the rubble. He saw the dust-covered, camouflaged-painted Jeep, Smith's head poked out the window and looking back, his black hair longer, his face unshaven, his signature ears sticking out, and his blue eyes wide—caught in the act. He jerked his head back inside the Jeep and tore off. Emerson immediately fired several shots, but he couldn't hit Smith before the Jeep raced off down the dusty, dirt road, and disappeared around a bend, past some more bombed-out buildings.

Emerson ran back to where Condor was before Smith called in reinforcements and tried to finish the job. "Remember, you have your sixth-maybe wife to get home to so don't you go dying on me."

"Hell no. Smith sold us out. We have a new unsanctioned mission—eliminate Smith for the team. I'm not dying today because of that traitor."

But this would be the last official Black Ops mission Emerson was going on.

Emerson called in a new pickup point. He had to. Smith knew the other one. Though Emerson realized the pickup point might have all been a ruse and no one planned to come for them—because they were all supposed to be dead. He told the crew that normally extracted them that Smith was a traitor and not to give him their new pickup location if he called them for it. Then Emerson lifted Condor in a fireman's carry, Emerson and Condor both groaning in pain, and he urged Kline up. They went to get Gardiner and Robertson, both of them taking care of a couple more shooters that had shown up from out of the blue. Gardiner had been shot again, this time in the chest. Emerson checked for a pulse. The ranger was dead, damn it. Robertson was looking worse for wear, his face ashen, but he and Kline managed to carry Gardiner while Emerson carried Condor as they headed to the pickup point.

"Did you get him? Smith?" Condor asked. "Hell, did you get shot?"

"Yeah. Arm. And no, I didn't. He tore off in a Jeep."

"I thought you were quicker on your feet than that."

Usually, Emerson was. "I was afraid I'd break a leg or ankle on all that rubble. Then where would we have been?"

"True, thanks for coming back for me. Did you change the pickup location?" Condor asked.

"Hell, man, how can you even talk with a bullet rattling around in your skull?"

Kline and Robertson chuckled. "Condor never shuts up," Kline said.

"The bullet didn't penetrate, I don't think. But I'm too dizzy to walk and my vision is blurred," Condor said.

"Yeah, yeah, any excuse." Emerson gave him a wry smile. "Are the rest of you okay?"

Kline was quiet. "Yeah, just pissed off," he finally said.

Robertson didn't say anything, but Emerson couldn't look back at him to check on his condition. He just had to keep moving forward, one foot in front of the other and pray that Robertson went home to his kids all in one piece. "I think that's how we all feel."

They finally reached the pickup point and Emerson was damn glad Smith hadn't learned of it or they probably would have been in another firefight. And this time he doubted they would have made it.

"We have to kill him," Condor said again as they got into the helicopter.

"Yeah, but we need to heal up first." Emerson would recuperate at his uncle's home at the Whispering Pines Resort and give Uncle Paul the news he wanted to hear more than anything else in the world—Emerson was quitting his dangerous job for good and helping him to manage the resort, taking over even, if his uncle was ready to retire.

He checked on Robertson who looked near death. A medic on the flight kept him alive though as Emerson and the others tried to help. He was thinking he'd send Christmas gifts to the kids, but they didn't know each other's identities. It was safer that way for just this reason. Smith would want them all dead still, and Emerson didn't want Robertson's family in the crosshairs.

Once Emerson was feeling better, he was going after Smith, with or without Condor and the rest of the men's help. At least with his faster cougar healing genetics, Emerson would be in good shape soon.

Condor could be another story if he really had a bullet in his skull—even as a wolf shifter. Kline appeared to be in stable condition. Robertson was touch and go. Emerson glanced at Gardiner's body and promised him, "Smith is a dead man walking."

* * *

JESSIE WHITTINGTON SAID goodbye to her mom and dad and took off from Loveland, Colorado to go to Whispering Pines Resort on Lake Superior. She'd made a special German chocolate cake for Mr. Paul Merriweather, who owned and managed the resort. He was sixty, a cougar, widowed and he had always been so kind to her. He gave her a discount on her stay at the resort and she brought him a special treat every time she visited —which was going on five years now. Her mom had a cake business and she made cakes for special occasions and Jessie was used to helping her with them, but this one she made herself.

In the car, she got a call on her dashboard from Deputy Sheriff Nina Hill, who had been sharing some psychic stories with Jessie for the romantic suspense novel she was writing. Jessie's story would be fiction, but Nina and her twin sister, Ava, were the real deal when it came to seeing future events from time-to-time.

"Hi, Nina, I'm driving up to the resort up on Lake Superior. Do you have another story for me to incorporate in my novel?" Jessie couldn't pass up the opportunity to get another story idea from Nina or her sister. Jessie found their stories fascinating, which was why she was writing about a psychic hero and heroine and villain this time.

"Listen, I talked to Ava to see if she had any visions about you but she hasn't had any."

"About me?" Now that wasn't what Jessie had expected to hear.

"I saw you chasing two bears while you were wearing your cougar coat."

Jessie smiled. "You must have been having a dream or nightmare like I have."

"Maybe, but if it's a premonition, promise me you won't chase after a couple of bears through the woods up there."

"All right, I promise. I've never even seen a bear out at the resort, mostly because I go up there in the winter and they're hibernating."

"Oh, you're right. I never even considered that. Forget what I said. It must have been just a weird dream I had last night then," Nina said.

"Do I win the confrontation with the bears?" Jessie figured

she might as well learn that, even though she didn't think she'd do well against two bears, even in a dream.

"I have no idea. All I know is that you were chasing them. Hmm, come to think of it, you were chasing them through the snow."

"See? I imagine, even if a bear woke up out of hibernation and went looking for a meal, there wouldn't be two of them. Not running together."

"You're probably right."

"Okay, anything else?" Jessie asked.

"The coffin will be empty."

"Pardon?"

"Sorry, I told you my visions could be mixed up, just like dreams are. They're not in any perfect story order. They're bits and pieces like in dreams."

"A coffin?"

"Yes, it's empty."

Jessie bit her lip. "Okay, I have no intention of checking out any coffins. Was it like I was thinking of purchasing one?" She wouldn't be, though it did make her worry that someone close to her was going to need one, and she didn't want to even consider such a possibility. That was the problem with having friends who had actual psychic visions if they were something ominous.

"No. You were just greatly relieved when you saw that nobody was in the coffin."

"All right. So was this before or after I was chasing two bears in the snowy woods?" At least this was giving Jessie some ideas for her stories, even if they weren't really psychic predictions but just a typical mixed-up dream. The characters in her story would still have the same issues as Nina and Ava did when it came to their sixth sense.

"Before, but you know my dreams or visions can be out of order."

Jessie thought it was interesting that Nina and her twin sister often didn't share the same visions concerning people. But they were fun to have at festivities, especially when running the fortune-telling booth. Most of the time, they tried not to tell anyone anything but good news. Sometimes it backfired.

Jessie remembered her twin sister, Tracey, telling her that Nina had congratulated a mother-to-be on her twins when it turned out the woman's husband hadn't been the father and neither she nor he had known she was pregnant.

"Oh, well, have a safe trip and forget what I said. You'll have a great time and you won't encounter any bears or coffins, empty or otherwise. Only I will—so it seems—in my dreams."

Jessie laughed. "Okay, thanks, Nina. I'll be seeing you sometime for the Christmas holidays when my family visits my sister and her family in Yuma Town."

"It won't be long."

"I agree. I can't wait." Yet, Jessie could. She was looking forward to her vacation at the resort.

Then they ended the call.

Chasing bears and checking for bodies in empty coffins at the Whispering Pine Resort in the dead of winter? That would be the day.

CHAPTER 1

"*W*hy did you choose Dr. Smith for your alias?" Reginald Bates asked Girard Smith.

"Did you ever watch 'Lost in Space?' Dr. Smith was intelligent, conniving, manipulative, and would sacrifice anyone who got in his way. I really respected him. The whole family that went on the mission with him were easily manipulated, despite supposedly being a bunch of brainy scientists. It goes to show deceptiveness can win over morality every time." Smith readjusted the plant lights on his indoor garden. "Not to change the subject but I've got to terminate Thor, Condor, and the rest of the team. They should never have escaped that mission."

Reginald smiled and lit a cigarette. "I really don't believe any of the team members knew you orchestrated the faux rescue of the college students. They saved them and were none the wiser that it hadn't been in the plans."

"Vengeance be mine. And put out the damn cigarette. How many times do I have to tell you I don't allow smoking in my home?" Smith was a cougar and with his sensitive sense of smell, he couldn't stand smoke. It reminded him of a forest fire out of control, and imminent danger to his kind in the wild.

"Sorry. I forget you don't like smoking."

Reginald was sorry, all right. "If Thor and his team hadn't gone in and rescued the hostages ahead of my well-planned schedule, the parents would have seen that their rescuers had died and they had only one option left to them—to pay up or lose their precious kids. When Thor changed the timeline, it made me believe he knew something was wrong when he ignored my carefully laid plans as far as the schedule went. I can't believe he got away this time."

"And most of the rest of the team. You should have finished them all off."

Smith cast him a cutting glower. Reginald could easily be replaced, but Smith still needed him to help him eliminate Thor and the others. Sometimes it seemed as though Reginald thought he was indispensable in this business. No one who worked for Smith was. He just needed to learn where the members of the team were hiding. Once Smith located them, he'd hire new mercenaries to kill them. Of course, Smith would be there—in the shadows—to see that it was done right this time.

"What about that other Black Ops team?" Reginald asked.

They were a thorn in Smith's side too. That group had gotten away with only a few injuries too. It had been the first time Smith had arranged a setup of a Black Ops mission like that. He was still learning how to do it so he got it right. Thor was a cougar shifter and he'd still walked right into his trap, so Smith knew it was doable.

"I'll get them too," Smith said.

"They're going to know you set them up. Thor especially since he saw you make your escape."

Smith usually didn't like Reginald's inferences and Reginald was being a lot more vocal about it of late. But that was just the way Dr. Smith was. Always coming out on top of the food chain no matter how wimpy Dr. Smith of "Lost in Space" fame seemed or how things didn't seem to work out his way. He had the intelligence and cunning to get things done eventually the way he wanted them to. *This* Smith wasn't wimpy in the least. Sure, he didn't fight the battles. That's what made him so cunning. He had everyone else do it for him.

Smith babied his indoor garden as the snow piled up outside of his Minnesota home.

He needed to think of something else while he was waiting to hear word about where Thor and the others were hiding out. Maybe it was time for Smith to look up one of his girlfriends and just have some fun. He had another mission coming up after the new year though. He really needed to get rid of the men on both those teams if he was to have any peace of mind. He couldn't think of a better Christmas present.

"You got a team in mind to take those guys out when you find Thor and the others?" Reginald asked, glancing out at the snow.

"Yeah. And you're leading them." It was time for Reginald to show what a badass he could be. Besides, Reginald knew Thor personally too. They'd served as army rangers together. Reginald was strictly human though.

Did Smith have any regret that he planned the demise of a fellow cougar? Hell no. Thor had loused up one hell of a payoff and he knew way too much. The team members had been wounded in the fight that should have ended their miserable lives. But since it had killed only one them, Smith knew they would be teaming up to take him down. They had to go.

Reginald looked a little surprised that Smith told him he would be in charge of the team.

"Are you worried they'll get the best of you?" Smith asked.

"Hell no."

Smith hoped Thor would, but only if another of Smith's hired killers took Thor out. Smith was thinking Reginald was getting a little too mouthy for his own good. He just couldn't afford any other mistakes. He pulled out his phone and checked out his girlfriends on Facebook. He would friend them and check their posts to see if they mentioned where they were at. None of them suspected what he did for a living or that he thought of himself as *the* Dr. Smith of "Lost in Space" fame. He was just a fun-loving guy, generous on a date and always running off on an important mission to keep entanglements down. None of them would ever guess he had a string of women all over the world at his beck and call either.

Now that was his Don Juan persona. The "Lost in Space" Dr. Smith didn't date.

* * *

EMERSON RETURNED HOME, still healing up from the gunshot wound. He fully expected to find his Uncle Paul at the resort, who would have been thrilled to learn that Emerson was done with the job and here for good—though Emerson had every intention of keeping the bad news from his uncle that Smith was still a threat to him and that Emerson had been wounded.

Instead, Emerson had learned his uncle had died of a massive heart attack. No one in his family had any issues with heart disease. Emerson couldn't believe it! And he was sick about it. He was finally going to be home for Christmas with his uncle, his last living relative. He closed down the resort, pending the transfer of title into his name, and refunded all the cabin renters' money, well, all except for one stubborn woman—Jessie Whittington—who absolutely wouldn't take a refund, insisting on coming. He had told everyone else that his uncle had died, and he would be opening up the resort again in the spring.

Except for Jessie. She had refused to take the refund and though he could have insisted further, something about her made him give in.

He didn't care anything about the resort right now. He felt bereft with his uncle gone. This had been Emerson's home for many years until he went into the army and then later was working Black Ops. He loved it here. He had always planned to take it over when his uncle wanted to retire, and before that, just to help his uncle run things as he got older.

A week after he'd returned home, Jessie Whittington was arriving. Emerson glanced outside at the snow-laden clouds, at the wintry setting, the snow a foot high and the drive and walk to Jessie's cabin cleared, but he was having a hard time putting on a good face for her visit when he normally would have been just like his uncle, cheerful that the guest had arrived, welcoming.

On top of that, his damn arm was aching where the bullet had been removed. It was getting better by the day, but it was still giving him grief. Most likely because he'd been chopping wood for the fireplace and doing a ton of other chores around the place, like clearing the snow before Jessie's arrival. He had promised his uncle he would stay here and run things, keep the place as part of their heritage, yet he was so upset his uncle had died, he didn't want to deal with it or anything else. And he was never like that.

If he had been firmer with Jessie, like he should have been, she wouldn't be coming here and he could take off and try and find Smith, though he had no idea where to look. He'd contacted several of his acquaintances, both former Black Ops team members and contractors who had given him missions before, but no one seemed to have a clue who he was or where he could find Smith.

He got a call where the caller said, "Red," and Emerson answered with, "Blue."

"Hey." It was Condor. Emerson hadn't heard from him since the mission and he was glad he still seemed to have his wits about him.

"How are you?"

"Healing. You?" Emerson asked, keeping the conversation brief for safety sake.

"Same. Potential wife number six dumped me."

Emerson smiled. "So, what's new?" The guy had a revolving door of she-wolves to date, though with wolves, Emerson had learned, they waited to consummate a relationship when they agreed to a mating and they were mated for life, so he understood why they had to be careful when trying to decide on a mate. With the cougars, they were more like humans. But Emerson and Condor were used to giving each other a hard time.

"Still looking. You?"

"No clue."

"Everyone's on this. R pulled through, divorced W. K is good. Keep looking."

"You too." Robertson had pulled through after all and divorced his wife. Emerson was glad for that and to hear that Kline was good.

That was good news. Then they ended the call. Emerson took a deep, settling breath. They didn't want to alert Smith if he should be trying to monitor their phones, though neither of them had the same phones they had used when he had been in contact with them for the mission. Still, they had to be careful in case Smith ever learned of their new numbers. But Emerson was glad Condor and the others were all right.

Emerson chopped some more wood. The snowstorm was coming in tomorrow, and so was his only guest at the cabin. He hoped she made it in time, but he wished she had just taken a refund for her cabin rental, like all the others had.

* * *

Hoping she wouldn't be sidetracked with the impending winter storm on its way, the author of ten photography books, Jessie had never written a novel before. She planned to write more of her paranormal romance book at the cabin on the North Shore of Lake Superior at Whispering Pines Resort soon. In her new book, the hero and heroine were both psychics and dealing with a psychic killer. She thought about writing a cougar shifter romance, but nobody would believe anything that far out, despite that she definitely knew her subject matter and editors always told her to write about what she knew. That wasn't something she could divulge to the rest of the human population though.

Every year, she stayed at Whispering Pines before Christmas to get away and work on a book, and every year it seemed she did so while she was getting over yet another tumultuous relationship. Her older twin sister, Tracey, who was a special agent with U.S. Fish and Wildlife Service (FWS), and Tracey's mate, Hal Haverton, a rancher and a part-time deputy sheriff out of Yuma Town, were always concerned with Jessie when she started dating again. In fact, they'd gotten into the habit of doing background checks on the guys she was seeing and that helped keep her from getting too involved with them if Hal and Tracey learned the cougars were rogues.

Jessie stopped overnight at a hotel and then drove the next day, finally reaching the Whispering Pines Resort and parking at the owner/manager's house to check in and get the key to her cabin before the sun set. She was glad to get here before the blizzard started. It was snowing already and the visibility with the wind blowing it all across the road was getting to be hazardous.

Paul Merriweather was always glad to see her. He was a widowed, gray-haired cougar who always had a smile for her and all kinds of advice of what to do and where to go when she visited. He had even given her dating tips, though he'd told Jessie he had only dated one cougar in his lifetime, and she had been the woman he had loved and married and lost. Jessie was always arriving after a breakup and so Paul would be waiting to see what had gone wrong this time with her former relationship and help her to see how much better off she was without the guy. She loved Paul for it.

Jessie went inside Mr. Merriweather's home to check-in and get her cabin key, carrying the German chocolate cake she'd made just for him as a fun treat. As soon as she did, she met a dark-haired man she'd never seen before. She was more than a little surprised. He wore all black—sweater, pants, boots. She swore if she saw his underwear they would be just as black—and why she was even thinking of that, she hadn't a clue—except he was drop-dead gorgeous, with an angular face and a scruffy beard that gave him character, *and* he was a cougar.

"Is the owner in? Mr. Merriweather?" Jessie asked.

"No, he's deceased. You're Jessie Whittington, I take it." He glanced at the cake box and took a deep breath, smelling the heavenly, sweet, chocolate aroma.

She felt her whole world crash into oblivion in that one little statement. Mr. Merriweather was dead.

The guy grabbed her arm and took the boxed cake from her hands and she was glad for his strength when she thought she would collapse from the news.

"Jessie Whittington?" the man asked, frowning at her. He set the cake on the desk, but he didn't release her as if he realized she was still shaken from the news.

She swallowed hard, fighting tears that threatened to spill. She felt horrible about it and she realized now why this guy, or whoever had sent her the email, had wanted to refund her money. "Uh, yes. I have a reservation for cabin five for fourteen days. I'm so sorry to hear about Mr. Merriweather. How did he die, if you don't mind me asking?" She so had wanted to see him. It was part of why she came here.

"He had a massive heart attack, but he died here, which was just the way he wanted to go. He loved the resort."

"He was always so nice." Like a father to her. "So you're the new owner?"

"Yes. Emerson is the name. You need to sign this contract." He handed her the paper to sign. He was strictly business. Not anything like Mr. Merriweather. He never made her sign a contract. Emerson started telling her some of his rules for the resort as she looked over the contract. "You can't have guests at your cabin. There's not enough parking space for everyone as it is."

She glanced out of the window of the office in his home to look at the parking lot and the five cabins in the woods overlooking Lake Superior. "Nobody's here. In the email the resort sent me, it said management would refund my money, that you— I guess—were renovating all the cabins and no one else was here. But I didn't want my money refunded and management, I guess you, said I could stay then."

"Right. But it's still the rule. I told the two men who came looking for you that I couldn't give out information about guests. You might tell them the cabins are exclusively for paying guests only, if they return while you're staying here."

She frowned. "Who were they? I don't know anyone up here and I didn't tell anyone but my parents and sister where I was going to be." She couldn't imagine anyone would be looking for her up here. Everyone who knew she was coming would have mentioned it to her if someone had queried them as to where she would be.

"Someone told someone. I didn't ask for names. Furthermore, there's not to be any wild partying..."

Really? "Like I really plan to do that. I'm here by myself. And I don't break the rules. Though I've had my fair share of trouble dating guys who were rogue cougars—to my surprise." And why she mentioned that to him, she had no idea. "My sister is a special agent with the U.S. Fish and Wildlife Service and her mate is a deputy sheriff of Yuma Town. My father is a retired special agent with the Cougar Shifter Force, CSF. I'm used to being around law enforcement types. So I don't have any issues with obeying rules."

"Just the guys you date do."

"Uh, yeah." Again, she wondered why she'd mentioned it to Tall, Dark, and Imposing. "Well, that's why I'm up here alone while I'm writing my book. So you bought Whispering Pines when Mr. Merriweather's estate was sold off?" She still couldn't believe he was gone.

"He was my uncle and I inherited it."

"Oh, I'm so sorry about that." That was worse since he had lost his uncle and it wasn't just a case of Emerson buying the estate. "I guess since you inherited everything and I wanted to give this cake to him, you're welcome to it, if you like German chocolate."

He gave her a hint of a smile. She took that as a controlling-his-enthusiasm yes.

"Are you keeping the resort?"

He hesitated to respond. Cougar shifters noticed things, scents, body movements that would indicate feelings—anger, frustration, interest, friendliness—in his case, mixed feelings. "Yeah. I like the solitude and quiet."

"When you're not renting out the cabins," she reminded him. When he didn't say anything, she said, "You're not renting out the cabins in the future? I thought you said you were renovating them. It's such a beautiful place. It's so nice that I've been here every year for the past five years at wintertime." And she wanted to come back again next year, even if someone new was running the place. But maybe he was distraught about his uncle's passing and the resort reminded Emerson too much of his uncle. Though come to think of it, she didn't remember Paul Merriweather ever talking about having a nephew. Maybe they'd been estranged, and Emerson felt bad that his uncle was now gone when they should have reconciled before this. She had to stop thinking too much into this. She could make up a hundred stories about what had gone on between the two men.

"With rogue cougars you've been dating?" Emerson asked.

She let out her breath, slightly exasperated, and was now thinking she should have kept the cake for herself. Though she knew she would eat too much of it if she had. "No, I've always come alone. I shouldn't have mentioned them. I always seemed to be dumping the current rogue cougar right before I come here. Though I guess in truth the term dumping them isn't exactly the correct word." Why in the world was she telling this guy anything?

He raised a brow, appearing to be waiting for clarification.

"They died. They couldn't be incarcerated—cougars, you know. Anyway"—she reached her hand out for the keys to her cabin—"I'm going to get settled in. I hear we're going to have a bad snowstorm and I want to get back to working on my book." She wasn't about to go into details about the rogues she'd hooked up with. She shouldn't have said as much as she had.

He handed her the key. "You're right. A snowstorm is headed our way. I hope you brought enough warm things to wear."

"Right." If she hadn't, would he loan her some of his warm things to wear? She preferred light and colorful to all black, but she doubted he would give her the time of day once she left here. "I did. If all else fails, I'll wear my cougar coat. Oh, and I'll take a couple of movies with me." She loved how Mr. Merriweather had movies on hand to borrow. He was always getting new ones too, but this time, since she was writing a Christmas story, she only wanted to watch Christmas stories.

Emerson looked like he was eager to send her on her way as if she were wasting his precious time. Or maybe he wanted to dig into the cake once she was gone. But she carefully perused the movie titles, longer than she needed to—and she wasn't sure why she wanted to needle him, except that she felt he'd been giving her grief for having come here and not taken him up on his offer to accept a refund. Then she chose two of her favorite movies. She didn't want to have to trek back through the snowstorm for other titles if she picked something out that she wasn't interested in watching.

"I love *A Christmas Story* and *Jingle All the Way*, don't you?" She figured he didn't. He didn't even have his home or the cabins decorated for Christmas. Then again, if he thought she wouldn't come and since the other cabins weren't rented, she could understand why he wouldn't decorate then. But his own place? Why not?

Well, he was a bachelor, and his uncle had just died, so she guessed that was the reason why. Because she was writing a Christmas story, she wanted to get into the Christmas spirit.

"I've never watched the movies."

Why wasn't she surprised? He didn't appear to be the type of man who liked more family fare. She was about to leave when she figured she might as well ask him about some holiday lights. "Do you or your uncle have any Christmas decorations that I could borrow?"

Emerson frowned at her. She wasn't going to ask him to put them up!

"I'm working on a Christmas story and it helps me when I'm writing to set the mood."

"No."

Of course Mr. Merriweather had them. He always decorated for Christmas. So did Emerson get rid of them? Or he just didn't want to accommodate her? She figured the later was true. "Okay, thanks. The movies should help." And she had brought fixings to make wassail and spiked eggnog that would get her in the right frame of mind too.

She said goodbye and got into her car parked outside his place, then drove the several hundred feet to her cabin in the woods with a view of the lake. It was beautiful. As a photographer and author, she couldn't think of a better place to spend the time before Christmas working on a book than here. When she returned home to Loveland, she and her parents went to stay with Tracey and Hal in Yuma Town at their horse ranch for Christmas because they had lots of room and four-year-old quadruplets they loved to play with. Having multiple births was the hazard of being a cougar shifter!

She thought again about how she hadn't known Mr. Merriweather had had a nephew. What was Emerson's deal anyway? Why couldn't he give her his first name? Unless that *was* his first name. He might be Emerson Merriweather, only she'd call him Stormy-weather instead. He appeared to be about the same age as her. She had felt more comfortable calling Mr. Merriweather by a more formal form of address since he had been her father's age and he'd never told her to call him by Paul, so that's the way it had been for them.

Was Emerson afraid she would come on to him? That would be the day. She went for rogue cougars, not on purpose, but it just seemed to be her destiny. And they were always super friendly. She couldn't abide by a man who was dark and foreboding. She wasn't interested in the least in Mr. Macho Cougar who didn't like wild parties or decorating for Christmas.

She carried her bags into the cabin. It had a screened-in porch that looked out onto the lake through the trees and a large wooden swing in the area next to it that would be great to use when it wasn't so cold. She'd always managed to come here in winter, but she vowed to come here either in the fall or summer one year. It seemed like she was always breaking up with a rogue cougar at this time of year and needed to get away from everything before she and her parents landed in on Tracy and Hal and the kids for Christmas. Maybe not now though. One of the reasons she came was because of Mr. Merriweather. Maybe it was time to move on and find someplace else to explore. Though one reason she loved seeing him was he was a cougar too. *Had* been.

A foot of snow covered the ground already. At least Emerson had cleared a path through the snow to her cabin and the stairs down to the rocky shore.

The wind was whipping up waves on the lake. Man, that would be cold out on the water about now. Still, she planned to walk down to the rocky shoreline before it was dark so she could take pictures of the sunset on the water and stack some rocks.

Then she would make some dinner and watch one of the movies while she wrote the next chapter in her book. Just from the skeptical look on Emerson's face, she knew he didn't believe she would finish it. But she had ten books to her name, so she wouldn't have any trouble with this one. Sure, she'd never written a book like this, but still, she was having a ball with it. And she was determined to finish it.

She got a call from her mom and smiled. "Hey, Mom, I just got in and unloaded my groceries from the car and was putting them away."

"Okay, good. We were worried about you."

"We"—as in her mom and dad. "Yeah, I was going to give you a call as soon as I put things away in the fridge."

"Of course, dear. We're watching the news about the snowstorm headed your way and were anxious that you reached the resort before that hit your area. Was Mr. Merriweather glad to see you again?"

Jessie unpacked a couple of her photography books that she was leaving at the cabin in their little library for guests. "No. He died. His nephew has taken the cabins over." She unpacked her laptop to work on her story later, and her sketchpad that she drew on sometimes—she had thought to draw a picture of her stacked rocks from a photo once she made them down on the shore and photographed them.

"Nephew?" Her mom acted hopeful that someone new might be just the right one for her. Like that would ever happen. "Is he your age?" her mom asked.

"He appears to be, but he's moody and barely aware of me. And I'm not interested in him. For heaven's sake, Tracey had to shoot my last boyfriend. I have no desire to date right now."

"Is he nice?"

"No, I just said he's moody."

"Maybe because his uncle just died."

Maybe. Jessie was usually more intuitive about people's feelings than that, but she was having a hard time coping with the fact Paul had died also.

"What did you do about the cake?"

"I gave it to him."

"Good. Maybe that will make him feel better. When you're down, chocolate always helps you. I'm so sorry about Mr. Merriweather. I know how much you enjoyed visiting with him and you were a bright spot in his life to be sure. Well, you tell us if you have any trouble with this storm. And we'll keep in touch."

Her mom was right about the chocolate! She shouldn't have given it to Emerson, or just left him half of it so she could drown her sorrows with the other half. "Thanks, Mom, sure." Jessie said goodbye to her mom after that. She was so looking forward to relaxing and writing, if she could quit thinking about Mr. Merriweather—and the brooding nephew. No interruptions. Just peace and quiet, like Emerson had said about this resort. Which made her wonder again just what his full name was.

When she was at home, her mom and dad thought she should do things with them all the time because she didn't have a "regular" job. She would just get into the zone, writing away at a scene —feeling one with the characters, and then her mom, or dad, would want her to go with them somewhere. Or talk. Or play a board game. Or watch a movie with them—as if she were bored and needed the entertainment! Or needed to keep them company while they entertained themselves.

She made up a hot grilled cheese and ham sandwich and mixed a little bit of rum in a glass of eggnog. She thought of turning on a Christmas movie while she ate her dinner, but she would get hooked on it and there would go her trip down to the shore.

She was so glad that Emerson hadn't just told her that his uncle had died, and he was refunding her money, period. She sat down at the kitchen table. Once she was done eating, she put on her coat, purple scarf, fluorescent pink gloves, and pink hat and grabbed her camera.

Then she walked to the stairs near cabin number four that would take her down to the rocky shore. Snow clouds helped to share the colors of the setting sun with the surface of the lake. It was just beautiful with its pinks and yellows and oranges. She hurried to take some shots. Afterwards, she found some stones protected by the cliff overhang that were not buried in snow. She stacked five of them, balancing them just so and took a picture of them sitting on the snow. A frozen cascade of water coming down the hill was the last thing she wanted to take a photograph of before the light was gone.

Now it was time to return to the cabin, get warm, watch *A Christmas Story*, and then she would run as a cougar through the woods when it was fully dark out, like she always did. Unless it was snowing too hard by then. She most likely would find her way back to the cabin, but if she didn't, that wouldn't be good.

She hoped Emerson wouldn't be peeved about her running as a cougar if he chanced to see her. Though he couldn't from the house. The cougar door was situated at the back door and she was surrounded by woods. She could see the house and cabins from the side door, which was the "front" door, but no one could see the back of her cabin unless they were standing in her "backyard." That was another thing she liked about her cabin. It had a backyard area, whereas the others just strictly looked off the cliff at the water.

Since Mr. Merriweather had always given her a discount when she stayed there because she was a cougar, she should have told Emerson about their arrangement so he wouldn't overcharge her. Mr. Merriweather had even put in the cougar door for her because she always stayed in that cabin. He had been such a sweetheart. She was sad he was gone.

Once the movie was over, she stripped out of her clothes and shifted into the cougar, loving this part of coming up here the best.

She tore out the cougar door and ran into the woods, racing through the snow. Man, this was the life!

And then deeper in the woods, she saw a cougar watching her from a distance and she stood stock still. His fur was a little redder than hers, definitely a larger male, beautiful amber cat eyes with a hint of green staring at her as if he was just as much in shock to see her as she was to see him. Then he prowled toward her in a cat's way that was very much predatory in nature.

But she stood her ground, hoping it was just Emerson and not a real cougar who was trying to defend his territory, or was interested in her as a potential mate!

CHAPTER 2

*E*merson was running as a cougar and had just come through the trees when he saw Jessie. He smelled her scent on the breeze. He growled low. He should have known she would be off running around as a cougar! Damn it! One cougar would probably never be noticed, but two? Then again, with the incoming snowstorm, probably no one would be out hiking in the woods, private property or no.

On his property though, it was fairly safe. But he had seen on the web where someone had set up a trail camera near a cave by the hills overlooking the North Shore near Castle Danger for bobcat activity and ended up capturing the image of a cougar! And that wasn't far from where his cabins were located.

The cougar caught on the trail cam wasn't anyone he knew, so he wasn't sure if it was one of their kind or a shifter he didn't know. Not that he would know many in the area. The only one he had known well was his uncle. Emerson hadn't even realized the pretty blond he'd tried to dissuade from staying here was a cougar until she walked into his office at the house.

He had so wanted to have the peace and quiet. He had felt lost. He'd always had a mission and coming home had been his new one. Though he still intended to find Smith and make him pay for what he had done to the team.

Adjusting to normal life would take some time. After everything that had recently happened, Emerson hadn't been ready to become the manager of the resort, visiting with people, putting on a cheery face, which was why he had cancelled any reservations for the winter holidays. Except in Jessie's case. She had made hers a year in advance and he had seen where she'd been coming here for years. When he'd tried to offer her a refund, she wouldn't take it. So he figured what the hell? One woman? He assumed he wouldn't see much of her at all. He never counted on her being a cougar.

When she had asked him about decorating for Christmas? Forget that. Christmas wasn't on the schedule this year.

He watched the she-cat observing him, indecisive, not smelling his scent—the breeze blowing the wrong way. She didn't know it was him. He sighed and headed for her.

As a cougar, she stood her ground, her ears twisting, listening to him moving toward her. She was sniffing the air, trying to capture his scent. And then she caught his scent and her wary stance eased.

He let out his breath and ran off. He loved running in the woods through the snow since he had returned here after such a long absence. If he'd known his uncle had been so ill, he would have left his covert job long ago and helped him to manage the place.

Then he heard the she-cat running after him, and though he didn't want to acknowledge that he really kind of enjoyed the company, he glanced at her and inclined his head.

She smiled at him, appearing pleased that he wanted to be with her. He thought he heard her purring a bit even.

He hadn't wanted to be with her, in reality, but they were together, so he would make do. At least he could show her the boundaries of the property and encourage her not to go beyond them. He didn't want her getting caught on any trail cameras.

They had a hearty jaunt and even saw an owl in a tree, but the snow and winds were picking up and he knew they had to return to the cabins before it got too bad. After showing her the boundaries, they turned to go back to the resort. It was nearly whiteout conditions on the way back and he didn't want to lose her in the snow either.

When they finally arrived at the cabins, she licked his face, startling him, and then she dashed through the cougar door of her cabin and was gone.

He stood for a moment, looking at the door as if he expected her to come outside again, which was crazy. Then in the wildly blowing snow, he turned and dashed for his home.

Before he entered the house through the cougar door, Jessie called out, "Thanks for running with me. I would have lost my way in the blizzard, I'm afraid."

That's what he had been afraid of too. He nodded and headed through the cougar door to his home. For the first time since he'd hoped Jessie would take a refund and not stay here, he was glad she was here.

Not that he planned to interact with her in any way any further, except as the manager of the resort. Though he realized he needed to thank her for the cake too.

He walked into his bedroom, shifted, and threw on a pair of pajama bottoms and his robe and slippers. Then he returned to the living room and glanced out his window at cabin number five and saw the lights on inside. His first thought was he should have reminded her not to keep the lights on when she wasn't using them. If she was going to be gone from the cabin, he meant. Not while she was inside the cabin, of course.

Yeah, he wasn't renovating the cabins. Not now anyway. Not in the dead of winter. Maybe not next year either. He would have to wait and see.

Christmas decorations? He sighed. He supposed if he could find some, he could give them to her tomorrow. He didn't have any idea where to even look. The attic? The storage shed out back? One of the four extra bedrooms? Would that really help her to write? He couldn't imagine it would.

He grabbed a beer and watched out the window at the storm, the snow sweeping in windblown torrents, obscuring cabin five, all except the light on in the kitchen like a beacon, beckoning him to find safety from the storm in *her* cabin.

He shook his head at himself. He was used to rescuing people, assassinating people. Romance? No time in the past or any real inclination. Of course now he would have the time, if he was interested.

He considered the TV, but he didn't feel like watching anything. Reading a book? No. Then he wondered what she was writing. A Christmas story. Something sweet and full of hope for the holidays?

He felt sort of like a Scrooge. But why decorate if he had no reason to? With only one guest here, why go all out to make it look like the resort was open for business, when it wasn't? Besides, he just wasn't in the mood for it.

He went to look at her paperwork where she had filled in her address, phone number, and license plate number. She was from Loveland, Colorado. A long way from here. Which told him right then and there he wasn't getting involved with the woman. Why do so if she was going to return home after her vacation here and they would never see each other again? Not if he planned to stay here.

Then he went to his computer, planning to play a game. He settled down and was in the middle of an epic space battle, the wind howling through the trees, the snow blowing against the windows, and about that time, he hoped they wouldn't have any downed electric lines. Just then the electric flickered, his computer cut out, and boom, the electric went out. Just like that.

He stared at his dark computer screen, figuring the electricity would come back on any second now. But it didn't. He walked over to the window and stared out into the blizzard at the dark cabin number five, as if he would see a light shining in the kitchen still. With their cougar eyesight, he could see movement in the kitchen and a flashlight turned on. He smiled. At least she was somewhat prepared. She had a woodburning stove in the living room, but he couldn't remember if he had left matches for it in the cabin, or if it even had any wood inside it. He'd been so busy trying to go through his uncle's papers and cleaning the walkway for her, he really hadn't made any other preparations for the only guest he was going to have, nearly forgetting all about her.

He watched her flashlight move about and again he felt it was a beckoning beacon, telling him to join her and stay safe. The generator automatically turned on in his home and he had power again. But it was only for the main house. Should he invite her to stay here until she got her electric back? She could freeze over there as cold as it was and with no heat, the temperature in the cabin would rapidly drop. He knew she said she could turn into her cougar, but he wanted her to enjoy her stay here without having to shift just to stay warm. That wasn't any way to spend her vacation, especially when *he* had power.

He kicked off his slippers, slid on his snow boots, and pulled off his robe. Then he dressed in his parka, hat, gloves, and ski goggles and headed out of doors. He kept his eye on the light that guided him to her cabin, trudging through the deepening snow, the gusts of wind nearly blowing him over they were so strong and icy cold. He finally reached the door of the cabin and banged with his gloved fist.

"Hey, Jessie! It's Emerson. I've got a generator, if you want to come over and stay in the main house until the electric comes back on."

He expected her to open the door and let him in so she could bundle up before she headed over to the main house. Instead, she poked her golden cougar head out the cougar door, her eyes squinting in the blowing snow. He smiled, not expecting that. Of course he hadn't expected to see her running as a cougar before the snowstorm hit either. He'd just had to run, to let out some of the pent-up frustration he'd been feeling. He'd seen her go down to the shore earlier even and had thought to make a trip down there when here he wasn't planning to do anything that would bring him into contact with her unless absolutely necessary. At least he had bit back the inclination to bother her when she was having a private moment to herself.

"Did you want to come with me and stay at the house until the electricity comes back on? The generator will keep you nice and warm."

She pulled her head back inside, and then after a couple of minutes, she opened the door wearing only a long sweater. "Come in. Hurry. It's cold!"

He smiled and entered the house and shut the door while she hurried to put on her clothes in her bedroom. Her cabin was already too cold. He had thought she might light a fire in the wood-burning stove, but she hadn't. "You didn't start a fire in the woodburning stove."

"No wood? It's all sitting outside under a pile of snow, I'm sure. No matches? No kindling?" She rolled her eyes at him as she shoved her feet in Mukluks, pulled on her parka, then her purple knit scarf, pink hat, and gloves. She grabbed a bag, which he was kind of surprised about.

Did she think she was staying with him overnight? He figured the electricity would be on in an hour or so. Maybe even sooner.

Then again, if it wasn't, it was a good idea to be prepared.

With her flashlight in hand, and her bag slung over her shoulder, she followed him outside into the blinding snow, stopping only to lock her cabin.

Startling her a little, he took hold of her gloved hand and led her to the house in the wind-swept snow so he wouldn't lose her. Even though he shouldn't be thinking of her as a prospective girl-friend, he couldn't help but think of the situation as two single cougars being alone together as opposed to if he had to rescue a family or a couple of men, or even a single human woman, staying at a cabin here on vacation.

As soon as they reached his place, he let her inside. "Did you want something hot to drink? Some cocoa?" He removed his hat and gloves and coat.

She stared at his bare chest and his navy-blue pajama bottoms. In his haste to check on her, he had forgotten he'd only thrown his parka on over his pajama bottoms. He noticed that his pajamas legs were cold and wet and he would need to change. Worse, her eyes riveted to the bullet wound injury on his arm. It was healing well, but he didn't want to have to explain to her how he got shot or any of the rest of what had happened or what he worked at. And he didn't want to make up stories about it. Maybe she wouldn't recognize that a bullet had caused the injury.

"Yeah, sure, thanks." She removed her gloves, then pulled off her hat and scarf, hanging them on his clothes tree. She stripped out of her jacket and hung it up. Then she carried her bag into his living room and proceeded to unpack her laptop.

Here he thought she had packed enough clothes and other essentials to stay overnight and longer, if the electricity didn't come on. He forgot she was writing a book. Though he thought everyone and their brother had a story idea, and it didn't mean she would actually be published.

"I'll be right back." He headed for the bedroom and pulled off his snow boots and wet pajama bottoms. He considered throwing on another pair of pajamas. But he didn't want Jessie to get the wrong idea—that he was coming onto her or something. He slid on a pair of boxer briefs, blue jeans, a soft black sweater, and sheepskin, booted slippers. Then he returned to the kitchen and made them both cups of hot chocolate. "Would you like a slice of

German chocolate cake to go with it? It sure looks good, but it's meant for sharing."

She smiled. "Yeah. I would have eaten it with your uncle, if he had been here."

"It looks too delicious not to share. Besides, I know I would eat way too much of it if I didn't." He took a slice of the cake and mug of hot chocolate over to her and she thanked him, drank some of the cocoa, and smiled.

"Hmm, double hot chocolate. That's my favorite," she said.

"Mine too. Double chocolate is always the best."

"Thanks. That really helps a body to warm up on a blizzardy night." She opened her laptop and began to type away. He had figured she would talk his ear off like she had done earlier when she first arrived and was checking in. He hadn't expected her to work on her story and completely ignore him. Which is what he had wanted, initially! So why did he feel a bit unnoticed? He was curious about the rogue cougars she'd dated that had ended up dead, that's why. He found her…intriguing.

She glanced up from her laptop and saw him studying her. Caught in the act.

"Don't mind me. I'll just work on this until the electricity comes back on and I can return to my cabin. I won't bother you at all." She took another sip of her hot cocoa.

He ate his slice of cake at the dining room table and drank his cocoa. "If it doesn't come back on and you want to get some sleep, you are welcome to use the first guest bedroom on the right down the hall."

She frowned at him. "My sister and brother-in-law haven't checked you out yet."

"Pardon me?" No way did he want her to think he was looking to date her. And he certainly didn't want anyone to check into his past. He was a ghost and that might look suspicious to law enforcement types.

She gave a cute little shrug. "They said if I stayed overnight with some guy, they wanted to check him out first. Sorry. Family joke. You know. Because I have trouble with picking up rogue cougars. If I have to stay the night, the secret will have to remain between you and me."

"Oh."

"You look a tad worried. Should I be too?" She smiled and appeared to be teasing him because she didn't seem concerned and wasn't waiting for an answer but began tapping on her laptop keyboard again.

"Do you need the WIFI password?"

"Not right now, thanks. You can give it to me on a slip of paper for later if I need it. Sometimes"—she took another sip of her cocoa—"I just need to disconnect from the world so I can get some uninterrupted writing done."

"Uh, right." He wasn't really connected to the world that much. And he realized his talking to her wasn't conducive to her writing either. He wasn't sure what to do with himself that wouldn't be a distraction for her. And that was something new to him. His place, his way.

He sighed and walked back to the bedroom, removed his slipper boots, and turned on the TV. The cabins didn't have a streaming service like he had. His uncle was of the notion that the cabins were a way of returning to more of a rustic way of life. Emerson had lived that way enough on the go, and he wanted to see all the latest movies, and those he'd missed while out on his missions.

He climbed onto the bed and flipped through the selections and found a funny, mystery, adventure, fighting movie about finding treasure in the Sahara Desert. He'd missed seeing it before, though it had come out in 2005. Then he thought some popcorn would be good while he watched the movie. He padded down the hall in his sock feet and glanced in Jessie's direction. She was frowning, staring at her monitor, then typing furiously away. He smiled and went into the kitchen that was open to the living room. He would offer her a bowl of popcorn too, but not until after it was popped so he wouldn't keep disrupting her work.

He stuck a buttery, salted version of popcorn into the microwave. Sure, he knew the unbuttered versions were better for him, but that's what made popcorn taste so good. As soon as it finished popping, he poured some into a bowl and glanced at her. She was watching him, looking hungry for popcorn.

"Would you like some?"

"The buttery kind? Yeah, of course. There's nothing better than hot popcorn on a wintery, stormy night. Except for double hot chocolate. And German chocolate cake also."

"The cake was really good, by the way. And thanks for my uncle and from me." He poured her a bowl of popcorn and was going to go back to his room to watch TV, a second bowl of popcorn in hand.

"What are you watching?"

"*Sahara.*"

"Oh, I haven't watched that in years. That's a great hot movie to watch on a bitterly cold night."

"That's what I was thinking. I never got to see it and it looked like it would be fun to watch."

"Would you like some company?"

He was so surprised, he just barely caught his jaw from dropping. "Yeah, uh, sure. I thought you were writing and I thought you wanted to watch Christmas movies."

"I'm at an impasse in the story right now and I'll watch the other Christmas movie later."

"Does that happen often with your writing? Writer's block?" He brought his bowl of popcorn and the rest of the bag in to share with Jessie. At least his uncle had a TV in both his bedroom and the living room. It would have been awkward having her watch TV with him in his bed, especially when she needed to have him checked out by her family first. He just hoped that would never happen. He might not be a bad guy, but he had a string of aliases. He realized he should have asked what she wanted to see—like the other movie she had intended to watch.

"Yeah. Sometimes I just get stuck and I need to do something else for a while."

"I hope I haven't been too big of a distraction."

"Are you kidding? Every time I see you, I get more material for my book."

He frowned at her. She was writing about him? "What are you writing about?"

"A paranormal romance where the hero and heroine are psychics. He's dark and brooding, and she's afraid of the psychic connection she has with a serial killer."

"I'm dark and brooding?" Maybe he was a little bit. After all the missions he'd been on and then his uncle's death had come as such a shock, reminding him that life was precious, and he should take stock and do something good with his own, he supposed he could be considered dark and brooding without too much of a stretch of the imagination.

"You wear all black," she said, motioning to his clothes.

Wearing all black had suited most of his missions. That's what made up the majority of his wardrobe. Basic. Black. "And I didn't decorate for Christmas."

"Right."

"So your story is set at Christmastime?" He ate some of his popcorn, delaying the start of the movie. He found her writing process fascinating for some reason. Maybe because he'd never known a writer before.

"At first it was autumn. Blustery fall, blowing winds, trees bare, chillier temperatures, apple cider, pumpkins."

"But?"

She smiled and got up to go to the kitchen. "I'm changing it to winter. Christmas. Snowstorm. Do you want some water? The popcorn is making me thirsty. I love the kind you got. It's just perfect."

"Buttery and salty."

"Right."

"Yeah, sure on the water, upper righthand cupboard for the glasses."

She brought two down and filled them with water, then carried them to the coffee table. "If I get an idea while we're watching the movie—"

"You'll want to write it down?"

"Uh, yeah. Will it disturb you if I work on the story while we're watching the movie?"

"Can you do that?"

"Yeah, sure, but only if it doesn't bother you. My folks hate it when I try to work on my story while we are watching a movie. I tried having a light on so I could write by hand instead, and my dad didn't like the light on because it caused a glare on the TV. No tapping on the keyboard on my computer either because that bothered them. So either watch the story with them, or don't."

"It's fine with me any way you want to do it."

She sighed. "You're losing your dark and brooding persona."

He chuckled. "I'll just frown the whole time while you're typing away."

"That's the spirit."

"What psychic powers do I have?" He really didn't believe in people having them. He wondered if she did or this was just all fantasy for her.

"You can read other people's minds."

"Hmm, that could be interesting. And you?"

"My heroine can also. So she's disturbed when he begins to speak to her in her mind."

"Okay, that would be spooky, but of course, psychics aren't real."

She smiled. "Go ahead and start the movie."

He began the movie, and for a while, she just watched the show with him, smiling and laughing and seeming to enjoy it. He hadn't done this with a woman since he was a teen. But then she opened her laptop up and began to type.

He didn't think it would bother him. Sure, their cougar ears were more sensitive to sound than a human's, so tapping the keys at a rapid pace did catch his attention, but he didn't think it would matter. But then he realized he wanted her to enjoy the movie with him. He glanced at her and he saw that she was watching the show and typing without looking at her monitor. Okay, that worked. He wondered how much she could absorb from the movie while she wrote her story though. He noticed when there was a particularly important scene playing in the movie, she paused her typing.

He couldn't write a book and watch TV at the same time. Hell, he couldn't walk and text people at the same time without making a ton of mistakes.

Halfway through the movie, she set her laptop on the coffee table and pulled a green and black plaid blanket off the arm of the sofa and over her lap. She looked cozy and comfy on the couch, like a sleepy big cat. In that moment, he had the strangest urge to pull her into his arms and cuddle with her.

"More popcorn?" He had to keep his dark and moody image for her, if it helped her with her writing.

She shook her head.

He poured the rest of the bag in his bowl and finished it off. When the movie ended, she yawned, stretched, just like a tired cat, and glanced out the window. "I left the kitchen light on. No light still."

"Why don't you sleep in the guest bedroom then."

"Thanks. I never thought I would end up at the main house and not the cabin for my first night here. Thanks for the popcorn and cocoa too."

"You're welcome. Thanks for the German chocolate cake. It

really hit the spot." He turned off the TV. "Bathroom's down the hall. I have one in the master bedroom suite also, so no worries about taking your time in the bathroom, if you need to."

"Thanks."

He heard a banging sound outside and he wondered what he hadn't battened down, particularly since nothing had been making that noise all along while the wind was whistling away. "I've got to go check that out." He grabbed his parka.

"Did you need any company?"

He smiled this time. "No, you stay warm. I'll be but a minute." He hoped.

He went outside to see what was banging in the wind and realized the door to his storage unit had blown open. That was a surprise. He normally locked it. He tried to recall the last time he'd been out there. Earlier, looking for a hammer and nails to hang some stuff in the house, and then again when he had the snowblower out.

He trudged through the blowing snow to reach the storage unit and saw something out of the corner of his eye.

It moved too fast for him to see what it was and then he was struck from behind, hard, and Emerson thought of the last mission he was on, right before he fell into a blanket of cold, wet snow, and blacked out.

CHAPTER 3

*O*hile waiting for Emerson to return to the house, Jessie was doing a sketch of Emerson on her sketchpad when she had an idea for her story, so she tucked her sketchpad back in her backpack and opened her laptop and began typing on her manuscript again. She had been writing for some time, really getting somewhere with a scene—excited about the hero and heroine hooking up, him in protective mode, staying with her, and his brother, who was a deputy sheriff, giving him a hard time—when she realized Emerson hadn't returned to the house yet. She hoped he hadn't gotten disoriented in the blizzard and lost his way, though she didn't really think he could have. Not as a cougar and being from here.

She got up from the couch and set her laptop on the coffee table, and then went to look out the window. The banging sound had stopped. Where was Emerson? She couldn't see him anywhere.

She pulled on her parka, hat, scarf, Mukluks, and gloves and went outside in the howling wind, the snow still blowing in her eyes. She squinted, wishing she had her ski goggles with her—though she never had figured she would need them on a trip up here—and started moving through the snow. In the snowdrifts near the large shed, she saw a body lying face down in the snow, wearing all black and partly covered by snow. "Emerson?"

Her heart racing, she hurried toward him, her only thought being that she had to go to his aid, and she was praying he wasn't hurt too bad. No way would he be lying in the snow if he hadn't been injured.

She reached him and tried to revive him, shaking him. "Emerson! Emerson, wake up!" He seemed to be out cold. She tried to move him, but couldn't. He was too heavy and the snow was too deep. "Emerson!" If he had a sled in the storage unit, maybe she could roll him onto it and pull him to the house. She opened the shed door and inside, the building had been trashed. Everything was thrown everywhere. She couldn't imagine the shed was usually like that.

She didn't see a sled but then she heard Emerson groan and she hurried back to see to him. "Emerson!"

His eyelids fluttered open and she saw his dark brown eyes staring up at her. He appeared to be disoriented.

"Come on. Let's get you into the house. What happened?"

He struggled to sit up and she had to help him.

"Do you need to see a doctor?" He seemed so out of it but the cougar shifters avoided doctors when they could, just because they healed twice as fast as humans.

"Slugged." He used her strength to get to his feet. He was still wobbly and she placed her arm around his waist and tried to move him toward the house. "Bear."

"A bear hit you?" She'd thought maybe something like a tree limb had broken loose and hit him and then the wind carried it away or it had been buried in the snow. She hadn't considered that coming to Emerson's rescue could mean tangling with a bear! Wait! She immediately thought of Nina's dream or vision that said Jessie was chasing off two bears in the snow. No way would she run off after a bear or two. Though, come to think of it, she would have done anything to fend a bear off to protect Emerson. Then again, Nina had said Jessie would be in her cougar coat and Jessie was definitely not stripping and shifting to try and find bears in this storm. "Or a tree branch hit you?" She thought he was kind of out of it and could be mistaken.

"A bear. I think."

She glanced around, but didn't see any sign of a bear, but the mention of one had her moving Emerson more quickly through the snow to the house. "You didn't have food in your storage shed, did you?"

He grimaced. "No."

"The shed looks like it was trashed. A bear could have done that. Do you need a doctor?" He hadn't answered her the first time she'd asked, and she was afraid he wasn't quite catching what she was saying.

"No. I don't think so. I just have a horrible headache. He bashed me good."

"A black bear? A grizzly?" She figured if it had been a grizzly, Emerson would have been dead.

"I don't know. I just saw something move in my peripheral vision and when I turned, he, it struck me on the back and side of the head, and I was out."

"That's not good."

It seemed to take her forever to get Emerson to the house through the blowing snow and with struggling to keep him on his feet. He was staggering like a drunk. She really was thinking she should take him to the hospital to get him checked out, though she wasn't sure it would be safe to drive in these conditions. Especially since she wasn't used to driving in a blizzard up here.

"Did he bite you?"

"No."

"That's good." She finally got him to the house and opened the door, then helped him inside where she could see better. Even with their cougar vision, having a little extra light helped her to see his injuries. She kept her arm around him until she reached the couch. He slumped onto it. He was such a virile man that he looked like he could tackle a bear and win so she was surprised to see how out of it he was.

Blood was trickling down his face and she realized the bear had actually clawed his cheek and the right side of his temple. "I'll be right back." She returned to the door and shut and locked it. If a bear was prowling around here still, she sure didn't want it getting inside the house where there was food and injuring Emerson further and tackling her too. She shivered involuntarily.

She carefully pulled the black knit hat off his head. He had claw marks across the back of his head also and was bleeding. "I've got to get some antiseptics and bandages. Where do you keep them?"

"The guest bathroom down the hall." He leaned against the cushions on the couch and closed his eyes. "And I've got antibiotics in there."

She raised a brow at him. Most people didn't have antibiotics on hand unless they were taking them for some kind of infection.

"Ear infection," he said.

She wondered about that and slapped his parka-padded shoulder softly. "Don't go to sleep on me." But then she wondered about the wound on his arm. It wasn't that old. It was still healing, which meant he must have been shot fairly recently. She'd seen gunshot wounds before and she knew that's just what it was. She wondered who had injured him—and when and where.

He smiled a little at her and she figured women he didn't know, didn't tell him what to do very often.

She headed for the kitchen first and grabbed some paper towels off a roll for him to press against the wounds until she could find the bandages. She returned to the living room and held the paper towels against his cheek and head. "Can you hold them there to stop the bleeding while I get the bandages?"

"Yeah, thanks."

"Make sure you're holding enough pressure against the wounds." Then she strode off to get his first aid kit. She hadn't wanted to take off his parka because he might be chilled from lying in the snow, dead to the world for the time he was out there. Whenever she was writing in the zone, time sailed by, so she wasn't sure when he had gone out to check on the noise exactly. She wished she'd found him sooner, but if she had, she might have been attacked too and wouldn't have been any help to him.

She rummaged through all the bathroom cabinets and found the one with a first aid kit and hurried back to the living room with it. "Do you need to be warmed up?"

He gave her a predatory smile.

He couldn't be that bad off if he was going to take her comment in a sexy way, for which she was glad. But the bear's wicked claws could have infected him and that had her worried. After she took care of him, she was going to call whoever the doctor on call was in Yuma Town for tonight. She carefully wiped his wounds with an antiseptic, and before she covered them with bandages, she took pictures of the wounds. It was harder to see the wounds on his scalp where the hair covered it. Then she covered his wounds with a couple of clean paper towels.

"Hold these in place." She hated to make him do it himself, but she needed her hands free. "I need to make a Zoom call to one of our doctors in Yuma Town."

He arched a brow.

"Yuma Town is cougar run."

"That's a great deal, but you're from Loveland."

"It is. My sister and her family live there." Jessie called the clinic and was transferred to speak with Dr. Kate. "Hey, this is Jessie. The cougar who runs the Whispering Pines Resort on Lake Superior was attacked by a bear. I figure it wasn't a grizzly or it would have killed him. I'm going to get on Zoom, if we can do that, and I'll show you the claw marks close up. I'm sending you pictures also." Jessie wanted to take a picture of his wound on his arm too and ask Kate what that was from, to verify it!

"Okay. Are you all right?" Kate asked Jessie.

"Yeah, I was inside his house when he was attacked. He was unconscious at first, but as a cougar he'll heal faster. I disinfected the wounds and applied pressure to stop the bleeding." Jessie removed the paper towels Emerson was using to apply pressure to his wounds and held up her laptop so Kate could see the wounds.

Kate said, "They look like the bleeding has stopped. They're nasty gouges, but it doesn't look like he needs stitches. Where are you again? Could you bring him here?"

"No, we're in Minnesota in the middle of a raging snowstorm up on the North Shore of Lake Superior. It would be more dangerous for me to try and drive him there, or anywhere, really. And it's way too far to drive. It took me sixteen hours to drive here and driving in these conditions would take even longer. He would know these roads better than me in any event."

He shook his head.

"Okay, he hasn't been here long and doesn't know them either that well. But he shouldn't be driving anyway."

Kate cleared her throat. "All right. Shine a light in his eyes. Let me see if they react to the light."

"Okay." Jessie hoped he didn't have a bad concussion. She turned her phone light on, shined them in his eyes, and saw both pupils react.

"Is he confused?" Kate asked.

"Oh, I hadn't thought of that. What's your name, Emerson?"

Kate smiled. So did Emerson. Jessie frowned. Yes, she goofed by telling him his name if he couldn't remember it, but she still didn't know his full name. Did he?

"Your full name? Your address? Do you know where you are?"

Jessie asked, flustered, not giving him a chance to answer any of the questions before she asked another.

"I'm the recent owner of Whispering Pines Resort. My Uncle Paul Merriweather owned it before that and willed it to me. I don't know the actual address off-hand. I am thirty-five, six-feet tall, have a heart-shaped birthmark on my left thigh"—he gave her a little wink—"and I'm a cougar. You're Jessie Whittington and you brought me in out of the snowy cold. Thanks. I'm fine. I'll be fine."

"And your full name is?" Jessie wasn't giving up on learning what his name was, now that she had a good reason to learn of it.

"Emerson."

Jessie scoffed.

Kate got back to the business at hand. "Are you feeling dizzy? Try and stand up."

Though Jessie wanted to reach out and help him stand, just a natural instinct, she didn't, knowing Kate had to evaluate how bad off he really was. Jessie would have to take him to a hospital, no matter the road conditions, if Kate determined he needed to have his head checked out. Then maybe Jessie would learn what his whole name was.

He struggled to get up, but he stood and didn't collapse. He didn't look like he was perfectly normal, and Jessie was ready to grab him if he started to fall.

"Are you experiencing any nausea?" Kate asked.

"No," he said.

Jessie thought he answered Kate too quickly, like if he said the word fast enough, Kate wouldn't realize he was feeling worse than he was letting on.

"Do you have any ringing in the ears?" Kate asked.

"No. Can I sit down?" Emerson looked ready to collapse if she didn't say yes.

"Yeah, sure, sorry," Kate said. "Are you having double vision or blurry vision?"

He sat down, but kind of collapsed, not like he was perfectly fine. "No, though I swear I thought there were two bears initially, but then the one that hit me hadn't struck me yet. I mean, I glimpsed the one, but the paw struck me from behind, so two bears? Or it just moved so quickly, it didn't register until I came to."

Jessie was thinking she would need to stay with him overnight, even if her electricity came back on. She definitely didn't want to go outside in the dark again and walk all the way to her cabin if there was a bear, or two, out there. And Emerson couldn't walk her to her cabin, not in his condition.

"Hmm. Are you having any loss of smell?" Kate asked.

Emerson took a deep breath. At least he was making an attempt to prove he was all right. "I smell a she-cat nearby." He cast Jessie a small smile.

She smiled back. She couldn't help herself. He could be cute, when he wasn't being all gruff and tough.

"If you aren't feeling sick to your stomach and you eat something, see if you taste it. Do you have a headache?" Kate asked him.

"Yeah. Some of that might be from the claw marks and the bleeding though."

"Sure. Okay, so, if the headache gets worse or doesn't go away, you end up with significant nausea or repeatedly vomit, you become weak, disoriented, experience numbness, and/or slurred speech, you'll need to see a doctor. You can feel some symptoms for several weeks before getting better, but if things go downhill fast, you need to have some tests run at a hospital," Kate said, all official business-like.

Jessie was so glad she could call on her like this. Both Kate and Dr. William Rugel made cougar house calls if they needed help. For that matter, so did their veterinarian, Vanessa Vanderbilt, since they were half cougar, after all.

"I'm okay, Doc," Emerson said.

"Oh, and also, about the claw marks. If you see red streaks near the wounds or begin running a fever, I know we fight infection faster than humans, but—" Kate started to say.

"He has antibiotics for an ear infection," Jessie said, sounding like she didn't believe him. She told Kate what his prescription was for.

"That should do the trick. What about a history of concussions? Sometimes repeat concussions can be bad news," Kate said.

Emerson glanced at Jessie and she had the sneaking suspicion he'd had them before, and she guessed he wasn't going to 'fess up.

"No, nothing major."

Nothing major? Jessie didn't believe him.

"Are you all right with watching him?" Kate asked Jessie and she got the distinct impression Kate figured the same—the cougar had had concussions before, and they hadn't been minor.

"Yes." Jessie was thinking she needed one of their veterinarian's tranquilizer darts to knock him out if she needed, and take him to a hospital if he took a turn for the worse, because she imagined it was the only way he would go along with the plan. Then again, tranquilizing him when he had this condition probably wouldn't be a good idea either. And if she knocked him out, she would never be able to move him.

"Let me know if you have any further trouble," Kate said.

Jessie thought Kate was saying that to her and not to the stubborn cat of steel. He probably had never admitted he ever hurt, except maybe as a young boy. She was surprised he had even gone in to get antibiotics for an ear infection. She glanced at the wound on his arm. Or had it been for a bullet wound? That sounded much more plausible.

"I'm going to end this meeting now, but I'm serious. If Emerson starts to feel poorly, call me," Kate said.

"Thanks, I will."

They ended the session and Jessie eyed Emerson warily. "No major concussions?"

He shrugged.

"And you don't remember your last name? Or is it your first?"

He smiled.

Jessie was serious. What if she had to take him to a hospital in the middle of the night? She hadn't a clue where the closest one would even be. And she would probably have to fill out his insurance paperwork for him. Though then she could learn his name. "And you're really not nauseous?"

He let out his breath. "Fix me a bowl of ice cream, hot fudge sauce on top, skip the cherry. I'll see if I can hold it down and if I can taste it."

She frowned. "Are you warmed up now?" She couldn't imagine eating anything frosty after being in what felt like a freezer outside for some time.

"I'm hot, sitting in the heated house wearing my parka."

"I'll bandage your head and then help you out of your parka. Are you sure you're not feeling feverish?" He was looking a little rosy-cheeked, not ghostly like earlier. "And are you sure you want to eat ice cream?" Or anything else for that matter. She didn't want to mention that she didn't want to have to clean up after him if he threw up! She would probably end up getting sick herself. She was a writer, not a nurse!

"Yeah." He began to pull off his parka before she bandaged his head. She tsked.

She helped him out of his parka because he was frowning something awful, and she figured his head was hurting. Then she bandaged his wounds. He looked like he had been in a war zone. "Do you really want ice cream?" She couldn't imagine eating anything cold right now.

"Yeah. You can fix some for yourself too, if you would like."

"During a blizzard, nah."

"Ice cream is good no matter what time of year it is. I should have had it on my cake, but I forgot about it."

"All right"—she shook her head—"one hot fudge sundae coming up." If it made him feel better, that was all that mattered.

She pulled the ice cream out of the freezer and the hot fudge topping out of the fridge. "Should we report to the authorities that a bear attacked you?"

"No. I was thinking about it. Bears would be hibernating right now, wouldn't they?"

"Uh, yeah, in these conditions, sure. Though I've read where they will come out of hibernation if they're old, disoriented, or sick, and they can be dangerous to both humans and themselves while searching for food." She put some of the hot fudge in a saucepan and put it on a burner to warm up.

"What if there is another reason?"

She finished heating the hot fudge and figured there was enough for two sundaes. She made up two sundaes and brought them into the living room. "How are you feeling?"

"Like crap."

"You didn't tell Kate that."

He smiled. "I shouldn't have told you that."

"Figures. So what other reason could there be that a bear would be tearing up your shed and injuring you?" She sat on the couch with him to eat her cold ice cream. The hot fudge was a really great touch though. She knew she shouldn't be having it too, but it sure was good.

"Someone like us."

"A cougar shifter?" She frowned at him. She hadn't smelled a cougar, other than them. "Or did you smell the bear?"

"Uh, come to think of it, I didn't smell him at all. The wind might have carried his scent away from me."

"But wouldn't it have left his scent on you?" Now that she thought of it, she didn't remember smelling the bear's scent on him. She leaned over close to take a deep breath and smell his wounds. He smiled at her as if he thought she was getting up close and personal for some other reason. Even though she had cleaned the claw marks with antiseptic and they were covered up in gauze, with her superior sense of smell, she should be able to tell if a bear's scent was on him. She didn't smell anything. No human scent either, nothing.

"He should have left his scent on you."

Emerson arched a brow. "Yeah. I agree. I figured I wasn't smelling things like I should because of the injuries." He gave a heavy sigh. "I thought you were just getting close so you could smell me."

She smiled. "You wish. Hmm, this is good. I'll need to run again if I keep eating all this fun stuff. Does it make you feel any better?"

"Yeah. It does."

She reached out and put her hand on his forehead. He was still feeling cool. She was glad for that.

"I'm fine. I told you I was. Aren't you glad you had a sundae too?"

"Yeah." Once she finished eating her sundae, she got up and looked outside to see if she could see any sign of the bear. Or bears. "So what would cause claw marks like that but not leave a scent?"

"A shifter wearing hunter's concealment," he said, and she wondered if he'd ever seen bear shifters up here!

CHAPTER 4

"A bear shifter? Hmm, maybe. One of our doctors ran into a wolf shifter in town. I mean, literally ran into him. We had heard they existed, but no one had seen any out there. I've never heard of bear shifters," Jessie said to Emerson in the toasty warm house.

"I've...uh, met a wolf shifter before. But I've never met any bear shifters either. Was the wolf okay?" Emerson immediately thought of Condor but didn't want to mention him. But if the bear had been one...hell, what did it want? He couldn't imagine his uncle having any enemies. If anyone knew who Emerson had been and that he was here, plenty of them would want him dead. Smith was on the top of his list because he knew Emerson would be gunning for him as soon as he could. Another attempt at ambushing him? But this time using bear shifters? But the bear could have easily killed him and it hadn't.

"Yeah. The wolf shifter returned home, right as rain," she said.

"That's good." He let out his breath. "A bear shifter. Okay, so let's say there's such a thing. It wouldn't be like a real bear, foraging for food then. And if it tore up my shed, the same thing.

It wouldn't be a rampaging bear, searching for something to eat. He would have to have been looking for something else."

"Hmm, okay." She carried their empty ice cream bowls into the kitchen and put them in the dishwasher. "Right. So then what? Like a robber searching for something and you got in his way?"

"Yeah, but what? And in the storage shed?"

"I can't imagine your uncle would have had anything in there that a robber would want. In the house, maybe. But not in the shed." Jessie frowned. "The announcement of his death was probably in the paper, right? Thieves have been known to break into residences while there's a funeral going on."

"That's true, but the funeral was a couple of days ago. Your vehicle is here. Mine's in the garage, but if there's a renter here, the thief would have to consider that the new owner would have to be here also. With the lights on in my house, they knew I was home." He figured with the electricity out, the generator on in just the main house, and the blizzard going on, the bear, or whatever it was, figured he could break into the storage shed without anybody being the wiser. Except Emerson heard the banging noise of the open shed door and the wind catching it. Why wouldn't the person have made sure the door hadn't banged like that? It didn't make any sense.

Jessie grabbed up a notebook and began writing some notes. "Is there anything here that belongs to you that someone might want to steal? I'm adding all this to my story. Not about shifters, but that the bad guys had tried to break in. Nothing like a real story to jumpstart my muse."

He wondered just what else she would include in her story that was happening in real time. "There's nothing in the shed that I can imagine would be worth anything."

She crossed the floor and peeked out the window and peered into the dark. "And the lights were on in the house because you had the generator—" She hesitated to say anything further.

"What? Do you think someone cut the power to the resort?" He tried to get up from the couch. He hated feeling this woozy. It was one thing to be injured on a mission—that was inevitable, but to be here where it should have been safe? That was another story.

"Where's the circuit breaker?" She had her hand on his shoulder in an instant and made him sit back down. "Stay. You're not going anywhere."

He couldn't believe she had enough strength to force him back onto the couch, though his arm wound hadn't healed all the way, either, which was the reason for him taking the antibiotics, not for an ear infection. He hadn't wanted to mention he'd been shot on his last mission or that his team had been set up. Smith didn't know Emerson's real name or where he lived now. Everyone had worked under aliases, so this probably had nothing to do with him, though a nagging worry still plagued Emerson. What if he had hired these men to come after him? But then again, they didn't kill him.

"The circuit breaker is outside. And you're not going out there." There was no way he wanted her out there if the bear was there. He still believed there might have been two of them, which, if they were shifters, would make more sense.

"The bear, or whatever it was, won't be hanging around. If I can check on the circuit breaker box, I can see if it's okay. And turn it back on. Then we can shut off the generator," she said adamantly.

"I'm going. I figured the electricity going out had to be due to the snowstorm." Which made sense. But now he wasn't so sure.

She placed her hands on her hips, her brow furrowed. "Do I have to tie you up or what? You are *not* going. After the injury you suffered and after you were in the cold for however long you were, you should stay right here."

He smiled. There was a lot more to little Miss Jessie than he had first suspected. Tie him up? Now that sounded interesting.

Not that he would ever be tied up willingly, even for fun. But the image came to mind of her trying and it amused him. "Do you know how to shoot a gun?"

"Uh, I'm a writer. I don't shoot guns. My characters do though."

He wasn't surprised. "You should. Just to add realism to the story. Okay, then that decides it. You're not going out there by yourself. I'm not going to risk you heading out there alone if the bears attack again." He might feel like shit, but he would never forgive himself if something bad happened to her because he didn't do the job that needed to be done and he sent a defenseless guest out to do it.

She let out her breath in exasperation. "You do know you're going to go in the book like that?"

"Like what?"

"Stubborn to the max."

"That's me." And he didn't think that was a bad thing. He stood up and walked into the kitchen and brought out a gun from behind the jar of sugar.

She bundled up and then brought his parka to him. He was amused she was taking her role as his caregiver so seriously and making sure he was thoroughly dressed, at the very least. He pulled on his snow boots.

"Is that your uncle's gun?"

"One of mine. He has some too." He hadn't meant to let it slip that he had several.

"Some?"

He set the gun on the counter and then began pulling on his parka. She zipped it up for him, whether he needed help or not. He smiled down at her, not minding being babied a bit. That hadn't happened to him since he was a little boy.

"Can you wear your hat?" she asked.

"Yeah." He figured it would hurt but if they had trouble

outside, a hat was some protection from the elements, and it probably had protected him some when the bear attacked him.

She hurried to get his hat, gloves, and found his scarf on the clothes tree and got it for him. She handed him his hat. He grimaced when he pulled it on. It hurt.

"What about a video security camera?" she asked. "We could check it out to see if it captured anything."

"I thought about that too. But my uncle didn't have any. He said he'd never had any trouble the whole time he'd lived here, and he wasn't about to buy something he didn't need. That's something I need to do too. Add some video security."

He hated that she felt she had to go outside with him in the blizzard, but he knew she was too worried about his well-being not to. After handing him his gloves, she wrapped the scarf around his neck and he leaned down and kissed her mouth, appearing to shock her as her eyes widened in surprise, yet, when she smiled a little, he figured she was pleased.

She kissed him back, and he wondered if she'd add this to her story also. He wanted to wrap his arms around her and kiss her until tomorrow. She was warm and sweet, the taste of vanilla ice cream and hot fudge sundae adding to her sweetness. He hadn't kissed a woman like this in forever.

Knowing this wasn't the time for this, if ever, he finally broke off the kiss. "Thanks for saving my life out there. It's a damn good thing I didn't refund your money for the cabin rental." He was trying to let on that he kissed her for saving him, but he took a little too much liberty to show that was all there was to it. He was truly intrigued with her.

"It's a good thing that I didn't take the refund." She cast him a wicked smile, and he thought she was telling him the kiss was the reason she felt that way and not because she could have saved his life. "Are you ready to go outside then and we can check the circuit breaker box?"

"Yeah. We stick close together." He got the gun, really wishing she'd stay safe inside the house. If she could shoot a weapon, that would be a different story. He never made the mistake of thinking a woman wasn't capable of defending herself though— not after the first time a woman tackled him in combat training and threw him on his back. That had been an eye-opener and game-changer for him.

"You don't have to tell me twice," she said.

He didn't want her to get clawed by a bear, even if she could write about it in her new book—if she survived a bear attack. He could just imagine what Dr. Kate would say if he had to call her about Jessie's injury next.

"Where did you learn to shoot?" Jessie asked.

"The army." Which was true. Black Ops came later.

He grabbed a flashlight for her to carry and they both had their cell phones with them. They left the house and he locked the door, then trudged out into the snow with her.

"Special Forces?" she asked.

"Ranger."

"I knew it. I'll have to add that to the book."

He was smelling the air, though it was blowing so hard, it would be difficult to tell where smells were coming from, but he didn't get a whiff of any sign of bears out here, just his scent and Jessie's. Maybe the wind had carried the bears' scents off, but Jessie was right. She hadn't smelled any bear scent on him and neither had he. He was sure the bear's claws or paws would have left their scent, just like he left his on Jessie when he kissed her and vice versa.

He couldn't believe he'd done that. Then again, he'd wanted to ever since she'd made the hot fudge sundae for him and had one with him. He'd been feeling somewhat revived and he was being truthful when he said he was thankful to her for saving his keister outside in the snow. Calling a cougar doctor for him really could have been a lifesaver also.

Though he hadn't been much interested in reading books of

late, he wanted to read hers, to see what she was writing—particularly about him.

He listened to sounds too, but all he heard was the wind blowing through the branches of the trees and the waves hitting the shore down below.

They were close to the overhang of the house, and they finally reached the circuit breaker box. It took him a few minutes to break it open because it was frozen shut, which made him think no one had messed with it during the snowstorm. He used his phone to flash the light into the box, but all the switches were on, none of them having tripped. The storm *had* caused the power outage.

He wasn't even sure which electric company serviced this area. He needed to check it out and report the outage. He should have thought of it earlier.

Jessie was shining the flashlight on the cabins and surrounding woods, making sure no one sneaked up on them as he closed the breaker box, then he headed back with her through the snow to the house.

"I didn't see any sign of anyone and no tracks either. Not even the ones we made earlier tonight, the wind is blowing so hard. I figured when this lets up, we could shift and check it out, but with no scents and no tracks to follow, I think it would be futile," she said. "Besides, you're not in any condition to run around in the cold."

"I agree." He wished he could have gone after them, right after he'd been hit, not that he would have been able to. He figured they would have killed him then. Still, they could have initially if they had wanted to and they hadn't.

As soon as they were back inside the cozy, warm house, he locked the door and she removed her parka, hat, and gloves and hung them up on his clothes tree as if she belonged with him there. He realized he kind of liked the notion, when here he had thought he would much rather be alone.

He removed his gloves and hat, but before he could do anything else, she was untying his scarf and then removing his parka and hanging them up. She pulled off her own scarf then.

"Okay, so I'm kind of relieved he or they hadn't messed with the electric box," she said.

"Me too," he said.

"I had a long drive today, and I need to get some sleep, but I want to make sure you're going to be all right too. Do you need me to do anything for you?"

"Does your caregiving include patient baths?"

She chuckled darkly, her face lighting up with amusement. He was glad he could lighten the mood. On her, the look suited her.

"It sounds to me like you're healing up nicely. How is your head?" she asked.

"I have a headache, but nothing worse than it was before."

"Good. Do you need help removing your snow boots or anything?"

She could undress all of him and join him in bed, he was thinking. "No, I'm good. You go and get your rest. If I feel worse in the night, I'll let you know."

She cocked her head to the side. "I doubt it."

She was right about that. He'd been wounded so many times in the line of duty, he certainly wouldn't let a little thing like being clawed by a bear get him down.

"If you hear anything in the middle of the night that sounds like trouble, shout out a warning, all right? Just in case I'm dead to the world, though I'm normally a light sleeper." Emerson turned on the light in the hallway and then he began rummaging through a file cabinet in the office that was open to the kitchen and living room.

"You need to go to bed."

He hated to admit he should have called the electric company before they ventured out into the snowy cold. "I'm looking for the name of the electric company that services the resort."

Her mouth dropped, then she smiled. "That would have been a good thing to do earlier."

"Yeah, I know." He cast her a little smile. "Neither of us thought of it."

"You're right." She grabbed her laptop and bag and headed to the first guest room. "Thanks for letting me stay here."

"I wouldn't have had it any other way. Sure, you might have been fine without heat in the cabin as a cougar, but you're still a paying guest. And at least you were able to watch a movie with me and write some more in your book."

"Would you have done the same for other paying guests? A family of five? Humans?"

He found a bill from the electric company that serviced the resort with the phone number on it for power outages, grabbed the paper, and turned off the living room and office lights. "Yeah. But it wouldn't have been half as much fun and I wouldn't have kissed any of them."

She chuckled. "You kissed me to thank me."

"True." As if that had been the only reason. "Night, Jessie. Pleasant dreams."

"You'll have to tell me your bear story again tomorrow so I can get more of the details for my novel, only you're human in the story and you wouldn't have smelled the scent of a bear."

"Just a plain human?" That wouldn't be much fun.

"Yeah, psychics are more real than shifters—to some humans. So that's what I'm writing about."

"You'll have to tell me more about it in the morning." He kissed her on the forehead and before he got carried away, he left her off at her room and then headed down the hall to his bedroom.

"And when you remember your full name, you'll have to tell me that tomorrow also."

He smiled at her and entered his bedroom. He turned on his lamp next to the bed, set his phone on the bedside stand, pulled off his clothes, and put on a pair of dry pajama bottoms. Then he climbed into bed and called the electric company's emergency number for electrical outages.

He got a recording saying that the electricity was out for 5,000 residents in the area. He really should have checked that before he and Jessie went out into the blizzard where a possible bear was lurking, but he was glad to get confirmation one way or another.

He turned out his lamplight when he heard light footfalls leaving the guest room and he suspected Jessie was going to the bathroom one last time.

But her footfalls continued to his room and he turned on the lamplight for her. As soon as she appeared in the room wearing hot pink, plaid pajamas and a hot pink robe and slippers, he smiled.

She looked like a vibrant flower on a gloomy, cold night.

"Too much, do you think?" she asked, motioning to her night-wear. She smiled. "My sister knows I love hot pink, but not like this. More as an accessory, like with my gloves. She got the robe, pjs, and slippers for me for last Christmas and they do make me feel cheery on a cold, winter's night. Like tonight."

"They cheered me right up."

She laughed. "You, who wear all black all the time?"

He pulled his covers aside as if inviting her into bed, which he would have, if she'd been game, but he'd only done it to show her he was wearing another pair of navy-blue pajama bottoms. "Blue."

"Almost black!"

"Isn't black basic for every wardrobe?"

She sighed. "Okay, so I was thinking about the shed door. Had you locked it? Was it damaged? As in the intruder had to break the lock to get in? I was too busy worrying about you to really check the door over to see if anyone had broken in. I didn't realize at the time that someone had hit you and I wasn't positive someone had trashed the shed either. It could have always looked like that."

"Hell, I don't know. I guess I was so out of it, I didn't even think of that." He started to get out of bed.

"Where are you going?"

"To check it out."

"Sorry. I shouldn't have mentioned it. You're to stay in bed."

"*You're* not going to go out and check it, are you?" No way was he allowing Jessie to go out there alone to see if the lock was broken. He really couldn't remember if it had been or not, just that the door was swinging back and forth and banging as it swung closed again.

She sighed. "No. I just wanted to see if you knew for sure, then I could go to sleep. I had to shove the door aside since snow was blocking it when I went to look for a sled inside, to haul you back to the house, but then I heard you groan. Sorry, now I guess you're wondering about it also."

"I would have after a bit. Once I shut my eyes and began to revisit what had happened again." He patted the bed. "Do you want to think about it with me?"

She gave him a mischievous, little smile. "No. Remember the part I was telling you about how my sister and her husband have to check out the guys I'm with, especially if I'm going to end up with some guy in his bed?"

He smiled.

"If you need me, just let me know. Good night." Then she left his room.

He really wished he could have convinced her to stay with him. After the night he'd had, it would end on a better note if she had climbed into bed with him.

He closed his eyes and envisioned the shed door banging and tried to remember if the doorknob had looked damaged in any way. Now, he wanted to go out and check to see if the lock had been broken on the shed.

* * *

REFLECTING on the kiss they'd shared and about his offer to join him in bed—to *think*, ha!—Jessie smiled as she climbed into bed. Emerson was such a cougar. She closed her eyes, but she couldn't sleep. The wind was whipping around the house and howling through the woods. She couldn't stop pondering about the bear in the woods, wondering if there were two and if they were shifters. If they were shifters, they had to be rogues and that wasn't good. She wondered if the Cougar Shifter Force would handle something like that. They took care of their own rogues, but if there were other kinds of shifters out there, who would deal with the rogues?

She gave her sister a call, even though she wasn't with CSF. Tracey knew the others well who were. "Hey, Tracey."

"Jessie, don't tell me we need to check on a new guy you're hanging out with," Tracey said, goodheartedly.

"No. I mean, maybe. But I don't know his last name, or maybe I don't know his first name yet."

"Jessie," her older twin said in a way that said she knew Jessie was heading for trouble already.

"I didn't call about that. Emerson, the owner of the resort where I'm staying, was struck by a bear and we think maybe it was a shifter."

"What?"

"Yeah, really. That's the way I felt about it. No self-respecting bear would be out running around in a blizzard, foraging for food and Emerson thought there might be two of them. Oh, and they didn't leave their scent on him, or any scent at all in the area —which spells rogue shifter to us. I was wondering what would happen if bear shifters were real and one was a rogue, who would deal with him?" That was the problem with being a shifter. They had to take care of them themselves and not turn them over to the police. They couldn't risk having a shifter incarcerated long-term if it got growly and wanted to shift to pay an inmate—or a guard—back.

"I don't know, but I'm sure anyone with the CSF could handle it. I was wondering the same about the wolves after we had that incident with William running into the wolf shifter. If the wolf had been a rogue, that would have been bad news. We could have incarcerated him, but I guess it's something we need to learn about for future cases," Tracey said. "How to handle other rogue shifters. Are you safe where you are right now? I can get hold of Leyton or Travis and see if they can go up there and meet with you and try to track a bear shifter down. If you feel you're in danger, though it's not our sheriff's department's jurisdiction, they'll be up there in a heartbeat to protect you and bring you home."

"No, I'm okay. As long as it's a shifter and not a real bear, you can ask someone from the CSF if they want to investigate this. I'll call you tomorrow with an update. We're having a blizzard right now. But when the storm settles and at first light, we can check things out."

"You be careful."

"Thanks, I will."

"Before I let you go, who is this Emerson, exactly? Paul Merriweather was the owner of the Whispering Pines Resort every time you went up there."

"Emerson's the new owner and manager of the resort."

"Last name? First name."

"Emerson. It's the only one he gave me."

"Okay, thanks. We'll check him out."

Jessie sighed. "Okay, maybe you'll have better luck learning his full name. I'm off to sleep."

"Let us know if anything else happens. You know you'll have a whole bunch of cougars up there to protect you, if you need them."

"Okay, thanks. Good night, Sis."

"Night, Jessie."

Jessie set her phone on the bedside table, sighed, and closed her eyes. And thought about poor Emerson lying on his stomach in the snow and the injuries he'd suffered. She couldn't believe a stay at the resort this time would lead to meeting an interesting character, and real trouble too.

CHAPTER 5

*T*he next morning, the bear was chasing Jessie through the snow and she leaped into a tree, but the darn bear started to climb the tree after her! She heard a metal "thunk," smelled eggs, fried potatoes and bacon cooking, and coffee brewing. The sound of sizzling made her tear her gaze away from the bear and she woke!

Jessie opened her eyes. No bear, no tree, no snow, just a warm cuddly bed and then she realized the food she'd smelled was cooking in the kitchen. She was out of bed in a flash, throwing on her robe and slipping her feet into her slippers. She was planning on making breakfast while Emerson took it easy. She should have told him last night that he was to rest, and she would fix him breakfast, though she suspected he would have beat her to it as tired as she'd been. She couldn't believe he was up already or that she'd slept in a little—not her usual style.

When she hurried down the hall, he smiled at her from the kitchen. "Now there's a sight for sore eyes." He was starting to serve up the bacon on a platter, dressed already in his signature black pants, boots, and sweater.

"I planned to make us breakfast while you took it easy." She found plates and set them out.

"I've got this. I know where everything is."

"I'm sure I could easily have found the bacon and eggs in the fridge," she said.

He offered her a smile. "I was feeling just fine. How did you sleep?"

"I woke, dreaming about the bear coming after me. I figured I was safe when I'd leapt into the tree, but he hesitated, then climbed right after me. How about you? How are you feeling?"

"I'm not feverish. I just have a slight headache. I still remember who I am."

"First name? Last name?"

He smiled. "Thankfully, I didn't have any nightmare about the bears. Are scrambled eggs okay? They broke when I cracked open the shells."

"Yeah, they're just as good any way you cook them."

"I agree. Would you like some potatoes?"

"Oh, yeah." She eyed him warily. "You haven't been outside investigating the shed or anything, have you? I can't believe I slept through you cooking breakfast."

"You must have needed it. And no, I haven't been outside yet. I wanted to fix breakfast for us first."

"Okay. Well, we'll do this together. Investigate the break-in, I mean."

"Yeah, sure. It's light out, lightly snowing, but not a blizzard now."

"That's good." She set out the silverware. "This looks great. Did you need a cup of coffee?"

"I already got a cup, thanks."

She added sugar and milk to her coffee and sat down with him at the dining table. "Thanks for breakfast. Are you sure you are okay?"

"Yeah. I'm feeling much better. I just needed a rest."

"I'll check your injuries after we eat, then we can get bundled up and look outside for any clues as to what happened," she said.

"Okay, we can do that." He served up some bacon on his plate.

She took a couple of slices off the platter and added them to her plate.

"I got a call this morning from someone you might know. A Tracey Haverton?" Emerson arched a dark brow.

Shocked to the core, Jessie looked up from her food. "Omigod, she called you?" She couldn't believe her sister would actually call Emerson! Jessie would give her grief big time. He wasn't supposed to know Tracey was investigating him!

"Yeah, she sounded just like you. She wanted to know what my whole name was so she could learn all there was to know about me." He ate some of his eggs.

"She told *you* that? She was supposed to do a background search on you *without* you knowing it."

"I thought that only happened when you were dating someone." His mouth curved up just a tad.

"Uh, I asked her to call some of the Cougar Shifter Forces special agents about coming up here to investigate if bear shifters hurt you. She wanted to know who I was stuck with by myself in a blizzard. And you wouldn't give me your full name. I'm sure she was immediately suspicious of you."

He chuckled. "You don't give up, do you?"

"No, and I'm writing it in the story. Not your real name, whatever the whole thing is, but just that you won't tell me what it is."

He smiled. "I could just give it to you. But what would be the fun in that?"

"I should have dug through your wallet and found your driver's license."

"While I was sleeping? You would never have managed to do it without waking me."

"You hide it in bed with you?"

"No, but I would have heard you slipping it out of my pants pocket. Cougar hearing, you know."

She wondered if it was more than that. The army? Combat trained? Listening for any signs of the enemy in the middle of the night? "You don't have a gun under your mattress, do you?"

"No. If I did, I would never get any sleep. Too lumpy, you know."

"You mean like the princess and the pea?" She laughed. "What about a gun in your bedside table?"

He shook his head, got up from the table, and refilled their coffee cups. She noticed he added just the right amount of sugar and milk to hers and realized he had to have watched her make her own cup of coffee. He was observant. She was impressed.

"So about this business of your sister investigating me—" He handed the cup of coffee to Jessie.

"You're not worried my sister will discover anything bad about you, are you?" She sipped from her coffee. "Perfect."

He only gave her a small smile.

"You know what they did to the last rogue cougar I dated."

"I didn't think we were dating," he said.

"You know what I mean." Of course they weren't dating. Emerson would have to live near Loveland, Colorado or Yuma Town for that to work out between them.

"They eliminated him. Does that happen to all the guys you date?"

"No. One of them got away." She finished eating her eggs.

"Only one? What did he do? Run away?"

"He was chasing other she-cats' tails, so he was a rogue but not in the terminal category. Though that could depend on the she-cat he cheated on, I suppose. So is my sister going to dig up dirt on you?" Jessie waited for a response before she grabbed another slice of bacon.

"That would put me on her terminal list? I hope not, since we're not even dating."

Jessie smiled, amused he kept bringing that point up.

"What if I have a bunch of aliases?" he asked.

"Hmm, that sounds like a rogue to me, though I suppose that *could* mean you were undercover for law enforcement and one of the good guys." She realized she had no idea what he had done before he had taken over his uncle's resort. "So what *did* you do before you quit your job?"

"Undercover work."

She laughed.

"Oh, and the electricity is back on." He took another bite of his bacon.

"Okay, that's good news. I'll move back to my cabin as soon as we do a little investigating."

"Are you sure you don't want to stay here, just in case the bears return?" He sounded serious now, as if he were worried about her safety, not as though he was making a play for her.

"I'm sure you have stuff to do. And I need to write. We're so close to each other, I can yell, and you can come rescue me." She really had to write or she would have loved to just hang out with Emerson. This really had to be a working vacation for her.

"All right. But if you hear *anything* while you're over there, even if you think it's nothing, call me and I'll come check it out."

"I will." She didn't believe in trying to manage bad guys on her own if she could have a hunky hero to help her out. She appreciated that he would open his house up to her to keep her safe. Especially when initially it seemed as though he didn't want to have anything to do with any guest staying at the resort.

After they finished eating, she grabbed the dishes to clean up. He came to help her.

She began scrubbing the frying pan. "I've got it. You made breakfast when I had planned to."

"I'm perfectly fine." He put the dishes in the dishwasher.

She finished cleaning the frying pan, then said, "I'll check your injuries, and then change to go outside with you. How's the weather?"

"It's snizzling, a light snow-ice mixture. Cold. But nothing major like last night."

"Okay, good."

She reached up to feel his forehead, not taking any chances that he wasn't running a fever and was too macho to let on. But his skin was nice and cool.

She made him sit down so she didn't have to reach up to remove the bandages and could get a better look at his injuries. "Oh, my, you're healing nicely." The skin around his scratches was pink now, not red. They were lucky they healed so fast. "I'll send pictures of your injuries to Kate, so she has a chance to look at your wounds and verify they're looking fine."

"Thanks, Jessie. You would make a good nurse."

"Ha!" But she smiled at the compliment. After she took pictures of Emerson's wounds, then sent them to Kate, she said, "I'm going to get dressed now. I don't think you need bandages again, but we'll let the doctor be the judge of that."

"I'm fine. Thanks."

"If she says you are, then I agree."

He chuckled. "All right."

Jessie hurried off to the bedroom and shut the door. Then she slipped off all her pink nightwear and pulled on panties and her bra. She tugged on a pair of fleece-lined pants, jeans over those, candy cane socks, her boots. Then a fleece-lined shirt to go under her sweater. She had considered searching for the bear or bears as a cougar, but, like she suspected last night, she didn't think that she would find any trail left by the culprit or culprits.

She got a call and grabbed her phone before she left the bedroom and smiled. It was Dr. William Rugel. She loved Yuma Town's doctors. They were great about making sure that their patients were taken care of, even if they weren't close by. Kate must have been busy with a patient.

William said, "Kate filled me in on Emerson's injuries. From the pictures you took, they look good, like they're healing properly, and you're doing a great job. No more bandages required."

"Oh, thanks, William. I'm so glad."

"Kate said to keep watching for red streaks or fever, or if he is continuing to have headaches, give us a call."

"He doesn't have a fever, there are no red streaks, and he said he is feeling fine."

"Okay, good. Just keep monitoring him. A concussion can come back to bite him, so just watch him. I don't mean you have to stay with him, but just check on him periodically," Dr. William said.

"Yeah, I sure will do that." She felt glad that Emerson was going to be okay—as far as the claw marks were concerned. They ended the call and feeling lighthearted, she left the bedroom. "Unless the concussion gives you trouble, Dr. William Rugel says your wounds are looking good."

"I told you."

She smiled. "Well, I'm thrilled. Are you ready to check out the shed?"

"Yeah, let's go."

They put their parkas, hats, boots, and gloves on, and then they went outside. "I thought of running as a cougar to see what we could find. It would be faster, and we could cover more territory in the snow," she said.

"If they had left a scent and tracks. With all the blowing snow we had, we won't find tracks, and they didn't leave a scent."

"I agree with you there."

They made their way through the deep snow to the shed and found the door lock mechanism had been broken.

"What I don't understand is why they would wear bear coats to break in. They wouldn't be able to carry off anything much that way," she said.

"We wouldn't guess who they were if we'd seen them as bears.

They might not realize we are cougars." He let out his breath in exasperation. "I'll have to replace the lock now."

"But they would have smelled *you're* a cougar."

"They might not know we exist, just like we're unsure about them and wouldn't know why I smelled like one. Maybe I'd hunted one while wearing this parka and carried the carcass off."

"Well, that could be." She tried to walk into the shed and found a box of Christmas lights and ornaments and one of several trees sitting way in the corner under a pile of stuff that had been tossed around. "Oh, yes! Can I use these to decorate my cabin?" She was so excited about it.

"For the time that you'll be here?" He sounded surprised she would want to go to all the trouble.

"Yes. I like having the ambience so I can write the story. I'll put all the decorations away before I leave so you don't have to deal with it."

"No, that's okay. I can do it after the holidays, and I'll carry them over to the cabin for you and help you set them up."

"Thanks. But *after* I help you straighten up the shed." And she was helping him carry the decorations over to her cabin since it was her idea after all. She so appreciated him for saying yes and not being such a Scrooge any longer.

CHAPTER 6

essie seemed so thrilled about the Christmas decorations, Emerson again felt like he'd been a Scrooge, so he was glad he'd changed his mind. He vowed to hang the Christmas lights up around her cabin, at the very least. He carried a box of decorations that was labeled cabin five and set it on the patio, then returned to get the small artificial tree.

She was trying to sort things out in his shed—which he appreciated—the tools, mainly, setting stuff back up on shelves and on pegboard where some of the tools had been hanging. His uncle had been so particular about everything being in its place that Emerson felt sick about how the intruder had broken in and trashed it. He appreciated that Jessie was trying to help him set things right. Though it was too cold out there to do it all at once. He would come out later and do some more straightening.

Once he deposited the tree on her doorstep, he returned to the shed.

"I was going to help you carry that all over there! You still are injured, you know."

She sounded annoyed with him, but she should have seen when he was *really* injured.

"Ahh!"

"What's wrong?" he asked, worried she'd hurt herself.

"Fur! Bear fur." Lifting it off a metal shelf, she showed it to him. "I can smell a hint of bear on it."

He joined her and smelled the fur. "Hell, it smells like one of the guys who came looking for you before you arrived."

"The guys you mentioned to me? No way. I told you already I didn't know anyone up here and if anyone was looking for me, they wouldn't be checking out the shed. The shed has nothing to do with..." She hurried out of the shed and Emerson raced to catch up to her.

He imagined he was thinking the same thing as she was—that they had broken into her place too last night while she was staying with him.

He pulled out the keys to the cabin and made her stay on the porch to ensure no one was in her cabin. The lock hadn't been touched. He didn't understand it. "Would they believe you had some kind of connection to my uncle?" Emerson unlocked the door and opened it.

"I've been coming up here for five years, but just to write and of course I visited with your uncle. I wouldn't believe anyone would think anything of it. He was a charmer, you know. You're nothing like him."

Emerson was amused at the jab. "He decorated for Christmas."

"Oh, yes, his home and all the cabins. He always had a special little tree in the living room for me decorated with cougars of all kinds—glass, plastic, wood, fabric. Every year there was a new cougar ornament on the tree. He went out of his way to find one for me."

Emerson smiled. "Hell, he had the hots for you."

"Don't be ridiculous. He was my dad's age."

Emerson knew his uncle had always wanted kids, but he and his aunt had been unsuccessful at having any. He imagined Uncle Paul saw Jessie as the daughter he'd never had. Emerson went through the house to ensure no one had been there or was still there when she came in with the box of decorations. He meant for her to stay outside while he checked the place over. Thankfully, both bedrooms and the bathroom were clear.

"I don't see any sign of bear fur and they didn't break the door lock," he said.

"Well, good. I just don't understand why they would break into your uncle's shed but come to the resort looking for me first." She frowned at Emerson as he carried the Christmas tree into her living room. "Are you sure they're not after something to do with you? I mean, since you said you had an undercover job." She didn't sound like she believed it.

"I got here just a few days ago."

"Okay, so it didn't happen until your uncle died and you arrived. You could have inherited something or moved something here from wherever you were before this."

He put the Christmas tree stand up and she helped him set up the tree. "That wouldn't explain why they were looking for you."

She began pulling decorations out of the box and setting them on the table.

"Can I help?" He told himself he had nothing better to do with his time right this instant, but in truth, he wanted to be here with her, enjoying her company, and watching over her. Besides, it would go faster with the two of them doing this and he figured she wouldn't mind the company either. Then when she sat down to write, he would get out of her hair.

She smiled up at him. "Yeah, sure, if you don't mind."

"Not at all." He strung the lights on the tree first.

She began hanging ornaments and he started to string red beads around the tree.

He was amazed at all the Christmas cougar ornaments his

uncle had bought that she was placing among the red, green, blue, and gold balls. He left the plaid green and red and gold bows to her to tie on the tree. "I'll hang the lights along the eaves outside."

"Thanks, that would be great."

He went to fetch the ladder, thinking this would have been easier to do before the snow came. Not that he had been here before the snow came. But he was actually enjoying helping out. He began stringing the lights and when he was done, he turned them on, the lights reflecting off the snow. It really was pretty and made him feel more lighthearted after being ambushed on the mission and returning home to learn his uncle had died. *She* made him feel more lighthearted.

Then he went inside to hang the lights around the windows. She had finally finished decorating the tree. Her little cabin in the woods was cheerful and it made him reconsider decorating the main house for Christmas.

"It looks great. Just perfect for setting the mood for writing. Especially with all the fresh snow outside also. Thanks so much for being a good sport and helping me with this," she said. "Are you ready to see if we can find any sign of the culprits in the woods?"

"Yeah, I am, and you're welcome."

They bundled up and went outside. She locked her door and then they headed off through the woods. They could have covered more ground by separating, but no way did he want to do that. They needed to stay together, just in case.

* * *

JESSIE FOUND MORE bear fur caught on a tree branch about a half mile from the cabins. She was glad they had found more evidence. At least they had a lead. "He, or they, came this way."

"Yes, I see. And some fur over here. The snow might have

covered their tracks, but they left evidence along the way that will help us to track them."

Jessie and Emerson had hiked two miles in the snow and woods when they finally came to a craft store on the main road, one car parked out front of the shop.

"How much do you want to bet they parked here and pulled off their clothes and shifted," Jessie said. "I can't imagine they would have run for miles as bears to reach us from some other location."

"Yeah. I agree."

They went to the door of the shop and Jessie opened it. A bell jingled their arrival. They went inside but didn't see any sign of bear fur, or a clerk.

A middle-aged woman dressed in a green and red plaid, wool skirt and green sweater, and a red Santa hat trimmed in faux white fur came out of a back room to greet them, looking thrilled to have some customers. "Welcome. Come in. Because of the snowstorm last night, things have been quiet today."

"Uh, yeah, I'm sure of it until they clear all the roads," Emerson said.

"You didn't have anyone at the shop last night?" Jessie asked, looking over the Christmas decorations on a tree, specifically for any cougars the woman might have.

"No. I had to close early because of the storm. No one came after about two."

"And no one broke in?" Emerson asked.

"Uh, no. What's this all about?" Frowning, the woman looked concerned.

"I inherited Whispering Pines Resort about two miles from your place as the crow flies." Or, in their case, as the cougars could walk through the snowy woods. "I'm Emerson, Paul Merriweather's nephew." He offered his hand, and she shook it.

Jessie smiled at Emerson, who cast her a smile when he didn't give the woman his full name as if she already would know it.

"I'm Jessie Whittington, a guest at the resort and come about this time every year."

"Jessie, oh, sure, Paul often mentioned you after you'd come for a stay. I'm Rachael Pringle, owner and manager of the Crafty Knick-Knack Shop. I knew Paul. I was so sorry to hear about his untimely heart attack. He was always so friendly, dropping by when he had a moment to chat it up with me." The shopkeeper glanced outside and saw they hadn't driven a car there. "You... walked from the resort?"

"It was a shock to me. I'll certainly miss him, and I wish I'd spent a lot more time with him these past few years." Emerson motioned in the direction of the resort. "And yes, we walked through the woods. Someone broke into my shed at the resort last night during the snowstorm. We tracked them here."

"We can have a look at the security cameras I have. What about yours?" Rachael asked.

"My uncle didn't have any, unfortunately."

"Oh, I have the kind that is power-generated if the electricity goes out."

"That's good. Our electric did go out last night."

"Same here," Rachael said, "both at my house and at the shop. The clocks were all wrong this morning when I showed up for work."

"I'll have to get some security videos for the resort. That's on my things to do list, including repairing the shed door."

"That's just awful. Even though I've never had any trouble, the security video just makes me feel safer. Did you report the break-in to the police?" Rachael asked.

"They didn't steal anything, so no. The police wouldn't do anything about it."

But Jessie was thinking about the bear injuring Emerson, so it wasn't just that the bears broke into his shed. Of course, they couldn't report that either, not when the police and local hunters might go on a bear hunt to shoot what had probably been bear shifters. Since shifters turned into humans at death, at least cougars did, that could put the bear shifter population at risk.

"All right. Here's the security video." Rachael showed them the monitor and played back the time last night that they'd had the break-in and the time before that.

A black SUV had parked in her lot, the snow blowing hard.

"Oh, I would never have checked my video since my place hadn't been disturbed. But the snow is blowing so hard, you can't see the people who left the vehicle. Only that they wore black and then headed into the snow. Two men though," the woman said.

"Yes. That's them," Emerson said.

Jessie wanted to see the license plate number, but the vehicle didn't have one on the front of the SUV. "We need to watch and see if the license plate is visible when they drove off." She was hoping they had changed into bears out of sight of the camera. But what if they hadn't? She glanced at Emerson.

Emerson had to be thinking the same thing, but he didn't seem concerned. It would be a disaster if they had to turn the shop owner into a cougar because she'd seen another shifter shift.

But the men hurried out of the vehicle and headed into the woods in the snow. Thank heavens.

She wished she could have seen them in their bear forms though, just so she would recognize them again. Though she supposed she would anyway because if they showed up, they would be the ones since all the non-shifting bears should be hibernating.

Then after some time, the men returned, the snow blowing even harder, obscuring the view of the camera. They got into the SUV and drove off, but they weren't able to see the license plate number. At least they knew it was two men, and they drove a black SUV. Though they hadn't really proven anything. This was all speculation on her part that they went into the woods and shifted and one of them had struck Emerson.

"Thank you," Emerson said, then he found a cougar ornament hanging on a little tree near the cash register. "I want to get this."

"Oh, I always pick up some for your uncle to collect, but he didn't manage to drop by before he died. I'm so sorry for your loss. He was always such a charmer," Rachael said again.

Emerson nodded. "He will be much missed."

"I hope that Emerson will stay here and carry on his work," Jessie said.

"Oh, I do too. I'm so glad to finally meet you. Your uncle was always talking about you and him. Whenever he heard you were returning home, he would pop in and tell me all about it."

Emerson looked glum that he'd lost his uncle before being able to say goodbye to him at the very least. She would have felt that about her parents if that had happened to one of them.

Emerson paid for the cougar. "I guess we'll head back to the resort. Thanks for letting us look at your video security."

"No problem. Do you think those men were the same ones who broke into your shed?" the woman asked.

"Yeah," Emerson said, "but there's no way to prove it." He gave the hand-painted, ceramic Christmas cougar to Jessie.

She kissed him on the cheek. "Thanks, Emerson. It's adorable." She tucked it into her pocket, and they bid Rachael goodbye, pulled on their gloves, and headed outside. "What do you think? I mean, they could have been anyone just taking a walk in the woods, not shapeshifting at all."

"I would venture to say they are the ones. They led us right here. Why else park the SUV here and then wander through the snowstorm on a walk in the woods?"

"I agree."

They began to walk back through the snow along the trail they had made.

"Okay, so the men who came to ask about me, were they wearing the same coats? Driving the same vehicle?"

"They were driving a dark blue pickup. As to coats, they were more like wool dress coats, not fur-covered parkas like the men at the shop were wearing. I'd say they were about six-two, both of them the same height. With their hoods up when they got out of the SUV, I couldn't see their faces though to identify them as the same men as the same ones who came to the house looking for you."

"I don't understand why they would break into your shed, unless it was a ruse. Beyond that, why show their faces to you and then return? If they were trying to do this in secret, why not just come back later when I was at the cabin?" She was leading the way on the path they'd made and moved a snow-laden branch aside for Emerson.

"How did they even know you were going to be at the resort? That keeps running through my mind. Maybe it has to do with one of the rogue cougars you were dating and who ended up dead. A relative or good friend with a vendetta."

She scoffed. "The key to that is that I wasn't dating a bear, but a cougar."

"True."

"Maybe it has to do with whatever your job had been or something that you had done that offended someone. You haven't told me what you worked at before you arrived here."

"But why come looking for you?"

"Do you have another question?"

He chuckled.

"It appears both bears are mostly black in color," Jessie said.

"I agree, or we would have seen some other color of fur. Sure, a few strands of brown, but mostly the coarse outer coat of black. What if it had to do with my uncle giving you a discount on lodging, and that you have been coming here for years? Maybe he had issue with someone and they thought you knew about it."

"Oh, you knew about the discount on my lodging?"

"Yeah."

"Oh, good. I figured I might have to have a fight with you over the bill when I went to check out at the end of my stay."

"I think I can do better than that. How does free sound to you?"

She glanced back at him. "Are you sure that's okay?"

"Are you kidding? You saved my life and you helped straighten out the shed after it was trashed. I wouldn't usually have guests do that when they stay here. At least, I hope not."

"Okay, thanks. I appreciate it. Do you want the CSF special agents to come up here and help us to figure this out? My sister is awaiting word on whether we want them up here or not." She wanted them to come, but she didn't know if Emerson would like the idea and want to deal with this on his own. She thought since they had gotten the best of him the one time, it might help to have some others up here looking for these men if they came here again.

"Yeah. They can stay in the other cabins. I thought of you returning home until I can figure out what's going on, but I don't want you leaving and having them follow you, if that's what they ended up doing."

"I hadn't thought of that. I would feel better if the agents were here. And I don't intend to leave. I have work to do. This is my one big vacation a year."

"All right, do you want me to call them to ask for their assistance since it's my problem, or do you want to call since you know them?" Emerson asked.

"I will." She pulled her phone out of her pocket and pulled off a glove, then called her sister. "Emerson says he wants you to send some agents to help us learn what's going on."

"Okay, I'll let them know."

"Thanks, Sis." They ended the call.

When she and Emerson arrived at the resort, she went into

his home to move her laptop and bag back to her cabin, but Emerson came with her to check things out, just in case someone broke into her place in the meantime.

But the cabin was clear, no sign of any intruders, for which she was glad.

"Are you sure you don't want to continue to stay with me until reinforcements arrive?" he asked, sounding hopeful.

"No. It's daylight. There's no snowstorm. You will be on high alert anyway." She was certain if she tried to write when he was in the living room where she was working, it would be like being with her mom and her retired dad and she wouldn't be able to get any writing done. Besides, the cabin was all decorated for Christmas, warm, welcoming, perfect holiday ambience.

"All right." He carried in some wood and kindling for her wood stove and left a lighter to light the fire if she wanted one.

"Thanks, Emerson."

"Did you want to have lunch at my place?"

"No, thanks. I write while I'm eating." She hated to keep turning him down, but she really did work better if she was by herself.

"What about dinner?"

"Same thing. I'm just here to write. Really." And she hadn't even started working on her word count yet today. Though she would love to have lunches and dinners and breakfasts with him on the days she wasn't decorating for Christmas and trying to track down bear shifters. "Maybe tomorrow, if I can get my word count done first."

"Okay, well if you need anything or feel that something isn't right—"

"Wait, I was going to see the lighthouse this afternoon actually." Which was one reason she was feeling stressed about not getting her writing started already. "If you would like to go with me, that would be fun. I'll be taking some pictures and using the descriptions for my story. But the company would be welcome."

"Yeah, sure. I've never seen it. I would love to join you."

"Never?" She was really surprised, but then again, he didn't seem to be the kind who liked family fare or resort stuff. Maybe hiking in the vast wilderness would suit him better. At least he seemed kind of like a loner to her.

"No. When I visited with my uncle, I just…visited. He didn't want to leave the resort in case anyone needed him for anything, and I wasn't interested in seeing the sights on my own."

"Well, you're in for a treat. Okay, I'll be over at one."

"I look forward to it." And he sounded like he really did and that made her glad she'd asked. He didn't have anyone that might need him at the resort so he might as well enjoy the time.

He had a spring in his step when he left the cabin, and she set up her laptop to work on the kitchen table. Then her sister called.

Jessie hadn't wanted to say anything to her sister in front of Emerson in the woods, but now, she had to have her say. "Tracey, you were supposed to investigate Emerson surreptitiously. Not go and call him about it! He told me at breakfast. Talk about a shock. You could have at least given me a heads-up!"

"His name is Emerson Merriweather."

"Oh, well, that's boring as far as the intrigue about his name goes, but it makes sense. I had thought he might have the same last name as his uncle, but then when he wouldn't tell me what it was, I figured it had to be something different."

"He was Black Ops."

Shocked, Jessie's jaw dropped before she could respond. "What?" Jessie couldn't believe it. Especially when he was willing to let others come to help them out. Still, when he went on missions, he would have a team, probably, to back him up and not have a civilian in the line of fire he would want to protect. She couldn't believe that's what his former job was though. He had been undercover! She smiled because he'd told her the truth and she had figured he was joking.

"Our retired resident CIA operative, Florence Fitzgerald? She knew he was Black Ops."

"Aliases," Jessie said. He'd told her he might have lots of aliases. He had been telling her the truth about that too, when she had thought he'd been teasing. Then she thought of his injury—the wound to his arm—a bullet wound, she was certain. He had to have gotten it on the job since it looked to be so recent. "So he's kind of a good guy?"

"That depends on which side he was on and who he killed, if he was assassinating people."

"Wow. Are you sure about this?" Already Jessie was wondering if he had anything to do with the bear that attacked him because of his former job. Here he was denying it would have anything to do with him.

Her sister sent Jessie a picture of him wearing a dress army uniform. He was a Ranger.

"Yeah, that's him." Black Ops. He looked utterly dashing in a uniform too. "What did Florence say about him? Exactly?"

"He was good at his job, and then on this last mission, she learned he just called it quits. She still has friends in high places. The mission had gone down badly, but she didn't know anything more than that. She even recommended to someone still with the CIA to recruit him for a mission after that because she knew he could get the job done, but he wouldn't do it, even though it was something he could easily have done and it would have been a good thing. But once he was finished, he was through with the business."

"Wow." He'd been shot during his mission! At least Jessie suspected that was what the wound on his arm was due to for sure now. "Then at least I should feel protected." But Jessie wondered what had gone wrong on his last mission, besides him being shot, if that's what had happened. Would he feel he couldn't talk to her about it? Maybe, because it was a secret Black Ops mission. She wanted him to know that he could. Not one word of his mission would be in her novel, nor would she tell anyone else about it.

"Yes. He's a weapons expert and knows all kinds of tricks when it comes to hand-to-hand combat."

"Does Mrs. Fitzgerald know anything about his personal life?" Tracey laughed.

Jessie frowned. "I was just wondering."

Tracey chuckled. "Yeah, right. I know you. Even if we weren't cougar shifters and I didn't know better, we're twins. I always know when you're interested in a guy." Then her voice turned more serious. "And this time, like the last times you got involved with a guy, you are headed for trouble. I mean, you already are in the middle of it!"

CHAPTER 7

"You're Black Ops?" Jessie said to Emerson after lunch when he collected her to drive to the Split Rock Lighthouse. She'd had the hardest time forcing herself not to call him as soon as she and her sister had ended their call once she had learned of it and grilling him about it, though she suspected he wouldn't fill her in on anything about his job.

"What?" He frowned at her, looking surprised that she would know about it.

"Don't tell me you don't know what I'm talking about." Even though he was probably indoctrinated with the notion that he couldn't ever tell anyone about it. "My sister—"

"Learned this through the Fish and Wildlife Services sources?" He sounded incredulous.

"No. We have cougars who are retired from the FBI and CIA in Yuma Town."

"No way could they have learned about me. It's ultra-secret. Unsanctioned. Very few know about it. And they're not supposed to be telling anyone about the missions in any event."

She sighed, hoping he wouldn't get mad if she told him who

had known and had shared it with her sister. "Florence Fitzgerald?"

"Hawk One?"

"Hawk One. Oh, that's so cool." Jessie smiled.

Emerson shook his head. "Nobody's supposed to know about what I do."

"We're a cougar family. We watch out for each other."

"And she had to sign a non-disclosure agreement like everybody else."

"She's a cougar. And if it means protecting the people she cares about…" Jessie shrugged. "She's going to do it."

He let out his breath in exasperation.

"I understand why you couldn't tell me before. But what if this has something to do with one of your missions?"

"The men were asking for you. Maybe you were writing about someone in one of your books and it hit too close to home."

They arrived at the lighthouse and parked. "I did mostly picture books."

"For little kids?" He sounded surprised.

"No, photographic books. Like of ghost towns, or coral reefs, of winter scenes in Colorado. This is the first time I'll be writing a purely fictional, paranormal romance. I wanted to do something different."

"I can't imagine books on photography would pose a problem."

"I can't either. And that they think any of my books would involve your uncle. Why not my parents then? I live with them all year long when I'm not gallivanting around the country working on a book."

She paid for their admission to the lighthouse, though he had his credit card out to do so, but she had invited him and she wanted to do this, especially since he was letting her stay at the cabin rent-free.

"Thanks," he said.

"You're welcome. After you helped me decorate for Christmas, it was the least I could do. Besides, I invited you."

"I have to admit, your cabin looks nice after we decorated it."

"It does." Just like when she'd visited the resort in the past.

They walked through the grounds until they reached the lighthouse and went inside. She took pictures of the original lantern in the lighthouse when it was completed in 1910 and the winding stairs and the view of Lake Superior from the windows while Emerson talked to the lighthouse keeper who was wearing the costume of the period. It had been restored to what it had looked like in the 1920s. Then they went to the lightkeeper's home to see the way they lived back then.

She hadn't thought Emerson would be impressed, but he said, "This is a pretty cool place."

"It is. I'm glad we came to see it together."

After that, they headed outside to take the path that would give them views of the lighthouse up on the cliffs from a distance.

It was beautiful. Emerson seemed to be enjoying it too and she was glad he had come with her. She hadn't been sure he would like seeing all this stuff, especially given what his job had been. It shouldn't change her view of him as far as her perception of what might or might not interest him now. He didn't need to be at the resort for other guests, and just in case the trouble followed her here, she was glad he was here with her.

"I guess you can't talk about what you did while on your job," she said as they made their way to the steps that would take them to the rocky shore. On the way down, she was taking more pictures of the lighthouse in the distance way high up on the rocks and the waves churned up down below, the snow and ice on the rocky shore.

"Nope."

"Not even if it's about this case and me knowing what had happened might help us figure stuff out?"

"No, I can't. I don't want you involved in any of that."

She glanced at his arm. "You were shot. In the arm. I knew it. That's what you were taking antibiotics for. An ear infection." She scoffed. "I knew you weren't taking antibiotics for an ear infection." She took some more pictures of the lighthouse and rocks.

He didn't confirm or deny it.

She glanced down at the rest of the stairs they had to walk down and could imagine leaping down the 174 stairs in a race to the bottom to see if she could beat Emerson. Since he was a bigger male cougar, he would probably get there first.

"I would beat you," Emerson said, as if he'd known just what she'd been thinking.

She laughed. "You read minds just like the characters in my psychic story."

He chuckled. "If we were here, alone in the dark after the place was closed, I would be willing to race you."

"I would love to prove you wrong."

They took a walk on the trail through the woods after that. Nobody was out here but them and she really was glad for the company. At least they were dressed for the cold, crunching on the snow, and then he wrapped his arm around her shoulders.

"Okay, so I already know you were wounded, shot probably, and that probably has something to do with the last mission you were on," she said, unable to let go of the notion that something bad had happened to him and what if it would help him get through it by talking to her about it? Or anyone, really. Maybe he would feel better.

"You're right." He sighed.

Ohmigod, she could not believe he would really tell her about it. She wanted to prompt him for more information, but she was trying to let him reveal what he felt comfortable in speaking with her about.

They walked for a long distance in the snowy woods and neither of them said anything. A hairy woodpecker was rat-a-tat-

tatting on a tree a few feet away high above and a red cardinal flew off nearby, his red-beaked mate flying off to join him, catching their attention.

"Most of the team I led were wounded on the last mission. One died. We were really close to losing another team member," Emerson finally said.

Instantly, Jessie glanced up at him, saw the sorry in the lines etched in Emerson's face and felt bad about it. She had thought he'd been wounded, and that maybe felt he'd let his team down. Maybe he had, but she'd never expected him to tell her all of his team members had been wounded and one had died.

"I'm so sorry."

"It was supposed to be a mission to rescue little kids at a school."

"Oh no." She could imagine the worst-case scenario—that the kids hadn't made it either.

"There was no rescue mission."

"What?" She looked up at him, but he was looking at the woods ahead of them.

"It was a setup. The man who contracted us to do the job set us up. We were ambushed. There were no kids, there was no rescue mission. It was all a ruse to get us there and eliminate us."

"Why?" She couldn't believe it.

"Maybe we'd made some enemies on an earlier mission. We really don't know. Smith, the man who sent us on the mission, no doubt would have been paid off handsomely. He knows he'll have to finish us off because we'll want his head."

She pulled Emerson to a stop. "Wait. You were on a mission where someone had a contract on your life and you don't think any of what happened to you at the cabins has anything to do with it?"

"No." He pulled her along to walk again with him. "They wouldn't have left me alive."

Okay, that made sense. "This Smith got away with it."

"I will find him and deal with him."

"What about the other team members that made it out alive?"

"We had secret identities. Smith isn't really his name. I didn't go by Emerson. We had made-up home addresses, we were all orphans, no families, no girlfriends—"

"Well, that's good to know," she said, matter-of-factly.

He smiled down at her and she was glad she could lighten the mood a bit.

"I mean, for any woman who got interested in you when here you might already have a family, girlfriend, whatever, but it was all a great secret. That means you and your team are going after him? Together?" She thought it would be safer if they did.

"I did some searching. I haven't come up with anything yet. But I have every intention of getting him."

She squeezed Emerson's hand. And then she realized the cougars coming to watch their backs could help him find this Smith. "The CSF! They go after, oh, he's probably human."

"No. You're right. He's a cougar."

"Oh, good. I mean, it's not good that a cougar would do something like that to you and your team mates, but that's just the kind of mission the CSF agents do."

"I don't know that they'd ever find him, but it wouldn't hurt to get them involved."

"I bet you couldn't believe you would come home from a dangerous mission like that and be attacked at the resort."

"You can say that again."

They walked in silence for a while.

"Do you have a picture of Smith?" she asked.

"No. But I can describe him. He has short black hair, blue eyes, a cleft in his chin, and ears that stand out."

"That sounds like a guy I've dated."

"A rogue who was terminated," Emerson said.

"No. He was a cougar I see every once in a while."

"Oh, the one that got away." Emerson smiled.

"That was a different cat. And he only got away if some other she-cat didn't do him in. You know some cougars can be mighty possessive of their man."

"Not you though."

She sighed. "He was so not worth it."

"Did you meet the one you were still seeing in Loveland?"

"No. The second time I met him, I was doing a book on the wildlife up here, the wolves of Isle Royale National Park, the bears in the wilderness, moose, deer, and I even had to feature the Bigfoot at one of the restaurants down south. Anyway, I met him there."

"You didn't warn the cougar who was seeing other she-cats what your family and friends do to rogue cougars?"

She smiled at Emerson. "He wasn't a keeper or worth it." But then she grew serious. "I'm so sorry about your team though. Is your arm all right?"

"Yeah, it's getting better daily."

"I hope it was okay for me to talk to you about this."

"Normally, I wouldn't have told you a thing about it. But I'm glad I had you to talk to about it."

When she had first arrived at the resort, she would never had thought he'd come home from such a horrible mission. Between that and returning home after learning his uncle had died, she understood why Emerson had seemed so dark and brooding.

She took a deep breath of the scent of pines and the fresh snow. It was a good hike, but as much as she ran as a cougar, she was in good shape. He seemed to be also—he must have had to be for the kind of work he was doing. It would be fun to run here as cougars when the place was closed.

"Thanks for asking me to come with you," he said again.

"I had to bring my bodyguard." She squeezed his gloved hand with hers. "When was the last time you saw your uncle?" She realized of all the years she'd been coming up here before Christmas, not once had she seen Emerson here, and Mr. Merriweather had never mentioned he had a nephew.

"Last summer."

"A year and a half ago?" She couldn't help sounding incredible. Family meant everything to her, though she guessed Emerson's work would preclude his taking off at any time he wanted to either to see his uncle, unlike if he'd worked at a normal nine-to-five job. He'd probably been all over the world, even.

"Yeah. When you do what I do, you have to work. Sometimes between assignments I would just say I had to take off and I would come in to see my uncle. He knew I could show up anytime because I never let anyone know where I was going to be."

"What about your parents?"

"They died in a boating mishap on Lake Superior when I was ten—it was an adult boating trip, and I was home with my aunt and uncle. They ended up raising me."

"Oh, I'm so sorry." She thought it was awful that he'd lost his parents too. "Do you have any siblings?"

"No. And my aunt and uncle never had any children. So I didn't have any cousins growing up either."

He had no family at all. No wonder Christmas wasn't a big priority for him. "Was your uncle's heart attack a surprise to you?"

"Yeah, sure. He never mentioned that he had any health problems."

"Were you on the mission still when you got word he had died?"

"I was just coming home from it, but it was already too late. I was going to surprise him with the fact that I'd left my work for good. I never expected him to die of a heart attack. I thought I would be living there with him, helping him with the upkeep and spending a lot more time with him." He shook his head. "I never expected this."

"I'm so sorry, Emerson. He didn't tell you about any concerns he had before he died?"

"When I was on a mission, he really couldn't get a hold of me. Of course now, I really regret it."

"He didn't leave you any cryptic notes before he died?"

Emerson paused on their walk to watch a black squirrel scamper up a tree and she watched it too. "I never suspected foul play," Emerson said.

"What if someone gave him a heart attack? What if it wasn't just fate?" she asked.

Emerson began walking again and so did Jessie, but this time he seemed to be pondering the notion.

"Okay, no. I'm used to freeing hostages, eliminating kidnappers and any other kinds of situations that required my training, but I'm not one to believe in conspiracy theories. No one would be after my uncle. He wasn't the sort of person who created enemies."

"I've read mystery stories for years. I'm used to thinking in terms of 'what if.'"

"Like Miss Marple."

"Exactly. There's probably nothing to it, but what if some men, the two in particular, were looking for me because they had learned I arrived at the resort at the same time every year and I am friends with your uncle. He's got something they want. A treasure? Evidence of a crime, something. They try to get it out of him and he had a heart attack. Were guests at the resort at the time?"

"Yes. Everyone had to leave since there was no proprietor at the resort any longer. I refunded everyone their money for their whole stay here, even if they'd been there for part of their vacation already."

"You couldn't have let them stay?"

"If I'd been back there, sure. I hadn't returned yet. The only recourse I had was to refund them their money."

"Okay, I understand. So the autopsy revealed he'd had a massive heart attack, right?"

"Yes."

"Had any of the guests witnessed it? Was he alone when it happened? At night? During the day?"

"It was at night. I don't know if anyone had seen him have it. After I learned about his death, I checked with the doctor concerning my uncle's heart condition. The doctor said my uncle hadn't had any trouble as far as he had known and then suddenly, he died of a heart attack. It happens."

"Right."

"Is this going in your book?"

She suspected Emerson was afraid she would be writing this about his uncle. "No. Not unless he was psychic and it has some resemblance to him. The main characters are psychic, and there's no uncle in the story. Even then, I'm writing fiction. Did your uncle have any idea you might be quitting your job and moving here for good?"

"No. I didn't even know until the last mission and what had happened there and then I was done with it all."

They were still walking through the pristine woods. It was so pretty out here, snow covering the sides of trees and sitting on top of shelf mushrooms and the sun glistened on the sparkling snowflakes.

But Jessie couldn't shut her mind down as she thought about when she first had arrived at the resort and immediately had noticed that there were no Christmas decorations in sight. It had been a vague thought at the time and the implication hadn't really fully registered until now. "I was thinking about something else that's bothering me about this whole situation. Why hadn't your uncle decorated the resort, the cabins, his house, everything for Christmas already?"

"Pardon?" Emerson sounded genuinely perplexed by her question.

"The cabins? The house? He always decorated everything before Thanksgiving even, he told me. He liked making the resort sparkle. Unless you took everything down after you returned home because he had died and nobody but me was going to be there." That to her was a big mystery. A clue? Something Mr. Merriweather thought his nephew should notice to indicate something wasn't quite what it seemed.

* * *

EMERSON COULDN'T BELIEVE the way Jessie's mind worked overtime to solve mysteries. She was really good at it.

"You're right," he conceded after he thought about it. "He would have decorated everything for the holidays, both for Thanksgiving and Christmas. He liked for his guests to feel they were enjoying their holidays just like if they were celebrating them at home. It was all because one year he had taken a Christmas cruise with my aunt when I came home from the army and I managed things for them. He said they hadn't decorated the ship at all for the holidays and when they got home, Uncle Paul vowed to always have the Christmas lights and trees up early for their guests so they would feel the special celebration at a home away from home."

"So don't you think that doesn't add up?"

"Yeah, unless he was feeling poorly."

"Did you talk to anyone who said he was?"

"No. I didn't think there was any reason to."

"Right. No foul play. Where would he have left a cryptic message for you if he had? That only you would think to find?" They were getting close to the walk up to the lighthouse and homes that the lightkeepers had lived in.

Emerson smiled at her and shook his head.

"Those men were after something. *That* you can't deny. What about money? In the estate you inherited? Do you know if it was all there?" Jessie asked.

"I didn't know exactly how much he had, but I thought he had about a million and a half more in stock, bonds, and mutual funds. I just wasn't sure. He could have lost money on the stock market, invested more into the resort property, I just don't know. Now, if the majority of the money had been gone, I would figure someone had given him a heart attack and stolen his money."

"How much was left? If you don't mind me asking."

"Fifteen and a half million. Some of the money I'd given to him, knowing my life could be cut short at any time in the work I was doing. I made damn good money for the hairy missions I was on. I thought he could use it if something happened to me. I didn't realize he'd built up quite a nest egg also. And seeing the funds in there was a reason I didn't suspect anything was amiss."

"Okay, so with that much money left, I doubt he was murdered for it. But here's another idea, just something that slipped into my head—"

Emerson guessed what she was going to say right before she said it. "He's not dead. I've considered that too since the heart-attack scenario just came out of the blue, though there weren't any real red flags that said anything bad had happened."

"Did you see his body?"

"No. The doctor was a friend of his and he identified the body."

"Was his doctor friend a cougar, perchance?" she asked.

"No."

"And you didn't see his body?"

Which was another reason he was beginning to have some doubts now that Jessie was raising them. "No. The family doctor told me my uncle had wanted a closed-casket funeral."

"Hmm. Maybe your uncle witnessed something and he's in witness protection? Or on his own in hiding?"

Hell, Emerson sure hoped not. He shook his head. "Here I thought it was a simple matter of a heart attack."

"It still might be."

"Except for the two men who came to the resort looking for you and something else." Though he was hoping beyond hope that his uncle was alive and well, and if so, he was taking down whoever was involved in his need to disappear.

"You're not going to exhume the coffin, are you?" she asked. "Well, I guess you might not have been able to do a winter burial though, were you?"

"No, he's in a family crypt, indoors, private mausoleum. My parents' coffins are also in the crypt." And that gave him the idea they had to check his uncle's coffin out.

"Ahh, okay, that means we can investigate it without anyone being there or seeing what we're doing." She let out her breath. "Are we going to check it out? I mean, if he is alive and he's trying to hide that fact, if we open up a tomb to find him, someone might learn of it and he could be at more risk."

"I have to. I need to know if he's alive or not. If he's in Witness Protection, I have to know that."

"If he is, you're back in the Black Ops business."

"Yeah. I didn't plan to ever get back into the business, but if my uncle is alive and someone is threatening his life? They'll pay." Emerson would do no less where his uncle was concerned.

She sighed. "I might have opened a can of worms over this. And so close to Christmas too. I'm sorry."

"Don't be. If I have a second chance at being there for my uncle, I'm taking it." Emerson was praying Jessie's hunch was correct.

"I'm going with you to the cemetery." She sounded like she was worried he would leave her behind.

"Yeah, because I don't want you to be alone at the resort."

"So that means you want me to stay with you tonight?"

He smiled down at her.

She sighed dramatically.

"Hey, your sister checked me out, remember? And she didn't say I was bad news, did she?"

"I would say you were bad to the bone, at least where the bad guys are concerned."

CHAPTER 8

*A*fter enjoying the visit to the lighthouse and the trail hike, Emerson drove Jessie in the opposite direction from Whispering Pines, to her surprise. She wondered if he had decided to go to the cemetery now instead of going straight back to the resort. "Where are we going?" Jessie was thinking that she really needed to get to work on her word count for her novel if she was to get it done today before they went to the cemetery.

"We're going to a tree farm to get a real tree for my place like my uncle always did."

She smiled, surprised about that, but she thought maybe she had made him feel more in the Christmas spirit and she was glad if that was so.

"My uncle always had artificial trees for the cabins, but he always had a real tree in his own home to bring in the scent of the woods inside. He felt it made it feel more Christmas like. After discussing how he always decorated the resort for the holidays, I feel the need to carry forth his tradition. It's only right."

"Are you sure you want to go to all that trouble?" she asked.

"Yeah, I haven't celebrated Christmas except every so often. It's about the Christmas cheer, not just about present giving."

"Seriously." She felt bad that he hadn't been able to spend that much time with his uncle and she thought it would be sad if he didn't have any family to celebrate Christmas with this year especially since he was finally home for the holidays and his uncle was gone. "Okay, sure. Listen, I was thinking, you don't have any guests at the resort for Christmas. I'll be gone before then. You need to come out to my sister and her mate's horse ranch outside of Yuma Town and enjoy Christmas with us—feasting, playing games, family and friends. I don't want you to be alone."

He smiled. "But—"

"My sister has already checked you out. You're good to go."

He chuckled, but he didn't agree or disagree. She really hoped he would join them for Christmas. It would be awful to think of him just sitting in the house at the empty resort all alone for the holidays. She was almost thinking of staying here with him so he wouldn't be alone, if he didn't feel comfortable about meeting her whole family for Christmas. Which could be understandable. That could be a little overwhelming, particularly since they weren't even dating.

They dropped by a Christmas farm and wandered through it until they found a six-foot tall tree, perfect to set up in the corner of his living room. She loved the artificial tree in her cabin, but a real tree was so nice and fragrant.

When they got home, she asked, "Do you like eggnog and brandy? I'll go get some and we can have it while we're decorating the tree and putting up the lights. It's one of our family traditions." She was looking forward to seeing all the Christmas decorations. Here she thought she would be working on her word count, but she couldn't let him do this alone. Not after he helped decorate her cabin so she could be in the Christmas spirit for writing.

* * *

"Sure, thanks, Jessie." Emerson couldn't believe how good he felt about the holidays with Jessie being here, though the downside of all this would be she would leave before Christmas actually arrived. He could only visit her for the next few days. And he realized how short that time really was. He wasn't sure about seeing her family for Christmas. He couldn't imagine staying with her protective family and being scrutinized.

Without Jessie asking him to do so, he started playing Christmas music and went out to the shed to get more Christmas decorations. By the time he arrived at the house with the box of decorations, he figured Jessie would have brought the eggnog and brandy and returned to the house. She'd turned on the Christmas lights at her place, the tree lit up in the window, and the ones hanging from the house shining brightly in a multitude of colors. She was probably using the bathroom or maybe she had gotten a call from her sister.

But after the bear incident, he couldn't take the chance that everything was all right.

He hurried to her cabin and knocked on the door. There wasn't any answer.

"Jessie!" He unlocked the door and tore inside. The eggnog was sitting on the counter, the fridge door wide open. Hell. He practically threw the carton of eggnog in the fridge and slammed the door shut, just in case he was jumping to conclusions and she was just fine. Then he saw her clothes on the back patio. She had shifted? That surprised the hell out of him.

He tore off his clothes and shifted, then raced out through the cougar door as a big cat. If the bears were back, at least they couldn't fit through the cougar doors.

His heart was beating pell-mell, worried she was in a world of danger. Why didn't she alert him? No time?

At least he could follow her scent easily, and he could see her trail, but two bears had made a path through the snow too. Or bear shifters, to be exact.

He snarled a cougar warning, telling her and telling them he was coming. A cougar would have to move quickly to stay out of the bears' reach, but with their springy action, they could do it. Then he thought of the nightmare she'd told him about this morning—how she'd been treed by a bear and leaped into a tree while the bear climbed up to reach her.

Two cougars fighting against two bears wasn't a real contest. If there had been only one bear, they could chase it off. He was afraid this was going to go only one way. Terminate them, when he hadn't wanted to do any more of that. Still, he wasn't about to let them hurt Jessie, if he could reach her in time. He was glad she was calling her law enforcement friends in Yuma Town to aid them when he'd never had to rely on anyone but himself and occasionally a small team of operatives, who he knew well—but only on Black Ops' missions.

He heard her call out to him as a cougar, not in fear or that she was hurt, but saying she was okay, safe, waiting for him. She was straight ahead. He ran in her direction and saw her sitting on a branch in a tree, but there was no sign of the bears. There was no scent from them either. They were still wearing hunter concealment. Which meant they had to know he and Jessie were cougars or they wouldn't have to hide their scent.

He ran to the tree and leaped up into it to join Jessie and nuzzled her face, both their hearts drumming like crazy. He wanted to reassure her in the worst way that she would be safe with him. Why had she run? Why had the bears returned?

They needed to get to the house. He didn't know what to think, but at least at the house he had an arsenal of guns. He wasn't letting her stay at the cabin on her own any longer. Not after what had happened. He even had it in mind that she should return home, but he was worried they would follow her there and run her off the road. What the hell did they want?

He coaxed Jessie to come with him and then he jumped down into the snow. He waited for her to come to him. She jumped down into the snow, licked his face, glanced in the direction the bears had taken off, and then she raced him back to the resort. He ran after her, glad she was safe, but he didn't want to let her out of his sight again.

As soon as they reached her cabin and went inside, they shifted and she shut the back door of her cabin. They both started dressing. Once he had on his boxer briefs and pants and she had on her panties, jeans and bra, she surprised him by pulling him into her arms and kissing him.

"Thanks, for coming to my rescue. I did have them just where I wanted them though."

Smiling a little, he arched a brow. "Really? Did I mess up your plans?" He couldn't imagine she could think she could take them down.

"No. I was glad you arrived when you did."

"So what happened? Exactly?" he asked.

"They were in the cabin. I had set the eggnog on the counter and was about to close the fridge door when the two of them headed outside. They'd been in the house."

"You chased after them? I thought they'd gone after you."

"No. I chased them."

"Jessie." He shook his head. He couldn't believe she was so fearless.

"No, I was okay. They didn't seem to want to hurt me."

"Really. But what if they had?"

"You were coming to my rescue."

He couldn't understand what was going on. "I want you to move in with me."

She laughed. "You sure move fast."

He smiled. "Well, I was going to say I would be there for your protection, but maybe I should say I need to be there for the bears' protection."

"Exactly." She smiled brightly at him.

"They couldn't grab anything as bears. If they were looking for something in your cabin, how could they?"

"They were naked first. Men."

His jaw dropped. "Hell."

"Yeah, I thought so too. A naked black-haired man with a beard, both about six-two or so. The other guy had brown hair and a brown beard, longer, shaggier."

"That sounds like the men in the blue pickup that I saw. Did you get pictures of them?" He didn't think she would have had time. He hadn't taken pictures of them either when he'd seen them in their human forms, but he'd had no reason to at the time, or at least he hadn't thought he had. He really thought she had invited them to visit with her at the resort.

She got her cell phone out and handed it to him. "I have to help my friends in Yuma Town to figure out who these guys are."

He eyed the photo of them. "Yeah that's them. And they didn't see you taking a picture of them?" He was surprised they didn't wrench her phone away from her and take it with them, at the very least.

"They were too busy trying to get out of the cabin. The door was locked and they had come through the cougar door as humans and left the same way, then shifted outside."

"Okay, well let's get you out of here. I'll help you pack everything and you'll move in with me. Remember, you've already had me checked out, so we're good for staying together."

"All right. You're Florence Fitzgerald approved, so that's important."

"She better have." He loaded up Jessie's food in a box and put it in the trunk of her car. Then he helped her with her bags. He was glad she was agreeable about coming with him, but he couldn't believe she had run after the bears! They could have easily killed her. Which made him again wonder what they were after and why they hadn't hurt her.

"They didn't even make an effort to stop and scare me off,"

she said as he got into her car and she drove it to his garage and parked inside.

"I just don't know what to make of it," he said.

"Well, for now, we're going to decorate your tree and put up your lights. And have cheerful Christmas thoughts. So what do you want for Christmas?" She grabbed a couple of her bags.

"I just get what I need when I need it. Christmas presents aren't necessary." He grabbed the big box of groceries.

They finished carrying in her food and other items. Then they put the perishable food in his fridge and her canned items in the cupboards. He helped carry her bags into the guest bedroom.

"I don't blame you. Sorry, I guess since you've been alone and haven't been celebrating a lot of Christmases, you wouldn't make any Christmas lists." She helped him set up the tree in the stand in the living room in one corner next to the fireplace.

Even before they began decorating it, it made the room seem more cheerful to him. Well, truth be told, Jessie was what made the whole place seem warmer and more cheerful.

"Yeah, that's about right. Uncle Paul would send a care package, and I'd send him some things he would like. I guess with him being gone this year, I just haven't really given it a thought." He had. Not in a Christmas gift-giving way, but that he would miss his uncle.

"I don't blame you."

Emerson and Jessie began to hang up decorations on the tree.

"I love the ornaments. When I'd come to get movies from your uncle, I always enjoyed seeing them." She made them some eggnog and brandy and gave Emerson a glass.

They clinked their glasses together. "To solving a mystery," he said.

"To making new friends," she said. "So what would you like for Christmas?"

He smiled.

She drank some of her eggnog and put the glass down on the

coffee table, then hung some more ornaments. "You have to tell me or you could end up with something you don't want."

"What do you want for Christmas?" he asked, not expecting this turn of events. He suspected she felt that he needed to have a present or two and she'd feel better about it. He would get her a couple of gifts also in the spirit of Christmas giving.

She pulled her phone from her pocket. "My list." She handed him her phone.

He laughed as he looked over all the gifts she had listed on her account.

"For birthdays and Christmas. I just put things on there when I need something important."

"A new laptop."

"Yes, like that. It's not that anyone will get it for me, but if family members went together to get it for me, I'd be all set. It beats just getting stuff you don't really need or want."

He hung up some ornaments. "Okay, then I'll have to think about it and add a couple of things to my list."

"Lots of things. Because you never know what people will be able to afford to get you."

"So I go for inexpensive things."

"No, just an assortment. What if they want to give you something really expensive? So give a list of all kinds of things. And not just stuff you need, but fun stuff you'd like to have."

"All right." He hoped she didn't plan to give the list to the rest of her family.

They finished decorating the tree, and he said, "I'm going to hang the lights outside."

"I'll help you."

"I was thinking you could work on your story, if you would like." After everything they'd done today, and with plans to go to the cemetery tonight, he was afraid she wouldn't have time to get all her writing in.

"I need to. I got part of my word count done before we went

to see the lighthouse. I'll do the rest after we get the lights up on your house. I want to help you with this." She was already putting her coat back on and there looked to be no dissuading her.

"Okay, thanks." He realized he really enjoyed decorating the tree with her. It wouldn't have been the same without her. He certainly wouldn't have bothered if it hadn't been for her coming here and wanting her cabin decorated for Christmas.

He also wanted to give her the quiet time she needed while she worked on her story and not disturb her, and he still wanted to go to the crypt and see if his uncle was really interned there. But he would have to take her with him. Not only wouldn't he risk leaving her alone at the resort, he would need her to help him remove the coffin.

"So when do we go to the crypt?" he asked her as he brought the ladder out of the shed and she untangled the outdoor lights.

"Tonight? We'll try to do it without anyone being aware of it." She finished untangling one strand and plugged it in to make sure all the lights were working.

"Yeah. When we get inside, we'll need to pull off the bronze rosettes, the decorative marble cover, and then unscrew the plastic cover and we're in. The coffin is on the bottom, so we can pull it out." He was glad he had watched them seal it so he knew what was at stake.

"Okay. I sure hope we discover he's not there."

"Me too." That was enough of a Christmas present for him. Well, and finding his uncle was safe somewhere was next.

They hung up the Christmas lights around the house, admired how pretty it was, though tonight it would be even better, and then they went inside to warm up.

"I'm going to fix us some dinner while you work on your story." He took their empty eggnog glasses into the kitchen, and he realized just how much he wanted to impress Jessie, even though he'd never worried about doing that for a woman—ever.

CHAPTER 9

*J*essie uploaded pictures on her laptop that she had taken at the lighthouse and on their walk. Then she began typing away on her story. She was so glad Emerson had wanted to decorate for Christmas since she was now sitting in his house working on her Christmas story. The tree smelled heavenly, and she thought he was so sweet to have put Christmas music on in the background.

"Do pork chops, mashed potatoes, and asparagus sound good to you for dinner?" he asked.

"Yeah, sure, that would be great." She got a call from Leyton Hill, Dr. Kate's mate, and she was so relieved, assuming he was going to tell her who was coming to help them out from CSF. "Hi, are you the one who's coming to aid us?" she asked Leyton.

"Yeah, and Chet Kensington is on his way also from Cheyenne, Wyoming. Jack Barrington's riding up with me. All of us should be there by tomorrow night."

"Okay, good. We had another incident. The bears were in my cabin and then took off."

"As bears?" Leyton sounded astounded.

"Naked men and then they shifted outside."

"Hell. Are you okay?"

"Yeah, thanks, Leyton. I'm staying with Emerson now, just for safety reasons."

"Okay, good. We've checked him out as much as we could, given his secret ops missions, but Florence vouched for him."

"That's good." She smiled, glad Emerson had given that job up. "You can stay in my cabin. It has enough room for all three of you. Oh, and we have another mission for you but this might wait until after Christmas." She explained about Emerson's last mission.

"Hell, Jessie. He sounds like a dangerous man to be around." Leyton sounded worried about her but she felt safe with him.

"Who? Smith? I'd say so." She knew he was talking about Emerson, but…

"No. Emerson. Tell him he'd better stay with you at all times."

"He knows to." Then they ended the call and she typed some more on her story.

"What do I know to do?" Emerson asked as he cooked the meal.

"Stay with me at all times."

"That's a given. Was that a call from our reinforcements?"

"Yeah." She told Emerson who all was coming.

"Three Cougar Shifter Force special agents?" Emerson sounded surprised that many would join them.

"Yeah. When it comes to protecting one of their own, and you now fall under that umbrella—"

"Because we're dating…"

She laughed. "Leyton said you were dangerous to be around. His boss, Chuck Warner, immediately sanctioned the mission. He's only three hours from here in White Bear Lake, so if we need his help, he'll be up here pronto."

"Oh, good. You mentioned Smith to him. What did he think about that?"

"They'll go after him for sure. They'll be here tomorrow night."

"You told them about the bears in your cabin, but you didn't mention the mausoleum visit tonight."

"No, they would probably want us to wait until they arrive. If you want to, we can, but I'm eager to check it out, aren't you?" She would think about it all night long if they didn't.

"Yeah, I want to look into it tonight. I wouldn't be able to sleep without knowing the truth."

"Okay, then it's decided." She went back to typing on her story, pausing to think of where she was going next with it, and typing more of the scene and starting the next. Before long, the aroma of the pork chops cooking made her mouth water. She stopped typing to help Emerson set the table.

"I was going to do that so you could keep working on your story," he said.

"I can't when the food smells so good."

He smiled and started dishing up the food.

"Thanks for dinner."

"Thanks for joining me and helping me decorate for Christmas."

"Well, once I ended up at your place, I needed the Christmas ambience over here, you know." They sat down to eat. "Are you prepared for what we'll discover in the mausoleum?" She wasn't sure that she would be. Find a body? Don't find a body? And if they didn't find a body, then what? Had Mr. Merriweather's body been stolen or had he never been in the coffin? Then she thought of Nina's dream about an empty coffin—and thought—it hadn't been a dream after all.

"Yeah. I'm hoping beyond hope he isn't in there."

She prayed Emerson could be reunited with his uncle, if he was still alive.

* * *

AFTER DINNER and cleaning up the dishes, Emerson grabbed a backpack with a flashlight, lantern, and other tools, and he drove Jessie out to the cemetery and parked. They walked through the snow to the granite Greek-style mausoleum where Barnaby and Melissa Merriweather and Family was engraved on the top, while beautiful Corinthian pillars framed the front.

"My aunt and uncle had decided to commission the mausoleum when my parents died, and so my aunt and uncle and parents are interred here, though they had never found my parents' bodies in Lake Superior."

"Oh, I'm so sorry." She wondered if Emerson ever felt his parents might still be discovered while he was growing up. She thought it was worse not knowing.

Emerson pulled out a lantern from his backpack, turned it on, and unlocked the door. Then they went inside and shut the door and he set the lantern on a granite bench inside. They pried off the brass rosettes first from the marble plate. Then they carefully removed the marble plate. He brought out a couple of screwdrivers from his backpack and they removed the screws securing the plastic cover.

"What are you going to do about putting this all back together?" She suspected they wouldn't be able to put it together again, so that it looked like it was professionally done.

"I've got the calking to use to reseal it if my uncle is in the coffin. If he isn't, I want to make it appear as though he still is, just in case anyone gets in here to check things out like we're doing."

They pulled at the coffin, though she was thinking that they should have waited for her friends to assist them. She struggled to help Emerson get the coffin out. Since this was a private family mausoleum, she was thinking they could get the guys to help them move the coffin back in place tomorrow, unless Emerson's uncle was in the coffin and he really felt he had to put him back in his proper place right after they discovered the truth.

Then they managed to pull the coffin out, set it on the floor, and they both took a deep breath.

Emerson said, "Unless I'm mistaken, it feels too light to contain my uncle's body."

"You know, I was thinking that too." Though she hadn't wanted to get her hopes up too much despite praying Nina's dream was truly a vision about this. Jessie didn't want to see Mr. Merriweather's remains if he was in there. She wanted to remember him as he was before, greeting her cheerfully at the resort whenever she visited.

"Are you ready?" Emerson asked, appearing as apprehensive about learning the truth as she was.

"Yeah. But I'm not going to look."

"Okay." He opened the casket. "Hell."

"He's not in there?" She had to look and peeked inside. The casket was pristine.

"Yeah, it's an empty casket. And from the smell of it, no body has ever been in it."

"Wow." She sighed. "It's empty." She really couldn't believe it. She'd been hopeful, but she hadn't believed it could be true or that Nina had predicted this. "And I agree—there's no scent or odor that indicates any body has ever been in there. So he's really not dead?"

"Hopefully not or he would be in here."

"Are you relieved?" she asked.

"Kind of. I am if he's alive and well, but if he's in danger, then no. What the hell is going on?"

"What if he's being protected? Then if we go searching for him, we could put him at risk." She hoped they hadn't done the wrong thing in trying to learn the truth. Not that she or Emerson would tell anyone but family and the CSF agents, but still, if someone was following them to see where they might go, then they might realize what she and Emerson had learned.

"What if he needs protection and he's not being protected well enough?" Emerson asked.

"True."

Emerson glanced down at the casket. "Your friends are arriving tomorrow night, right?"

"Yes."

"Do you think they would mind if we ask them to help us with putting the casket back in place?"

"Oh, no, they wouldn't mind at all. I was hoping that they could." She was relieved. The coffin might be empty, but it was still unwieldy.

"Sorry. I should have considered that before I had you help me with this."

"I was like you. I couldn't have slept tonight without knowing one way or another either."

Then they left the crypt and locked the door and headed through the snow to his car.

"I should call Leyton, who is in charge of their little team of CSF agents, to tell him what we found," she said, as she got into Emerson's car.

"Sure," Emerson said as he drove them back to the resort. "Do you want to use my Bluetooth and we can listen in together to see what he has to say?"

"Yeah, that would be great." She gave him Leyton's number and then Emerson called it.

"Hey, this is Emerson Merriweather."

"Leyton. Is everything okay?" He sounded darkly worried.

Jessie didn't blame him. She was worried too. "We checked out Emerson's uncle's coffin. It's in a mausoleum, but the coffin was empty and there has never been a body in it. The funeral had a closed casket."

"He's alive?" Leyton asked, sounding incredulous.

"Hopefully," Jessie said.

"We're going to need to talk to the doctor again about the

supposed surprise massive heart attack my uncle had. He had no history of a heart condition, according to the doctor. I thought maybe my uncle had been hiding it from me. But the doctor said he hadn't known about it either," Emerson said.

"Okay, the doctor's name?" Leyton asked.

"Dr. Hennessey Jones. He's human, but he's been the family doctor for years, since before I was born even."

Leyton cleared his throat. "All right. We'll check it out."

Jessie glanced at Emerson. He was frowning. She was certain he wanted to be involved in the research every step of the way. But then he'd want to protect her too, she figured. Or maybe not. Maybe he would be just as content for one of her friends to look out for her while he went sleuthing with the other men. That would be fine with her.

"If you guys don't mind too terribly much, Emerson could use your help putting the coffin back in place tomorrow," she said.

"We can sure assist with that. See you tomorrow."

Then they ended the call, and she relaxed a little against her seat. "Leyton doesn't mean to exclude you from investigating this. It's not like you're just a civilian or anything. If you want to team up with a couple of the guys, they would welcome you. One of them will stay with me to watch over me while I write. Not that I don't want to help you solve this mystery and locate your uncle if he's still alive. But I don't want to be in your way either."

"We'll play it by ear."

"Okay, that works for me." She fully intended to stay at the house and write.

"If the guys need more room, they can stay at another cabin. There's plenty of room," he said.

"We can let them know when they get here, but I imagine they'll want to stick together."

"Yeah, with three of them, sure. You don't think they'll want you to move in with them, do you?" Emerson sounded like he was hoping that wasn't the case.

She patted him on the thigh. "Sorry. You have Wi-Fi. You're stuck with me."

He chuckled. "I couldn't have been stuck with a nicer person."

When they reached the house, he pulled into the garage. She was hoping they hadn't had any further break-ins while they were gone. From the outside, everything looked fine, the Christmas lights all reflecting off the snow, just beautiful.

Before they went into the house, Emerson pulled out a gun and she realized he'd been armed the whole time. Which she understood, she was just surprised.

"Just stay here for a moment, okay?" he said.

"Uh, yeah, sure." She was going to say she didn't smell anything, but then again, the bears had been wearing hunter's concealment. She listened for any commotion inside his house while watching for any sign of movement outside. Other than the shadows of the tree branches dancing on the snow as the wind blew through the woods, she didn't see anything moving out there.

Emerson came back to the door. "It's all clear, no sign of anyone entering the house while we were gone, but you know how it is with them wearing concealment."

"That's just what I figured." She walked into the house and began taking off her warm-weather gear.

"Thanks for coming with me to see if my uncle was in the mausoleum." Emerson locked the door. "I couldn't have done it without your help. Would you like some hot cocoa?"

"Double chocolate? You don't have to ask me twice." She sat down to work on her laptop and once she had started it, it wasn't long before Emerson was bringing her a hot cocoa and some chocolate chip cookies. "Hmm, thanks. Okay, I'm going to work on my story now that I've had some chocolate fortification." She started work on the story again and he went back into the office and was rummaging around. She thought he might be searching for clues about his uncle. She sighed. "If you need any help, let me know."

"Thanks." But he didn't ask her for any assistance and she wasn't surprised.

If she hadn't been writing, she was sure he would have welcomed her aid. Once she finally had her word count, she walked into the office to see if he'd discovered anything. He was sitting at the desk, papers strewn all over it, but what he was concentrating on now was a photo album showing pictures of a man she thought was his uncle in his youth, a boy of about ten, and a woman who was probably Emerson's aunt and a couple and a young boy. The boy looked like Emerson, and the couple might have been his parents.

She felt bad for him. He seemed lost in thought and she didn't think he even realized she had joined him. She didn't want to disturb him, but she said, "Is that you as a little boy, and your aunt and uncle and your parents?"

"Uh, yeah." He looked up at her and his eyes were misty with tears.

She felt her own eyes grow misty and she leaned down and hugged him. "We'll find him and we'll make sure he stays safe."

"Yeah, we will."

"Did you discover anything?"

"No. Except the paperwork showing him withdrawing funds before he supposedly died of a heart attack."

"And all the rest of the funds are still there, as if he wanted to leave them for you." She frowned. "You don't think this was a ploy for him to get you to leave your job, do you?"

Emerson didn't say anything for a minute. "Hell."

She smiled. "It might be a far-out notion, but your uncle was a character, you have to admit."

"He was."

"What do you think? Could he have staged this whole thing just to get you to quit your dangerous missions so that *you* would be safe?" It just kind of hit her all at once that he might do something like that in an effort to protect his only nephew.

"He was relentless about me quitting the job. Every time I returned home, he would start in on me again about it. Maybe... maybe he thought I would meet you and we might hit it off, mate, settle down, and have a family."

Jessie's jaw dropped. "No. He never once mentioned you to me. I didn't know you existed."

"I didn't know about you either, but it doesn't mean he couldn't have come up with the scheme. He knew you were coming at your usual time every year. He just had to ensure word got to me so that I would return home when you were here."

"Hmm, okay, well, that's something else to consider. I'm going to take a shower and if the offer still stands, I'll join you in bed to talk about the case a while longer."

He smiled. "We would both be safer that way."

She laughed. "I'm not so sure about that." She found that lots of times while she was in the shower or lying down in bed and not distracted by emails and other stuff, she would start to think about issues with her story, or like right now, with the business with Emerson's uncle. It didn't mean she was staying in bed with Emerson. Just that they could lie there in the dark and toss some ideas back and forth to see if they could come up with what was really going on.

She finished her shower and put on her pajamas, then headed for Emerson's bedroom. When she reached the room, she found him slipping on a pair of pajama bottoms.

He was so fit, sexy, and his charming smile just won her over. Did his uncle really plan this whole situation?

Could she really fall for a cougar who wasn't a rogue? Her family would never believe it!

Then again, neither would she.

CHAPTER 10

*E*merson couldn't believe his uncle would go to such lengths to bring him home and set him up with a mate at the same time, if that was the case. But what about the bear shifters? What were they here for then?

He smiled at Jessie as she came into his bedroom and knew the way her mind worked over problem-solving, she wasn't jumping into bed with him to have sex. Still, he couldn't help think about kissing her and running his hands over her soft pajamas and feeling her soft body against him.

"My side?" she asked, moving aside the covers on the right side of the queen size bed, pulling him from his thoughts.

"Yeah." He climbed into bed and so did she. "So what do you think? Was my uncle right in thinking you and I might have a chance to be together?"

She laughed. "Only time would tell. But you would definitely have to come and see my family for Christmas then."

"Okay. I will." His declaration seemed to have shocked her into silence. "But we still need to find my uncle." Because he wanted his uncle to share Christmas with them too if he could.

"Absolutely, and give him the devil for upsetting the both of us."

"I agree with you there." If his uncle was truly among the living.

"Where would he go? Did he ever tell you of a place he would want to live if he wasn't running the resort?" She rested her head on the pillow next to Emerson's.

He liked the idea of her staying here and sleeping with him, even if they didn't go any further than that. He'd heard that wolf shifters mated for life. Cougars were more like their human counterparts. Some stayed with their mate forever, others weren't in it for the long run. He had never given a woman the idea he was interested in a lifetime arrangement, not with the kind of work he had done. Now, things could be different, he realized. He'd never even considered settling down before he met Jessie, in truth.

"Uncle Paul expressed an interest in living in Florida, where mountain lions live naturally, near Big Cypress National Preserve, possibly so he could still run as a cougar and not create a bad situation for shifters. They call them Florida panthers there, but they're cougars just the same. Real ones, maybe a few shifters too that everyone thinks are just real cougars. He had said he wanted to get away from the snow and cold in Minnesota when he retired. Maybe he was tired of taking care of the resort all these years, especially with my aunt gone. But when I'd pressed him about it, all he would say was he would like to retire sometime in the future."

"And there were no other cougars to meet here that were more his age."

"Not that he ever mentioned. He had always wanted me to take over the resort at some point in time, though I was too busy with my own—"

"Very dangerous work and he was afraid you would be killed before you ever returned home."

"He was worried about that. He didn't say it in so many words. I think he didn't want me to believe he didn't have faith in my abilities, but the nature of the job was dangerous. Still, what about the two bears?"

"I have no idea. We need to tell the CSF agents what we suspect might be another version of what's going on—now that we know your uncle's body isn't in the coffin." Jessie frowned at Emerson. "Did you see anything in the items you were sorting through in the office that would indicate Paul had left for Florida?"

"A brochure on the Big Cypress National Preserve."

Her lips parted in surprise. "Okay, that could be evidence that he went there. Do you think he would have gone to such lengths to convince you to come home?"

"Come to think of it, he did once tell me he would have to keel over dead to bring me home for good, he believed. I never thought he would pretend to do it."

"But how could the doctor friend be in on the deception, if he is?" Jessie asked. "Unless your uncle told the doctor the dangerous work you were doing, not exactly what though, and somehow he convinced him to go along with the plan."

"That would be unethical. Besides, I'm here now. And I quit the job."

"Your uncle wouldn't know that. He could think if he showed up to see you at the resort, and you realized he was still alive, you would just return to your old job."

"Okay, that's true."

"All right. I think we have enough to think on." She leaned over to kiss Emerson's lips, and he thought the way she was kissing him gingerly good night, she was leaving the bed. Unfortunately.

He kissed her back, her mouth warm and soft against his, his hands on her shoulders, gently massaging. Man, he hadn't had a rampant need for a woman like this in forever. He was hoping she would stay, but if she wasn't ready for anything more than that, he didn't want to push his luck. His uncle might think Jessie was the right one for Emerson, but that didn't mean that either he or Jessie would feel the same way about each other.

She pulled away from him and smiled. "Uhm, I had another thought."

"You got that from a kiss?" He had figured she would have been thinking *only* about the kiss and more, like he had been doing.

"I often get all kinds of wild ideas when I go to bed." She smiled at him. "What if your uncle has a girlfriend in Florida?"

"Hell, I never thought of that." Emerson tried to recall anytime his uncle might have revealed he was interested in a she-cat, but he couldn't remember any. He suspected his uncle might not have wanted to mention one, worried Emerson would feel he was being disloyal to his mate's memory. But Emerson knew his uncle had loved her with all his heart and if he was ready to fall in love again, Emerson was all for it.

"Can you access his emails? We could look through his rental agreements and see if anyone had come here from Florida. A single woman, maybe? A cougar, though we wouldn't know that for sure. But it's just another idea." Then Jessie slipped out of bed. "Good night. I'll see you in the morning, but then I need to write."

He sighed. "What if you get more wild ideas tonight?" Maybe another kiss would do the trick.

"I will write them down in my notebook." Then she slipped down the hall and he sighed again.

* * *

THE NEXT MORNING, Emerson bundled up to check on things outside the house, but peeked in the guest room to see if Jessie was all right first. The guest room door was open, which made him think Jessie had wanted to hear if anything was going on in the house that could give them trouble in the middle of the night. She was sleeping soundly, her head resting on one pillow and her arms wrapped around another, as if she was holding him tight. Wouldn't the real deal be even better? For him, it would. He smiled, then headed outside to make sure they hadn't had anyone return in the middle of the night.

After investigating each of the cabins and the shed, he didn't see anything amiss and returned to the house where he heard Jessie in the bathroom.

"Would cinnamon pancakes work for you?" he called out.

"Oh, yes, thanks!"

He made them cinnamon pancakes while Jessie came out of the bathroom, dressed in jeans, slipper boots, and a red and green-striped sweater, her blond hair curling about her shoulders. She looked huggable and kissable.

"Hmmm, those smell great." She smiled.

"Yeah, perfect for Christmas." He hadn't planned to make any for himself, but then with Jessie here, he was really getting into the Christmas spirit.

She set the table for them, though he was going to suggest she just work on her story. He didn't want her to feel she needed to move back to the cabin because she couldn't get anything done on her book.

"How's the story going?" He served up their pancakes and she poured them both cups of coffee and then they sat down to eat.

"Good. I am a little bit ahead on my word count as of yesterday, though I try not to let myself backslide on reaching my daily goals and just figure I've written some bonus word count in case something comes up and I can't get in my regular day's work. I heard you go outside to check things out and watched you from the bedroom window. You should have waited for me to get dressed. You don't have any backup yet." She raised her hand to stop him from commenting. "I know, I can't shoot a weapon, but I have 911 on speed dial." She pulled out her phone.

He laughed. Then he thought about her book and realized he should have asked more about it. It wasn't that he wasn't interested, just that other things had been taking his focus. "What are you writing, exactly?"

"In the book, if you're interested and I don't bore you, it's a dark and stormy night when she 'meets' the hero telepathically at a club and he ends up dancing with her. Then later, someone breaks into the heroine's home and she communicates with the hero telepathically to tell him she's in trouble."

"Does he save the day?" If it had been Emerson, he sure would hope he would be there to save the woman.

"They are in this together, so not exactly. But he stays at her house to protect her for sure. He has to teach her how to deal with the voices in her head though."

Emerson smiled.

Jessie pointed her fork at him. "I know you don't believe in them, but psychics are real. At least in Yuma Town, they are. Bridget, also a CSF agent, can read minds."

He couldn't help smiling again. He just needed proof that such a thing was possible for him to believe in it. He'd never known anyone who had that kind of ability.

"I would just love to see Bridget read your mind sometime." Jessie smiled, then took another sip of her coffee. "And Leyton and his twin brother, Stryker Hill, who is one of our deputy sheriffs, can see ghosts. Not all the time, but sometimes. Like when they were at a ghost town. They just are more attuned to things like that when the rest of us aren't. Stryker's mate, Nina, and her twin sister, Ava, can see future events. Nina is also a full-time deputy sheriff and Ava works in a bakery."

"Uh-huh."

"Just you wait. When you meet the rest of the cougar family of Yuma Town, you'll see. Besides, who knows? Maybe we are all capable of having a sixth sense but we're in such denial, we don't even realize it."

"Okay."

"You don't believe me, but we can make a believer out of you. Most others who don't have any psychic gift in Yuma Town felt the same way as you until they saw what they could do."

"I'll keep an open mind. Not to change the subject, but in the book you're writing, do they learn who the housebreaker was?"

"Not yet. They're still working on it. She's sure her parents were murdered. The police and everyone else believe the car accident was just that. An accident."

"But you know the truth."

"Only that it wasn't an accident. But not who, when, or why. Yet. But it will all come out in the end." She sighed and praised his pancakes then, which delighted him. "These are delicious. I need to make them for the family for Christmas morning. You and I could make them together."

"We can sure do that." Which sounded a lot like she would be letting on to her family that they were dating. "Okay, so I have a question." He leaned back in his chair. "If my uncle wanted me to mate you—"

"Get to know me," she corrected him and took the last bite of her pancakes.

"Court you. What would we do about living arrangements? Let's say he's in Florida with a girlfriend. I'm here at the resort, managing things. Your family is in Loveland and Yuma Town, Colorado."

"I was thinking about that. Hypothetically, of course."

"Of course."

"I live with my parents and with the kind of work I do, I could actually live anywhere. And if I start writing novels, rather than publish books of photos like I used to do, I'll want to be in one place—writing. Living with my folks is *not* conducive to writing. My mom always thinks that if I'm doing research on the internet —and that can be anything from checking out clothes the characters are wearing to the homes they're living in—I'm just playing around. She has a cake business, and she expects me to help her bake or decorate them if I have nothing better to do with my time. She doesn't understand that my time spent researching things is just as important as the time I spend writing on the story. It gives me more things to write about. Nor would living near my sister, with all their kids, work well for writing. I could just see me offering to take care of the kids now and again, since I have no willpower when it comes to my nieces and nephews."

"This is a great place to set the mood while you're writing your stories."

"It is. That's why I come here every winter. I could see getting snowed in and just—writing."

He raised a brow, smiling. "I could think of *other* things to do."

She chuckled. "I just bet you could. Not only that, but when family wanted to visit, we would just make sure they had a cabin or two to stay at."

"We could even block out times for them to visit every year."

"Yeah, right. Hypothetically."

He smiled. Things were looking up. He loved it here, but he'd had the thought that living here alone all the time, except when he had guests and even that wouldn't be the same as having a family in his life, could be...lonely. Especially since his uncle wasn't here any longer, unless they could resolve that issue and he returned to the resort. But being with her, well, Jessie would sure liven things right up. If they were snowbound? Hell, no way would she spend all the time working on her story if he could convince her otherwise. Besides, she would have to take breaks and she *was* writing a romance. He could certainly give her some ideas in that regard.

"I'm going to clean up the dishes and try to access my uncle's password again," he said.

"Okay." She began to help clear the dishes, even though he wanted her to concentrate on writing her book. He could take care of all this.

Still, he enjoyed having her bump elbows with him as she loaded the dishes in the dishwasher next to the sink, and he began cleaning the frying pan. It made him think of hearth and home and really settling down with a mate. He'd never even thought in those terms before.

"Thanks for breakfast. It was so good." Then she kissed his mouth, which gave her an advantage as her hands were free, and his hands were holding the soapy scrub brush and the other, the dirty frying pan.

Still, he kissed her back, telling her he was willing to see just how far he could take this—but later. She had to work and so did he. He had to discover what was going on with his uncle—and the bears. And the way she pulled away, he knew she wanted to get to writing too.

"Okay, I'm off to work," she said and headed into the living room where she sat on the couch and began typing away on her story on her laptop.

He finished cleaning the frying pan, set it on a mat to dry and then headed into the office, determined to get into his uncle's computer.

All morning, Emerson searched for notes that his uncle might have made of his passwords. He found no sign of them. Emerson thought Uncle Paul might have had them on his computer, but he just had to get into the computer first. He wondered why his uncle wouldn't have taken his laptop with him, if he was still alive. But both his laptop and main personal computer were on his desk. Then again, if his uncle was trying to hide the fact he was alive, he would know Emerson would assume something was wrong if one or both had vanished.

Emerson tried every date he could think of—birthdays, weddings, deaths—in combination with every family name, just anything, but nothing would work as a password to get him into the computer. He tried to think of any time his uncle might have hinted at his password. Emerson didn't remember a time when

Uncle Paul had told him what it was outright. But people changed passwords, so whatever he might have told Emerson years ago could have been changed at any time.

Emerson left the office. "I can't get into the computer to see my uncle's emails and accounts. I'm going out and try to straighten up more of the shed before your friends get here."

"Do you want me to help?" Jessie got up off the couch and stretched like a sexy feline.

"How is your writing coming?"

"I've got my word count and I need a break."

"Okay, yeah, sure. I figured I would look and see what I could find that might be missing. Then we can have lunch. Do grilled ham and cheese sandwiches appeal? I have the bread and ham sliced off the bone and I saw you have the slices of sharp cheddar cheese."

"Yeah, absolutely."

They bundled up and went outside. When they reached the shed, he turned on the light inside and they began to pick everything more of the stuff and hang tools on pegboards on the walls.

"They didn't really break anything," she observed.

"Yeah, they just made a mess of things like they were trying to make it appear that they were looking for something, when they weren't," he said. "I don't see anything missing from here."

"Well, like when they came to my place, as bears, it would have been hard to grab anything important and take off." She hung up two rakes. "Hey, at sunset, I want to take more pictures on the water, if you don't mind coming with me."

"Sure. I'd like that."

"We could do that before the guys arrive." She found a brand-new doorknob still in its package. "Hey, can you use this to replace the other?"

"Oh perfect. It's got the keys and everything. I'll change that out."

She continued to straighten up the shed and when he finished changing out doorknobs, she said, "By the way, I'm officially hungry. Are you ready to make sandwiches for us?"

"I am. And we'll get warmed up in the house."

"Yeah, good idea. It's cold out here. You need a heated shed."

They went inside and he made the sandwiches while she made them hot cocoa.

While he was still making the sandwiches, she went into the office to try and figure out a password to get into his uncle's computer. She looked through all the drawers, but didn't see anything that looked like a password.

"Lunch is ready," he called out.

"Coming. I couldn't figure out a password either." She left the office.

They ate their sandwiches and drank their cocoa and then she went back to working on her story, and he started checking records in the file for reservations. He knew his uncle also had files on his computer, but his paper registrations when guests checked into the resort were in the file cabinet, and at least Emerson had access to that.

He just had to find the files. He kept searching through drawer after drawer until he found the one that contained the cabin registrations for the last five years and he began searching through them until he came up with a registration this past summer, right after he had chanced to see his uncle and then returned to work to take on a mission.

Guests had come from all over, but these guests were from Naples, Florida, which happened to be near the Big National Cypress Preserve. A coincidence? Robbie Randall and two female companions, Drew and Candice Cramer from Naples, no phone number though.

"I might have found something." He took the registration form into the living room to show it to Jessie.

"Oh, more than a coincidence, don't you think?" she asked, looking at the registration.

"Yeah. Come to think of it, his cell phone was missing."

"So you can't check texts."

"And we can't check his emails if he's been emailing her."

Jessie's lips parted. "Phone bills."

"Okay, I'm checking." He went through the files and found some for earlier years while she helped him look through some of the papers. "There is nothing here that would indicate he was in contact with anyone from Florida earlier on. There are no paper bills for the last two years, so I suspect my uncle went to online billing."

"Which means we still need to get into his computer," she said.

"Exactly. Hacking into computers wasn't anything I ever did on the job though." He tried calling his uncle's cell phone but it had been disconnected.

"Me either. I still say that brochure on the preserve and the fact that three women from Naples near there were visiting here in the summer could mean something. I have an idea." She went to her laptop and looked up the names for the Florida area. "I have a home listed in Naples here under the one woman's name, Robbie Randall. Now if only they would say if she was a cougar or not."

"Is there a phone number listed for her?"

"No. Of course not. Otherwise, we could just call her and see if she abducted your uncle, if she was a wild cougar woman."

Emerson smiled at Jessie. He couldn't imagine a wild she-cat seducing his uncle. "I'm back to sorting through papers. I need to make some order out of this and hope the CSF agents can help us unravel what's going on."

"I agree. I'm back to writing." But she was taking some notes from the website that had Robbie Randall's address. Then Jessie opened up Facebook and began searching for someone with that name. Jessie sighed. "There are tons of women by that name on Facebook. Four-hundred and thirty, to be exact."

"I'll start checking them out to see what I can find. If she lists Naples, Florida as her home, it could be our woman. Of course if I try and contact her, she might be concerned."

"How many times has she been here at the resort?" Jessie asked.

"Just the once."

Jessie shook her head. "That doesn't sound really promising as far as a relationship goes."

"Yeah, I agree. But they could have been corresponding all this time through text messages, phone calls, and chats."

"Can you check with the phone company and see if you could get printed phone records if we can't get into his computer?"

"The CSF agents might be able to. I wouldn't be able to because I would need police authorization."

"Okay, well, that's something else they can look into. But hopefully, one of them can hack into your uncle's computer and you'll find all kinds of information you were looking for. I'm kind of surprised he would take his phone and not his laptop, even though you think he might have left it to not arouse suspicions about his death."

If Mr. Merriweather was alive and well and he wasn't totally committed to a she-cat in Florida, or anywhere else, what about enticing him to visit Yuma Town? That's what Jessie was beginning to think about. They had single cougars: Florence Fitzgerald and Mae Sorenson, affectionately known as the cat lady, both who were widowed, and a couple of others Jessie knew of. Jack's wife, Dottie's widowed Aunt Emily Hamilton, for one. Florence would probably put him to work in the bakery. If he were to get to know Mae, he would have to like cats for sure. Aunt Emily doted on her great nieces and nephews, so he would have to like kids. Jessie didn't think that would be difficult because when kids arrived at the resort, he often would go out and make snowmen or build snow forts and play with them.

He would have a whole family of cougars to make friends

with. And if Jessie and Emerson ever really hooked up, when they visited her family in the area of Yuma Town, they would be able to get together with Emerson's uncle and his mate.

She made the proposition to Emerson and he smiled that kind of smile that said he was ready to take her to bed because she was saying all the right things that told him she was thinking of making this a more permanent relationship between him and her —forget his uncle and whoever he might get interested in!

"I'm just saying," she said.

"I know what you're saying. You want to keep my uncle close to your family so when we visit, we can see them too."

She smiled. "I'm saying that he might find a mate for himself and make someone else just as happy and he'd have the backing of a whole lot of cougars if he lived in Yuma Town." She planned to go back to writing, but she couldn't quit thinking about finding a phone number for Robbie. One call might solve everything for them.

She wanted to give Mr. Merriweather hell for scaring both her and Emerson, but she also wanted him to join her and her family for Christmas. Everyone would make him feel welcome and hopefully, he would make a connection with one of the single ladies.

"Besides, if he is in Witness Protection and needs to cloak his identity, Yuma Town is the perfect place for it. We have so many cougars who are with various law enforcement agencies, he would be safe." She continued to do searches, trying to find a phone number for Robbie, then figured the CSF agents could probably get one from their connections or databases. But they were still driving here.

She thought of the next best thing. Florence Fitzgerald. Ex-CIA, Wonder Woman in the flesh. When Jessie called her, Flo's phone went to messages, but her messages were full and Jessie couldn't leave one for her. Darn it! Flo had to be busy at the bakery and wasn't able to answer her phone.

CHAPTER 11

*B*efore sunset and the CSF guys arrived, Emerson grabbed a lantern and Jessie had her camera slung over her shoulder. They headed across the snow-covered parking lot and down the wooden steps that turned into stone steps as they made their way down the cliff to the rocks. He hadn't remembered doing this since he was a kid in the summer and skipping rocks on the lake water.

She took him over to see the standing stones that she had set up on the shore, but her mouth was agape.

"What's wrong?"

"There are two more here, two more on top of mine. No one comes to your shore except your guests and you don't have any, well, except for me. There's no way to get down here except by using your stairs, and then down to the rocky shore, the water reaches the cliffs and no one can go either way."

"The bears?" Emerson asked, surprised.

"Well, when I stayed here before, there were always other guests. The cabins were always full and people would mess with my stone creations. But whoever did this was creative, not just knocking them over and spoiling things for me."

"And bear paw prints are here in the snow," he said, peering down at tracks left around the area and then headed up the steep embankment.

"More bear fur was caught on a branch here, and then they climbed up through the trees." She took pictures of the bear paw prints and the fur. "It's the same fur as the type we found earlier."

Emerson rubbed his whiskered chin. "They would have smelled your scent down here and though you were wearing gloves, your scent was the only one down here."

"They knew I would return and find this like this?" Jessie asked.

"There was a good chance of it. They might have even watched you stacking the rocks and taking pictures of the sunset earlier."

"And then came down to do this after I left?"

"Possibly."

She frowned as she picked up an even smaller smooth stone and set it on top to make it eight stones. "It's almost as if they're trying to tell me they're not my enemy."

Emerson lightly patted his injured head, though it was feeling better now. "They might be okay with you, but I still don't think they like me."

She smiled. "They just need to get to know you."

"Like you do?"

"I'm working on it."

"I can sure help you out there." He sat down on a boulder and she sat next to him and took some pictures of the sunset. "It's beautiful."

"It is. More so because I get to share it with you. I never thought I would be sitting around enjoying a sunset over the lake on a winter's day at Whispering Pines Resort." He'd never really paid attention to sunsets. The sun set and he was on a mission in the dark—that was the importance of the setting sun.

"Not something that you were interested in doing on your missions, I take it."

"Right, and as a kid, it just wasn't that important. We used to come down here and roast hot dogs and marshmallows over a firepit. That was the fun of it. Or the sun would go down at Halloween time and we could trick-or-treat."

She smiled. "So what were you?"

"For Halloween? A vampire." He shrugged. "Batman one year. I look good in black."

"I bet you look great in other colors too."

"What were you at Halloween?" he asked, unable to guess what she might have been.

"A black kitty cat, one year, princesses, most years."

"Looking for a prince?"

"Heaven's no."

He laughed.

"So have you ever stacked rocks on the shore?"

He smiled and put his arm around Jessie's shoulders. "I might have to start doing that now that you've shown me how it's done."

She chuckled and motioned to the rocks. "The next one is yours."

"That's the hard one."

She laughed.

"All right." He wouldn't be outdone and picked a bigger rock than she had and set it on top.

She smiled and took a picture. "That's great! Come on, let's get back up to the house and warm up a bit before the guys get here."

"Yeah, let's go." He chased her across the snow-covered boulders and up the stairs, ready to catch her if she slipped. But she was as agile as if she were wearing her cougar coat and she was soon up to the top. He was right behind her.

He figured if they went to the lighthouse as cougars and ran down the steps, she might just have beat him! When they arrived at the house, they warmed up inside by the fire and she turned on the Christmas tree lights. She took off her Mukluks and parka, hat, and scarf and left the living room while he hung all his outer wear in the coat closet.

"Cocoa?" he asked.

"Yeah, I would love some since we didn't have s'mores down on the shore." She returned to the living room wearing a pair of booted slippers, then sat down on the couch and opened up her laptop.

"Next sunset."

"I'm keeping you at your word."

"We'll do it." But the guys would be there by then. He supposed he would have to invite them all, though he liked the intimacy of sharing the time on the shore during the sunset alone with her.

He made up the hot cocoa, added mini marshmallows, and brought it over to her.

"Thanks so much. I'm going to just work on the story for a bit. Did you want to watch something with me while we're waiting for the others to get in?"

"Yeah, sure. There's a comedy, western, or thriller we could watch."

"Christmas comedy."

"Okay." He put it on and sat next to her on the couch. If his uncle had the notion that he and Jessie should be together, Emerson could sure see the merit in it. He envisioned being with her during the spring and summer and fall too. And seeing more of the sights here with her. He just wondered if she would miss her family too much, or if her family would miss her too much. But this was sure nice.

She soon closed up her laptop and snuggled with him to watch the movie, the fire going in the fireplace, the Christmas lights on the tree twinkling.

"Did you finish what you needed to?" He was surprised she wanted to snuggle and not continue to work on the book.

"No, I just wanted to enjoy watching the movie with you."

"Well, this has really been a pleasant change in what I thought would happen before Christmas." He put his arm over her shoulder.

"I sure didn't expect to be dating someone new for the Christmas holidays either."

"We're dating," he said. Hot damn!

"We sure are. You didn't think it would happen? You ought to have known better."

He chuckled darkly. "I thought you only dated rogues."

"I'm willing to give you a chance. Who knows? Maybe the last bad guy finally did the trick and broke me of my bad habit of going out with rogues."

He sighed and squeezed her shoulders lightly. "Well, I'm not all that good." He had always just done a job and thought he was doing right, but if she'd been in his life before he would have seriously reconsidered the kind of work he had done.

"That's probably why I'm so fascinated with you."

He was glad for that at least and that she hadn't been turned off by the kind of job he'd done.

* * *

AFTER ENJOYING the movie with Jessie that night, Emerson headed into the kitchen to make beef stroganoff for dinner for everyone before the CSF agents arrived.

"What can I do to help?" Jessie asked.

"You can work on your story, if you would like." He wanted to prove to her that he could handle everything else so she could write.

She watched him bring out the steak, mushrooms, and onions. "Hmm, I think this meal will go in the story. I've never made it before, but you know what they say. Write about what you know. What do you need me to do?"

Later, while the dinner was simmering and ready to eat, two vehicles drove up into the parking area next to the house and both Jessie and Emerson went to check to see who had arrived, assuming it was the guys from CSF, but they had to make sure.

Both vehicles were black SUVs and Jessie verified that they were the men they were expecting. Emerson went out to greet them while Jessie hurried to remove her booted slippers and throw on her Mukluks and parka.

"Leyton Hill," Leyton said, offering his hand and Emerson shook it. "And you must be Emerson."

"I am. Welcome and thanks for coming." Emerson was sure that the men would like to wrap this up and be home for the holidays with their own families.

Jessie hurried outside and smiled at everyone.

"This is Jack Barrington"—Emerson shook his hand as Leyton introduced him—"who works for me in Yuma Town, and—"

"I'm Chet Kensington. I had worked *with* Leyton out of Cheyenne, Wyoming, before he kidnapped Dr. Kate Parker. Though I had been partners with Travis MacKay and Bridget Sinclair also." Chet shook Emerson's hand. "Leyton mated Kate. Then somehow, after all that, he managed to talk our boss, Chuck Warner, into allowing Leyton to open an office in Yuma Town and head the unit out there, taking Travis and Bridget with him."

Emerson smiled. Leyton sounded just like him. He liked the guys already and couldn't wait to hear that story. He motioned to cabin five, formerly Jessie's cabin. "That's your cabin over there. You're welcome to any of them though since they're all vacant. But that cabin has a cougar door in case you want to run as cougars. Why don't you come in to eat before I help you unload your gear?" He was thinking that if her family came up here, he would have to install cougar doors in the other cabins also.

"Yeah, sure, that would be great." Leyton locked his SUV's doors and Chet locked his.

Leyton was definitely the one in charge of this mission, even if he wasn't Chet's boss, though Emerson could tell Chet was getting a kick out of it and wasn't miffed.

The three men all gave Jessie warm hugs, and instantly, Emerson wondered if either of the other two guys were mated. She had to stay with someone while she was writing, but he wanted to make sure the agent staying with her didn't have any designs on her. He realized the rabbit hole he was quickly falling into.

Inside, he served up plates of beef stroganoff, while Jessie made everyone spiked eggnog.

They all took seats at the dining table and Leyton said, "Okay, tell us everything that's happened so far—even if you have told me already—for Chet and Jack's benefit."

Emerson was impressed that the agents were ready to work on the case tonight and not wait until tomorrow after they had rested up. He explained everything that Jessie had already told Leyton. He knew they would be considering all the angles like he and Jessie had been doing. With three more investigative minds on this, hopefully they would figure out what was going on pretty quickly.

"So why would they break into the shed?" Leyton asked Emerson.

"I have no idea. My uncle wouldn't have kept anything of value in there. Well, tools, but nothing anyone would want to break into the shed for and steal. It didn't make any sense that they would break into Jessie's place either. Why not the main house?"

"Did they steal anything from your place, Jessie?" Leyton asked.

"No. But I might have startled them before they could grab anything. Though as bears, once they left the cabin and shifted, I don't know how they would have managed to carry anything much. We did have another thought. It's probably too farfetched, but what if Mr. Merriweather had faked his death to get Emerson to return here and take over the cabins? So he could retire. He didn't know Emerson was already planning to leave his position. The other possibility, just as far out, is that maybe he wanted Emerson to meet me—a single she-cat."

The agents all looked at Emerson, as if they thought *he* had planned all this! He hadn't even been thinking of dating cougars when he learned his uncle had passed away and he arrived here.

Leyton smiled at Jack. "We were actually discussing that on the way up here when you told me Paul Merriweather's body wasn't in the coffin."

She sighed. "Good. I thought you would think it was too farfetched."

"We try to keep an open mind in any case we're involved in. We need to speak with the doctor and find those bears," Leyton said.

"Had your uncle ever mentioned friends he might have in the area that we can talk to?" Chet asked.

"He was friends with everyone. And his guests returned year after year because they liked it so much here," Emerson said. "Come to think of it, he always kept a little black address book of addresses and phone numbers. I couldn't find it anywhere. I was going to let his friends know of his demise if any of them didn't know about it. It should have been in his upper righthand desk drawer. I was trying to hack into my uncle's computer to check on his emails to see if they would give us any clues about anything, but I couldn't."

"We might be able to help you with that. You said the two men showed their faces to you as if they had nothing to worry about when they asked you about seeing Jessie, but they were wearing hunter concealment," Leyton confirmed.

"Yeah. It doesn't make any sense. If they're going to break into the places, why show their faces at all," Emerson said.

"What if it was just a ruse?" Jessie asked. "I was staying at my own cabin until the electricity went out and you took me to your home because you had a generator. The men/bears attack you, only enough to make me worried about you, but not enough to kill you. I mean, why not break into the main house? Breaking into the shed and cabin didn't make any sense to me."

"But the electricity had returned?" Chet asked.

"Yes, sometime during the night and I was planning to move back to the cabin the next day. Though I kept wondering why they hadn't broken into my place while Emerson and I were visiting the Split Rock Lighthouse during the day. Why wait until I return to the cabin to get eggnog for us to drink while we're decorating the tree and then hit the cabin? Speaking of which, would you guys like a refill on your eggnog?"

"Yeah, sure," Jack said, the others agreeing.

She refilled each of their glasses.

"Maybe the men's visit to your cabin ensured you would stay with Emerson that night." Leyton raised a brow at Emerson. "Are you sure this isn't any of your doing?"

Emerson smiled, but he didn't answer him right away, then finally said, "Well, I wouldn't have ever thought my uncle was capable of such a ruse, but maybe so. Would the bears have been friends of his? Or just hired to do the job? My uncle never mentioned knowing any bear shifters."

"You weren't in touch with your uncle that often, from what I understand," Leyton said.

"That's true. It was hard to keep in touch while I was on the kind of missions I was on and in the places I ended up."

*a*fter dinner, Emerson helped the CSF agents carry their luggage into their cabin. Jessie came with them, for her safety.

"Tomorrow, I want to talk to the doctor who said your uncle had died of a heart attack," Leyton said. "Jack can stay with Jessie. I want you with Chet and me because you know the doctor. In the meantime, Jack can try to hack into your uncle's computer."

"Yeah, sure."

Leyton looked at Jessie and she smiled. "I'm going to be writing. I hope Jack has something to do so he's not too bored, if he can't get into Emerson's uncle's computer."

"He's happy to help with protecting you."

Jack nodded. "Yeah, that's my real job. If you need help with brainstorming for ideas, I can do that too."

She laughed. "You're on."

"And I'll see if I can access Mr. Merriweather's computer."

They all said good night, then Emerson and Jessie headed back to his home. "You know, I can help you with brainstorming."

She chuckled. "Oh, that's great. Be forewarned, I'll take you up on it."

"Did you want to do any more brainstorming in bed?" He was hoping one of these nights, she would just give in and stay with him.

She patted his chest. "Not tonight. Night, Emerson. I'll see you in the morning." She kissed him but she was quickly pulling away. Maybe with her friends here, she suddenly felt uncomfortable about acting too intimate with him. They would be sure to tell her sister, he suspected.

"Night, Jessie." He kissed her tenderly and then they went their separate ways. He sighed as he undressed for bed.

* * *

THE NEXT MORNING, the guys joined Jessie and Emerson to have eggs and sausage for breakfast. Then Emerson left with Leyton and Chet to see the doctor, leaving Jack with Jessie as she worked on her story. Emerson had taken his bag of tools to use on a return visit to the mausoleum after they finished questioning the doctor.

When Emerson and the agents arrived at the clinic where the family's doctor was working, he had a patient he was seeing. Leyton hadn't wanted to make an appointment with him. They had badges and they said they were with CSF, and it sounded to Emerson like they were a special unit that was with the FBI.

The receptionist called the physician and he had them come back to meet with him.

Dr. Hennessey Jones was white-haired now and he still had the kindly face Emerson had remembered when he'd seen him on doctor visits when he was young.

Emerson shook his hand and so did the CSF agents.

"I know why you're here," the doctor said, taking a seat while the men sat opposite him.

Emerson wasn't sure if the doctor would try to cover up what he'd done or figure the gig was up, but he was kind of surprised that he would just come out and open up to them.

Before Emerson could ask him why in the world he would falsify his uncle's death, Leyton said, "Okay, tell us what you have to say."

"Don't tell me you people don't talk to each other." The doctor folded his arms across his chest.

Leyton opened his mouth and then smiled. "Witness protection. The U.S. Marshalls got here before us then. So Mr. Merriweather didn't come to you to make up this story about his heart attack?"

The doctor looked aghast. "No. He would never have done such a thing. He knows I wouldn't do that."

"Had he ever approached you about doing that?" Chet asked.

"No."

"Can you give us the name of the agents who needed the report that said Mr. Merriweather had died?" Leyton asked.

"No. They produced badges like you did and then they said they had to protect his identity. They wouldn't give me any details why he had to go into Witness Protection or I would have to be in it too."

But Emerson was thinking that the men who visited the doctor weren't from the U.S. Marshalls Service. That the Marshalls would concoct their own story and not involve a local doctor.

"I'm so sorry," Dr. Smith said to Emerson.

"Don't be. I just hope he's alive and well." Emerson wasn't about to say he had opened the coffin and found his uncle's body wasn't in there. "Thanks, Dr. Jones." Emerson rose from his chair and the doctor and the agents all rose at once. He shook the doctor's hand and then the other men did the same and they left the clinic after that.

"Hey, before we do anything else, we'll help you set the coffin back into place at the mausoleum," Leyton said.

"Okay, thanks. So what do you think about the Witness Protection scheme?" Emerson asked.

"They weren't U.S. Marshalls," Chet said. "Not that I want to go there, but what if they were somehow involved in his death and made up the story that they were with the U.S. Marshalls Service? Then everyone who knew your uncle would believe he died of a heart attack and there was no foul play."

"Hell." Emerson really didn't want to believe his uncle was dead.

"Another thought I had, would your uncle be capable of pretending to you that he was dead just so he could retire? What if you came home, but decided you didn't want the headache of the resort and went back to your line of work?" Leyton asked.

"We had discussed it. I had told him when he retired, I would take over the resort. I had always loved being up here when I had the chance to visit him and while I grew up here while living with my aunt and uncle."

"Would he have known what you were really doing?" Leyton asked. "It's supposed to be top secret."

Emerson raised a brow at him.

"Okay, so we have our own ways of learning of things. But you know what I mean. Your uncle ran a resort. He wouldn't have the databases or connections to learn what you truly did. At least I don't think he would," Leyton said.

"I came home in pretty bad shape a few times and had to convalesce, so he didn't know what my job was exactly, but yeah, he did know it was dangerous."

"Okay."

Emerson directed Leyton to the cemetery and once they arrived, he told them where to park. Then he grabbed his bag of tools and they crunched through the snow to the mausoleum. He was almost afraid they would find his uncle's body in the coffin this time!

Then Emerson wondered—would Leyton say he could see his

aunt's ghost in the mausoleum? Not that Emerson really believed he could.

* * *

JESSIE WAS TYPING AWAY on her story while Jack was watching out the window for signs of trouble. "Do you want some hot cocoa?" she asked.

"Yeah, sure. So what's going on between the two of you?" Jack asked, but he remained at the window on the lookout.

"Emerson and me?" She shrugged and pulled her milk out of Emerson's fridge. She found his double chocolate cocoa mix and made up two mugs of cocoa and brought them over to Jack and then sat down at the coffee table with hers. "I like him. A lot. I never thought I would like a good guy, but he's a lot more fascinating than most of the 'nice' guys I've met who didn't interest me."

"Thanks for the cocoa." Jack stayed at the window and drank his hot chocolate. "What if he goes back to his former occupation?"

She sighed. "It's possible." What if the thrill of excitement, adventure, and danger were what he really lived for. Then there was the matter of Emerson wanting to go after Smith for setting Emerson and his team up to be ambushed and slaughtered.

"Are you going home for Christmas?" Jack asked.

She smiled at Jack. "Okay, yes, I plan to and I asked Emerson if he would come too. And if his uncle turns out to be alive and he'll be safe coming out there also, we'll want him to. But it doesn't mean anything for us as—well, I guess we're dating. But it doesn't mean a mating for us for sure." She didn't want the word to get back to her family that she was close to settling down with a guy finally. Her mother would be preparing a wedding cake for them pronto. "Emerson's here by himself, his uncle is gone, he has no other family, the cabins are vacant, so there's no reason why he shouldn't come down and spend Christmas with a cougar family."

"I agree with you there. Especially since *he* is a cougar."

She got a call from Emerson and she was eager to learn what they had learned. "Hey, what happened with the doctor?"

"He said U.S. Marshalls put my uncle in Witness Protection."

"Really? The doctor was duped!"

"You think so too? We suspect they weren't really U.S. Marshalls. We're just at the mausoleum getting ready to put the coffin back in place."

"Okay, good. Nothing is going on here. Jack couldn't access your uncle's computer, but he has been helping me with my story."

"All right. Well, we'll be there soon."

Then they ended the call and Jessie told Jack what they had learned from the doctor.

Jack shook his head. "I'll go back and try my hand at getting into Emerson's uncle's computer again."

* * *

"Hey," Emerson said to Leyton, after they got the coffin and covers back in place. "Jessie was telling me that you have the ability to see ghosts."

Leyton smiled at him. "Oh."

"Yeah. She said you would make me a believer."

Smiling, Chet shook his head.

"Are you really sure you want to learn the truth?" Leyton asked.

"Yeah, sure." Emerson just couldn't see that any of it was real, but he was game.

"Your aunt was named Elise, her given name, Givens. She married your uncle thirty-five years ago when she was twenty-one. She loved you like a son," Leyton said.

"You could have looked that up anywhere." Emerson wasn't convinced that easily, not that he really thought Leyton had looked into all of his past, but then again, he might have considering they worried about who Jessie was seeing, given her propensity to date rogues.

"Your aunt said after your parents went missing, you stole a boat and went out to search for them all along the rugged coastline. It took them three days to find you, but even then you had provisioned yourself with food and water and clothing to last for a week or more. They knew you would turn out to be a survivalist."

"That was in the news." Even though it would be something Emerson figured would be a little harder to discover since it happened so long ago.

"Your aunt said you would be a skeptic."

"Why is she here? I would think she would have moved on."

"She returned when she heard her husband had died. But he wasn't here."

"Also known."

"She said you loved chocolate, and would never eat her pumpkin or apple pies. But if she made you a chocolate cream pie, chocolate cheesecake, or chocolate mousse, you were all over it."

Emerson smiled. No one knew that but his aunt and uncle and his parents.

"She also said you went through a phase when you were eleven where you ate only pizza or peanut butter and jelly sandwiches. And you wore only black. No patterns or anything. No other colors. Just black."

Again, Emerson smiled. That was something else no one but his aunt and uncle knew about.

"Does she know what Uncle Paul was planning to do? This charade with his death?"

"She won't say, but she did say that she approves of Jessie—for you. That you make a cute couple."

Emerson chuckled. "That could be coming from you."

"She says you were always hardheaded."

Emerson laughed. "What did I destroy of hers when I was eleven?" No one but his aunt and uncle knew about that either.

"A wind-up clock. You took it apart because it wasn't working and then you couldn't put it back together again."

"Yeah. I didn't think she would ever let me live that down. But my uncle saved the day by taking me to the store to get another one. I had to work it off even though I already did a lot of odd jobs around the resort." And he realized then, he did believe Leyton had connected with his aunt's spirit.

"I miss you," Emerson said to his aunt. "I miss Uncle Paul too. I wish I could let him know I quit my job for good and am ready to manage the resort if he wants to retire for good in Florida, but I want to know if he's all right. That he's truly not in trouble and having to hide his identity. And that if he wants to stay at the resort and just have fun while I manage the day-to-day business, I would like that too."

"She can't say what's going on. But she says she loves you both." Leyton took a deep breath. "She's gone."

Emerson let out his breath. "She wouldn't say what had happened to my uncle."

"He would visit her though. She said you always came with him when you visited and spoke with her."

"Yeah. But wouldn't he have said something to her about what he was doing before he left?"

Leyton nodded. "I'm sure of it, but she's keeping his confidence."

"She would. I can't believe you can speak to ghosts."

Chet said, "Yeah, it took a lot for me to believe in it too. Then I learned Bridget, who I had worked with and wanted to date, could read minds. Except she couldn't read Travis's, another one of our special agents, whom she mated."

Emerson laughed. "*That* could be a problem." He was thinking about Jessie and if she could have read *his* mind.

"Jessie can't read yours," Chet said, "I suspect, it's probably a good thing for you."

Emerson only smiled, but then he recalled the picture Jessie had taken of the two men in her cabin. "I have one other idea. Jessie took a picture of the two shifters. What if we run those by the doctor and see if he recognizes them as the men who went to see him about my uncle, who claimed to be with the U.S. Marshalls."

He showed the picture to Leyton and Chet.

They both laughed. "They're naked," Leyton said, stating the obvious.

"Yeah, I'm sure that will shake up the doctor if it turns out the men he saw were the same men who broke into the shed and cabin five."

"Let's go," Leyton said.

When they went to the doctor's office again, the receptionist looked surprised. "He's in with another patient."

"We'll wait," Emerson said.

When the doctor learned Emerson and the CSF agents were back, he shook his head. "You all don't watch the old "Columbo" series, do you?"

They all smiled.

"We have a picture of a couple of men who dropped by the resort and wanted to know if they might look like the two U.S. Marshalls that came to see you," Emerson said, showing the doctor the picture on his phone.

The doctor's jaw dropped for a second. He glanced up at Emerson and the other men.

"Were they?" Leyton asked.

"Uh, yeah. What's going on?"

"We're investigating the case. That's all you need to know," Leyton said.

"Thanks, Doc." Emerson shook his hand again. Okay, this was really bizarre.

After saying their good-byes again, they headed out to the car.

"Okay, well, that's a new one on me," Leyton said.

"More of the puzzle to decipher," Chet said.

When they arrived back home, Jack and Jessie greeted them.

"What did you find out?" Jessie asked, sounding eager to learn what they had discovered.

"The naked men in your cabin? They pretended to be U.S. Marshalls to get Dr. Jones to say my uncle died of a heart attack."

"So he's alive," she said, hopeful.

"We hope so. Leyton spoke with my aunt."

"Wait, she's deceased—he spoke to her ghost in the mausoleum?"

CHAPTER 13

*J*essie couldn't believe that Leyton saw Emerson's aunt's ghost. She knew Leyton could do such a thing, but she hadn't thought Mrs. Merriweather's spirit would be hanging around the mausoleum.

"Yeah, Leyton said he saw her and conveyed some of her messages with me," Emerson said, smiling at Jessie.

"Oh, so did he convince you he can see ghosts?" She was hopeful.

"My aunt did."

Jessie smiled. "Good. That could be an issue between us if you didn't believe, when so many of my friends have special psychic gifts that I believe in."

"That would never have been an issue between us."

"That's good to know."

Then Emerson got a call and he answered it. "Fitzgerald?"

Florence Fitzgerald of CIA fame? Jessie wondered why she would be calling Emerson, and then she wondered if Flo had any idea where Smith was. If Emerson took off to chase Smith down, then what would happen to the resort? Even though no one was here—except for her and a couple of troublesome bears.

"Uh, yeah. Okay." Emerson glanced at Jessie.

He looked so serious, she was certain he had word of where Smith had gotten off to and Emerson would be on his trail as soon as he could. But Jessie didn't want to leave the resort until her time was up, and she was enjoying being here with Emerson.

She couldn't be selfish though. Smith could very well be out to kill Emerson and the others on the team. And she knew Emerson had to take Smith out if he could.

* * *

EMERSON COULDN'T BELIEVE Flo was calling him, especially after she told the cougars of Yuma Town that he was Black Ops. "Yeah?"

"Hey, I know you're probably pissed off at me for revealing what you do to some of the cougars, but we've got your back. Tell me what had occurred on the mission."

Emerson explained all that had happened to him and his men.

Everyone was listening to him in the meantime, waiting to hear what was going on and she said, "Okay, I'm trying to discover where he's gone to. I've got all kinds of sources, but I haven't found anything yet. I will let you know as soon as I discover where he is though. I'm sure you know as well as I do that he missed all but one of his objectives. And he will be out to terminate you, knowing that you will be planning the same thing for him."

"Correct."

"But you're in your own home territory now. And if he learns where you are, then someone else could get hurt."

"Jessie."

"And I hear your uncle isn't dead either."

"But he's not here." Emerson was rethinking having Jessie stay here any longer. She could go back with the CSF agents to either Loveland or Yuma Town, out of harm's way.

"Right. We need to find your uncle also and make sure he's protected until this is done," Flo said.

"The CSF agents can take Jessie home."

"No, they can't," Jessie said. "While the guys are here, I'm staying here. If Smith shows his ugly cougar mug around here, you all can take him down."

Emerson frowned at her. "If he pulls what he did the last time, he'll hire someone else to do his dirty work and just watch to make sure it gets done."

"And you took care of them, didn't you?" Jessie said, irritated.

"All but Smith, yeah."

"Well, this time you'll take care of him too."

He appreciated that she thought he and the others could handle this, but she didn't know how ruthless men like that could be. Not like he could be either. That wasn't something he wanted to share with her.

"Staying or leaving?" he asked Leyton.

"If Jessie is staying, we are too. And we still have a mission we're here for. To determine who the bears are who broke into your shed and Jessie's cabin and where your uncle is," Leyton said.

"Okay." Emerson said to Flo, "We're staying. We'll resolve this business with the bears and my uncle and then after that, we go to Yuma Town for Christmas."

"Good. Then everyone in Yuma town will be ready to take care of you."

Emerson smiled. He was used to having a team back him up, but this time he would have a whole town to watch his back? Not to mention he was going to enjoy Christmas with Jessie and her family.

"Oh, ask Flo if she can discover a phone number for a Robbie Randall in Naples, Florida," Jessie said.

Emerson repeated the request to Flo.

"Yeah, sure."

Jack said, "We could have found that information out for you."

Jessie smiled at him.

"Thanks, Flo," Emerson said. Then they finished the call.

"She's looking into the situation with Smith," Emerson told everyone.

"We'll definitely be looking for him too," Leyton said. "Any rogue cougar who murders, or attempts to murder our kind, will meet his end."

Jack and Chet agreed.

"So back to the situation with your aunt's ghost. Why hasn't she moved on?" Jessie asked.

Everyone turned to see what Leyton had to say about it.

"She doesn't want her mate to be alone. She wanted to see Emerson return to the resort for good and be there for Paul since Emerson has been the son they never had," Leyton said. "I imagine she'll hang around until Paul returns."

"Oh," Jessie said, sounding disappointed.

Emerson knew why she sounded that way. She was hopeful Uncle Paul would find a mate in Yuma Town.

The guys all looked at her to see why she would be disappointed about that.

"Jessie wants to play matchmaker," Emerson said, smiling.

"With whom?" Leyton asked, appearing curious.

"We have any number of single women around Mr. Merriweather's age who would be just delighted to meet him," Jessie said.

The guys all smiled.

Chet said, "He might not want to be found if he learns that's what you're up to."

"Nonsense. I imagine he was quite lonely while being here all by himself, no one to talk to at night, no one to snuggle with. Though we do have the problem with this Robbie Randall, if he has taken a fancy to her and she to him."

Emerson chuckled.

"Well, it's true. I mean, if he's all the way out in Naples, and we…" She bit her lip and smiled. "Does anyone want lunch?"

Emerson smiled at her and went into the kitchen with her. He knew what she was going to say. With her family and his split up like that, they were going to have a time seeing everyone, but she probably didn't want to let on to the others that she was even thinking about that.

After everyone had grilled cheese and ham sandwiches, Leyton and Chet tried to crack into the code to get into Uncle Paul's computer, Jessie was writing, and Jack and Emerson checked around the property to see if they could see any sign that the bears had returned. They didn't see any bear tracks, or human ones either, except for the ones they had made, but then Emerson thought to go down to the shore and just on a hunch, see if anything had happened to Jessie's stack of rocks. Sure enough, another rock was sitting on top of his.

Emerson explained to Jack that they figured the bears had stacked a couple of rocks on top of Jessie's.

"Okay, so we watch for them out here tonight," Jack said.

"It looks like they came down the hillside over there. It's steep, but the bears can climb. That way they're not visible from the house or cabins."

"A game?" Jack asked.

"Yeah, I think so, to show us they're harmless."

"They hit you and knocked you out. It was bad enough that Jessie had to call Dr. Kate about it."

"I'm sure they're not used to knocking a man out as a bear and didn't know their own strength. They got what they wanted, I believe and that was for Jessie to stay with me so I can protect her. Now I have you all as backup too. I can imagine they're trying to maintain a low profile, but they're still trying to show us they're not the enemy."

Jack shook his head and carefully balanced another rock on top of the stack. "If we had a wildlife movement camera, we could set one up out here. I never thought we would need some-thing like that."

"Me either." That was something Emerson needed to do though. There was no hardware store close to here, so he would have to mail order some security cameras and maybe they would get here before the guys left, and they could help him set them up. He never considered setting up his own wildlife cameras to capture another kind of shifter on it. Emerson used his phone to take a picture of the stack of rocks.

They returned to the house and he showed Jessie the picture. "The top rock is Jack's."

She laughed.

Smiling, Jack shrugged. "It's a challenge."

Emerson showed the stack of rocks to the others, to let them know to watch it should anyone come down there to stack any more rocks. Maybe they'd catch them at it.

"Let's go for a run tonight," Jessie said. "If they're coming down at the same place, we might catch them at it."

The guys all agreed.

"And we'll catch the sunset."

"Stack more rocks?" Leyton asked, as if he'd missed out on the challenge.

"From the looks of that stack, I doubt you could get one more rock on top before it topples completely over," Jessie said.

Emerson agreed with her there. "Any luck on getting into Uncle Paul's computer?"

Chet smiled. "Yeah, I just found the password."

"You hacked in?" Emerson asked, impressed, since no one else seemed to be able to.

Chet waved a piece of paper in the air. "It was tucked into a secret panel in the desk."

"Ah hell." Emerson had found it when he was a kid, and he'd forgotten all about it.

"Did that jog a memory?" Chet asked, typing in the password.

"Yeah. When I was twelve, I was trying to fix my uncle's stuck drawer. He'd had some bulky items in there and it jammed the drawer good. My hands were smaller than his, so he asked if I could unstick it. He went out to talk to some guests and I worked on the drawer until I finally managed to get the stuff out of there and open it. That's when I found the wooden inlaid panel. Of course I'd peeked, but there hadn't been anything under it, so I just figured it wasn't a secret hiding place like I thought it was."

"He probably didn't have a computer back then either," Chet said.

"He didn't." Emerson came over to the desk and sat down. He realized Jack and Jessie had joined them in the office too.

He clicked on the tab for the email, but he had to sign in and that meant sending a code to his uncle's phone, which Emerson didn't have. Then he realized if it did and his uncle was perfectly alive, he would get the code to change the password on his email account and he would know Emerson was trying to get into it. Was that a good or bad thing?

He didn't believe the bears knew he realized his uncle wasn't dead, or at least wasn't in his coffin. If they were in cahoots with his uncle, would he tell them what was going on? Emerson felt he was playing a chess game but didn't know all the proper moves.

Everyone was staring at the computer when it asked Emerson for the phone code.

"Okay, does anyone know how to change this, like if I'd lost my phone?"

"I do," Jessie said, as she switched places with Emerson. "Yes, I've lost my phone before, climbing into mines and lost it down the shaft. Pain in the butt. Losing a phone can be the problem with using phone verification for identification then." She changed the phone number to Emerson's. "You do realize if your uncle is still monitoring his emails, he'll see in an email that you changed the phone number for verification purposes."

"Yeah, well, he should have left all the information for me

since I needed to get access to the resort information and he shouldn't have made it such a hassle." Emerson folded his arms.

She let Emerson sit down to get into his uncle's emails. Everyone was delighted, expectant, hoping to learn more of what was going on.

Emerson opened up his uncle's email to find nothing. Everything had been deleted. Everything. No inbox messages, trash, spam, drafts, sent messages, nothing.

Leyton laughed. Emerson gave him a dark look. Leyton shrugged. "That's what I would have done if I had wanted to disappear."

Emerson couldn't believe his uncle would do it. This was a side of him he'd never known. Still, Emerson couldn't help but admire his uncle for it. He wondered if someone else had told him to do this though.

There were no links on the tool bar to pages his uncle normally accessed either, like the weather or his emails, or other important sites his uncle accessed regularly accessed, all but the resort website and the online reservations link to all reservations made, including Jessie's with a special note that said: one sweet, little gal, half off for any stays at the resort. Emerson smiled. He knew his uncle wouldn't need to make a note of that to himself. He was making it for Emerson so he would know just what the setup was.

"You'd better honor that," Jessie said, looking over his shoulder, "I mean when I come up for future visits."

Emerson laughed.

Leyton asked, "Jack, do you want to take a hike through the woods and see if you can see anything?"

"Sure."

"I'll go with him to keep him safe," Chet said and then the two of them put on their parkas, hats, and gloves and left.

"I'm going to make some inquiries," Leyton said. I'll let you know if I discover anything." Then he left for his cabin.

"I'm working on the story," Jessie told Emerson.

"Okay, I'm updating the website."

She smiled. "So you are going to rent out the cabins."

"Yeah. Next year. I do want to do some renovations, provide the cabins with Wi-Fi and some other amenities. I need to order the security cameras also."

"Okay, sounds good." Jessie sat down on the couch and opened up her laptop.

Emerson ordered some security cameras online and decided to get some wildlife ones too and see if he could catch any bears in the act of trespassing.

* * *

THAT NIGHT, Jessie and the guys all went down to the shore to set up a couple of fires near each other and roasted hot dogs, to be followed by s'mores, courtesy of Jessie, who had bought all the fixings with her to share with Emerson's uncle, if he'd been here. Emerson realized she really had spent some time with his uncle and wished he'd been more like that in recent years. That would change if he could locate him.

Leyton began taking pictures. "Kate and the others wanted pictures of us, if we did anything fun. In fact, she insisted on it. We don't share our photos with the outside world, so don't worry about Smith seeing where you are, Emerson."

"After this, we need to build a snowman," Jessie said.

Emerson glanced at the other guys who didn't jump at the chance to agree. They didn't seem all that interested in making a snowman. He hadn't made one since he was a kid, and he was all for it.

Smiling, Leyton was shaking his head.

"And we'll take pictures," Jessie said.

Emerson figured their families would tell the guys they had to help them build snowmen, once they returned home, if they hadn't made snowmen yet that winter. "We'll make the snowman tomorrow. Once Jessie is done with her word count, unless something pressing comes up."

"We can do it first thing after breakfast," Jessie said. "That way if it takes us longer than we plan, we'll have the time to work on it. I can get my word count done after lunch. Besides—"

"It will go in the story," Emerson finished for her, knowing just what she was going to say.

"Absolutely."

"We can do the snow angels later," she said.

The guys all smiled at each other.

"What? You don't think you should be making snow angels?" Jessie laughed. "Fallen snow angels then."

"I can agree with that," Leyton said.

Leyton started to stack up some rocks near Jessie's. Chet had to get in on the act, then all of them were. He was glad the guys were here to protect them and were having some fun at the same time.

"Hey, so what's the story of you kidnapping Dr. Kate, Leyton? Speaking of fallen angels," Emerson said.

"I was chasing after a rogue cougar and was shot. I had been running as a cougar, so when I broke into the clinic, I had only intended to get some bandages and antiseptic. I didn't realize the doc was napping in the clinic."

"So naturally, you took her hostage." Chet shook his head. "I keep saying that he didn't have to take her hostage."

Leyton smiled. "It was a good way to get the lady's attention."

"There was a whole manhunt after him too," Chet said. "Guess who wanted him the worst."

"Leyton's twin brother, Stryker Hill, though they didn't realize they were brothers," Jessie said.

"Yeah, it all worked out for the best though," Leyton said.

They watched the sun set, the yellows and purples and pinks reflecting off the water, making it the prettiest sunset ever.

Emerson wrapped his arms around Jessie as they were seated next to the fire with the others and listened to the lake water lapping at the boulders. The breeze stirred the branches of the trees, but they didn't hear any other sounds.

It was beautiful like this, but especially because Jessie was enveloped in his arms. He would never have been down here cooking hot dogs, or enjoying s'mores, stacking rocks, or watching the sun set if it hadn't been for Jessie.

CHAPTER 14

hat night, as Jessie and the men headed up the stairs from the shore to the cabins, she decided to stay with Emerson in his bed. There wasn't any reason to hold back. They were single, adults, had no other attachments, both wanted this and even if they had sex, it didn't mean they were committed to each other forevermore. But she wanted it and she was certain he did too.

"Night, all," Jessie said to the others as they moved off to their cabin and everyone said their goodnights. She and Emerson headed inside the house.

"Are you sure you don't want to stay with me tonight?" Emerson asked Jessie as they pulled off their hats, gloves, parkas, and boots.

"About that...yes. I mean, I do."

He smiled. "Now you're talking."

"I'll just take a shower and I'll join you in a little bit."

"Okay, I'll keep the bed warm for you." He looked so happy, like she had given him the best Christmas present ever, but she was hoping he would give *her* an early Christmas present!

Once Jessie had showered and dried her hair, she threw on

her black top and buffalo red and black plaid pajamas and when she entered the master bedroom, she found Emerson waiting for her in bed. He smiled at her, looking devastatingly handsome, very much like a hungry cougar, hungry for her, his dark brown eyes gazing at her with admiration.

"Black," he said, motioning to her shirt, sounding amused that she had been giving him grief about wearing black and she wore it too.

She smiled. "Yeah, I thought you might like that."

"I like anything you wear. It all looks great on you."

"Better than hot pink though, right?"

He smiled again. "You may be surprised to hear this, but I would welcome you in my embrace no matter what you're wearing." He pulled the covers aside for her to join him where she had climbed into bed before. As soon as she was in bed, he pulled the covers over her and she slipped into his arms.

"You don't think we're rushing this a bit, do you?" she asked, kissing his bare chest, hoping he wouldn't want to hold back.

"Not at all," he said in a rush. "The whole time you've been here, I've wanted to give you the time you need to do whatever you need to, but I've been enjoying every minute we've spent together. Believe me when I say I didn't expect that at all. I didn't think I would meet such a fascinating she-cat shortly after I returned home. Tonight, I was going to do anything I could to convince you to stay with me."

"Hmm, did I make it too easy for you then?" She smiled at him.

He ran his hands over her arms. "I've had so many battles to fight, I'm glad you made this easier for me."

"I care for you too much to want to play games. I have to admit, given the choice, I want to be doing things with you instead of writing and I have to make myself do the writing instead." She sighed. "You are just—"

"A bad influence?" He kissed the top of her head.

"Oh, yeah, you're just too irresistible." Then she slid her body up his bare chest to kiss his lips, his gaze on hers—ravenous, just like she imagined hers was as she considered his face, the little dimples in his cheeks, the hint of a smile playing on his lips.

"When it comes to you, *I* can't resist temptation. I feel this deep-seated yearning in my blood for you. I just can't help it." Sealing his lips with hers, he kissed her back in a way that mirrored just what she was feeling. That he wanted to deepen the relationship in a hurry.

And she was all ready for that.

Their hands were all over each other, and the kissing was heating up. Her blood sizzling with desire, she slipped her leg between his, her needy body pressed against his thickening arousal.

"Hmm, so hot," she said, rubbing her body against his, loving that she could arouse him so quickly.

His hands slid up the front of her shirt and cupped her breasts. His warm hands felt so good on her breasts, massaging, his thumbs moving to her nipples, peaking to his touch. He moved lower on her body, pulling her shirt up to expose her breasts. Then his mouth was on one of her breasts. His tongue teased and tickled her nipple while his free hand caressed her back.

He was a lover like none other. She felt like she was in heaven, the way he coddled her and lathed his hot tongue over her nipple. And then he moved his mouth over to her other nipple and suckled. She felt a feminine wetness and the sensual ache growing between her legs.

He moved his mouth from her breast and slid her pajama top over her head and tossed it aside. She'd undressed before in front of him to shift, but this was so much more intimate. His hands again cupped her breasts and massaged. Heavenly, dreamy. She leaned down and kissed his mouth, and his hands went to her back and rubbed her skin with a heated touch.

Tongues tasted and tarried, lingering in a slow, long kiss. She loved this with Emerson, loved how he was so sensuous and didn't rush making love to her as if this was a race to the finish. She rubbed against his arousal again and he growled low in a hungry, needy way. Then he pulled at her pajama bottoms and she kicked them off.

She didn't hesitate to begin pulling off Emerson's pajama bottoms. Then they were naked together, rubbing against each other like big cats, sharing their musky scent, claiming they belonged together at least in the short run. Tonight. For this moment.

Tension filling her, her body was so attuned to his, so desperate for his penetration. And then he moved her onto her back and began to stroke her clit with desperate deliberation, as if he couldn't wait to go even further. Shockingly intense need ricocheted through her every nerve ending.

She moaned and ran her hands up his chest, her thumbs stroking his nipples, loving the sensation of his flat nipples pebbling to her touch. His finger was doing an erotic number on her. She wanted more, everything, him inside her, pumping, thrusting, to climax, to come at the same time he came.

Soft kisses, soft touches, then he was stroking her again, dedicated to bringing her to climax and she treasured him for it as she arched against his touch, yearning for the pinnacle. He kissed her hair, her ear, her chin and throat. Whisper-soft kisses that made her feel cherished. She wanted everything he had to give and she wanted to give him the same in return.

She licked his mouth, then kissed it with heartfelt meaning and he kissed her back with the same passion and intrigue. She saw the darkened desire in his eyes and was glad she hadn't delayed this.

She was kissing him and ran her hands over his taut body, but all her concentration immediately again was directed to the feelings he was coaxing out of her as he stroked her. She felt like she was teetering on a climax, holding, holding, needing, wanting, and it hit. "Oh—my—god." She was so ready to tell him she was keeping him, but she knew it was a *lot* premature. She could imagine him applying for his old job back in a hurry if he thought he was going to be tied to a mating just because they were having sex one time.

She kissed him again, then pulled at his hip. "Join me."

She suspected he needed the encouragement that she wanted him to go all the way. It wasn't a mating, for heaven's sake.

Then he moved between her legs and centered himself, and pushed into her, stretching her, and she loved the way he filled her. Then he was thrusting, long, slow, deliberately, his body moving against hers, rubbing against her body, his mouth on hers, tongues touching and teasing. Oh, he was good. *Really* good.

Being with him in the throes of passionate sex was sheer joy and made her whole trip up here one of unexpected delight. He nuzzled her throat and kissed her, tongued her and she met her mouth with his and they tasted each other again. He continued to thrust against her, sliding his hand beneath her buttock and pressing her tight against him, his muscles tensing with his thrusts, perfection, taut, tight, carved in granite.

"Oh, honey, you're…mine." And then he let go and thrust again and again until he was finished and she smiled up at him as he rested his body on hers, covering her, heating her, possessing her, still filling her with his masculinity. And he wasn't letting go.

His solid, muscular body felt good on hers and for a moment, he gave her a long-lingering, soulful kiss. It was as if he really needed this after the attack on his last mission—a spectacular sexual release, a she-cat's attention. Here she had only been thinking about setting the mood with Christmas decorations when he set her world on fire with making love to her.

"We're going to have to think of some other arrangements," he said, kissing her forehead, her nose, her mouth.

"Other arrangements?" She couldn't keep her hands off his skin, sliding them over his muscular shoulders and back.

"About you leaving so soon."

"I have to go home for Christmas."

"Okay, and I'll go with you." He kissed her breastbone. "And then you'll need to return here with me so you can write even more."

She smiled. "And do more of this?"

"You might get some story ideas."

She chuckled. "You know me too well."

He moved off her and pulled her into the crook of his arm and rubbed her shoulder with a light touch. "My uncle should have told me about you sooner."

"He might not have felt you were ready to change."

"He might have been wrong."

She was beginning to think Emerson was right. One visit with her while she'd been staying here, even with his uncle in residence, and Emerson might have been rethinking ever going back to the job.

* * *

"HMM," Jessie said, waking in Emerson's arms the next morning. Now this was the life and she could envision doing this on a more permanent basis. "You know, I think your uncle really had the right idea. I hope we find him and he's safe and sound and not in any trouble, but we owe him the biggest Christmas present ever."

Emerson caressed her arm and smiled down at her. "I was thinking the same."

She sighed and kissed his bare chest. "We need to get up and get ready since the guys will be coming over to eat breakfast with us and then build a snowman. I'm so glad you want to do it too."

"Yeah." He kissed the top of her head. "Doing things with you is lots more fun. I'm glad you suggested it. The guys weren't all that enthusiastic, but you know they'll have a good time once they get going on it."

"They will." Then she finally pushed her lazy bones out of bed and got dressed.

"If they weren't here though?"

She smiled as she pulled on her sweater. "We would have spent more time in bed."

* * *

AFTER A HEARTY BREAKFAST OF EGGS, hash browns, and sausages, everyone put on their winter gear and headed outside to work on the snowman. Jessie looked like she was thrilled to begin working on it as Jack and Chet began wheeling a wheelbarrow load of snow from between the shed and the cabins to bring to the snowman in progress. Emerson couldn't quit thinking about being with Jessie last night and was beginning to believe his uncle was an intuitive matchmaker himself and did a great job at it.

Jack and Chet dumped the snow on the base and took off to gather more snow. Emerson helped Leyton with the sled, shoveling snow on top of it, then pulling it together to the snowman site. Jessie was trying to form the base while everyone was gathering more snow.

This was the way to go. No little balls of snow but using tools to create the snowman at a faster pace. Emerson had never expected to be doing this with Jessie and a bunch of CSF agents! It was fun and it made him forget about the bad mission he'd been on or searching for his uncle for the moment.

Leyton said to Jessie as they unloaded more snow for her to work on, "You know, I told Kate what I was doing up here and she wanted us to do the same thing in the courtyard between the clinic and our home when we return."

"Good, then you will have more fun when you go home."

Leyton added, "And she wants us to have hot dogs and s'mores over a fire pit since we proved we could do it in the snow."

Jessie smiled as she patted more snow onto the base. "See all the inspiration you're getting while you've been up here? Did you mention about doing snow angels?"

About that time, Emerson and Jack were back with another load of snow and waited to hear what Leyton had to say.

Leyton shook his head. "No pictures. No sharing about that."

The guys all laughed. Emerson wondered how long keeping the snow angels secret would last before someone shared that with the folks in Yuma Town.

Much later that afternoon, they were done with their snow-man, making him in three parts and then adding one of Emerson's uncle's red and green scarves and his black furry hat, they found a drawer full of buttons—black ones for the eyes and mouth and his chest. Then they added a traditional carrot for the nose and branches for the arms.

They took pictures with the snowman, including one of Jessie giving the snowman a smooch on his icy cold cheek. Emerson kissed her mouth to warm her up and they had some pictures together with the snowman. Jack had to have some to send to his wife and kids. Leyton, also.

Chet didn't want one taken of him with the snowman since he said he had no one to send it to, but Leyton said, "Your mom would love it. And if you don't send it to her, I'll send it to the big boss."

Chet laughed and got with the program.

Then they went inside for hot cocoa and Leyton said, "This seems to be a good day to have the ribeye steaks we brought up for everyone."

"Sounds good to me," Emerson said. "I hadn't expected this much company, or I would have had enough steaks on hand."

"No problem. That's what these are for. Where's the grill?" Leyton asked.

That surprised Emerson. He figured they would cook inside.

These guys were the ultimate grill cooks to cook out in the snow. "What can I do to help?" Emerson headed outside to help them get the grill out of the storage shed.

"Help Jessie fix the rest of the meal, if you don't mind." Leyton and the other men carried the grill to the covered back patio and started getting it ready.

Jessie was still in the house getting warmed up.

"Will do. Thanks." Emerson went on inside and Jessie was just getting the potatoes out.

"How about mashed potatoes and I had brought asparagus with me we could grill," she said.

"Yeah, that should be good."

"I hadn't expected the guys to bring steaks with them, but they will grill practically in any weather."

"That's hardcore, grilling in the snow." Emerson started peeling potatoes.

"Don't you?"

Emerson smiled. "If I had someone like you here that I could grill for, sure."

"Okay, I just wanted to make sure."

"That sounds encouraging."

"Not panicking yet?" She smiled at him.

"Should I be?"

She laughed. "This is the perfect way to celebrate creating a snowman."

Though he knew she still wanted to do the snow angels next. For now, she and Emerson started boiling the potatoes and grilling the asparagus.

"I like your friends. I hope they're okay with us being together."

"They're watching you, though, as long as you don't turn all rogue on me, they will be thrilled for us," she said.

* * *

"Taking down Smith doesn't count, does it?" Emerson sounded so serious Jessie thought maybe he was worried about how she viewed his past assignments, or this future one if he could nail Smith, even though she didn't really know what all his assignments had entailed.

She pulled him into her arms and kissed him. "He's the rogue and you and the others have every right to eliminate him for the good of our kind and for the others on your team." She mentioned them because the rest of the team members hadn't been cougars.

Jack opened the door and bringing in the cold air with them, Leyton came in with the steaks on a plate, Chet following behind Jack and Leyton.

Leyton said, "I hope we're not interrupting anything." But he didn't sound like it at all, which amused her. "Hey, Emerson, I want you to know that I would hire you in a heartbeat to join our CSF unit in Yuma Town, if you were interested in the job."

Chet scoffed. "Cheyenne, Wyoming. That's the place to be. I could use another partner now that Leyton, Travis, and Bridget teamed up together. Then they added Jack. But we figure you're going to continue to run the resort. So we don't have a chance at convincing you to be one of us."

"Yeah, I'll be running the resort." Emerson glanced down at Jessie, as if saying she was the reason he wanted to stay put and settle down, if she were interested. She figured he had spent plenty of time running all over the world and even though the CSF handled regions in the U.S., not everywhere—particularly because they didn't have cougars everywhere—he wasn't interested in chasing down bad guys any further.

"Of course, what we could do is hire you for contract work," Leyton said. "You could be our point of contact up here if we learn of cougar rogues creating problems in your area."

"Yeah, my boss could hire you." Chet turned to Leyton as they all sat down to eat. "Are you trying to raise an army?"

Leyton laughed. "We'll get you down to Yuma Town to work with us before you know it, Chet."

Emerson didn't say anything, but Jessie sensed he was intrigued with the proposition. She could understand his desire to fill that adventurous part of his psyche, but if he was working to take down rogue cougars on occasion, maybe that would satisfy his need to fight the good fight, if he still felt like he needed that. She thought she could manage the resort for him so he could take on some of the missions to help if he wanted to.

And yeah, she couldn't believe she was even considering doing that, as if they were going to be mated cougars! Yet, she wanted to help him. She seriously wanted to be part of his life. Sure, she'd dated lots of guys before, either ones who hadn't interested her all that much, or ones who were rotten to the core when she learned more about them.

But she felt really good being with Emerson—his teasing her by not telling her his full name, thinking it was funny, amusing her. His protectiveness when he wanted to keep her safe from the bears and the like. His conscious efforts to allow her the time to write—and she'd gotten much more done while she'd been here, much more so than when she was at home—despite all the stuff that was going on here. His wanting her to join him in bed, so they could talk about what was going on, when she knew he just needed someone in his life. And she didn't think he would react that way with just anyone who had waltzed into his life. The guys she had dated hadn't had any romantic bones in their bodies either. Sunsets? S'mores? Visits to scenic vistas in the area? Yeah, she could envision it and more.

"This is just delicious," she said. "Outstanding. It will give us a lot of energy for making snow angels next."

The guys chuckled.

She figured they had thought she'd forgotten about that! Or at least hoped so. But when she wanted to do something fun, she didn't forget. Besides, it would go in the story. Rough and tough special agents and a Black Ops guy, all former military, making angels in the snow. How fun was that?

"Your families will get a kick out if," Jessie said.

"And make us do it when we get home," Leyton said.

"Naturally. You should be doing that." Jessie served up slices of German chocolate cake for everyone after the meal and before they dressed warmly to go outside and play some more in the snow.

"I can just imagine Kyle and Noah piling on top of me while I'm trying to make a snow angel, just like when I roughhouse on the floor with them. Five-year-old twins can be a handful," Leyton said.

They all laughed.

"Make that five for me, one pair of twins, aged nine, and triplets that are three," Jack said. "Knowing Dottie, she'd join them."

"That would be fun." Jessie was having a ball with the guys and was glad that they had joined them, not only to try and figure out what was going on but were enjoying themselves.

"And you can send the pictures to your mother, Chet," Leyton said, rubbing it in that he didn't have a mate.

"She would wonder what in the world I'm doing on this mission," Chet said.

"Working and having a good time. You can do both." Jessie finished her cake about the same time everyone else did and she and Emerson began clearing the table.

"We'll clean up the grill," Leyton said.

"We'll get the dishes," Emerson offered.

Once Jessie and Emerson were done, they headed outside to make snow angels and take pictures with the guys. Leyton and the others had just put the cleaned grill back in the shed. As they were making snow angels near the snowman, everyone was laughing so hard that she thought this was good for Emerson after what he'd gone through, both on the last mission and here at home when he was knocked out on his own property. She thought *she* was making him feel better too, just by being here.

She was already thinking of bedtime and joining him in bed again. He was totally addictive.

Once they were done, she said, "Okay, I'm off to write and you guys do whatever you need to in solving the mystery."

Leyton saluted her and he and Chet and Jack returned to their cabin. Emerson went with Jessie to the house. "What are you going to do while I'm working?" she asked.

"I'm going out to the cabins and check them over to make a list of what repairs and updates I might need to do."

"Okay, if you need my help, let me know."

He smiled. "You have work to do. You need to write. I don't want anyone to accuse me of not letting you have the time to get your work done."

She smiled and wrapped her arms around his neck. "You are so good for me. I might just stick around. You know, go home for Christmas and then return. It just depends on how we both feel after Christmas. What if you feel like you can't handle all the family members being there? What if you and my dad don't get along? Or my sister thinks you might not be as good as you appear to be?"

He kissed her. "I'm going to fit in just fine and if you have a mind to do it, you're coming back with me. You can help keep me from getting lonely, but I'll be sure that you have plenty of time to work on your stories without interruption and we can do a lot of fun stuff too when you need a break."

"Hmm, that sounds inviting." She hadn't moved out of her

parents' home because there wasn't any reason to do so before now, not with all the traveling she'd been doing for photo books, but she was thinking this would be perfect. And if things didn't work out between them, no problem. She would just return home and continue on as before. Though she might get an apartment so she could write in peace. Particularly if she was starting to write romance novels and sell them and needed to keep up with deadlines. Though staying in her own place wouldn't be half as much fun as staying with Emerson.

"You staying with me would be a Christmas present I would never forget," he said.

Then Jessie's phone rang and she checked the caller ID. It was Flo. "Hi. Did you learn anything about Robbie Randall?"

"Yep, I've got a phone number for you."

"Oh, fantastic." Jessie knew someone would come through for them.

"Is there anything else you need?" Flo gave her the phone number.

"Pumpkin and pecan pies for the family for Christmas."

"I'll make them for you. Good luck with finding Emerson's uncle."

"Thanks!"

When they ended the call, Jessie smiled at Emerson. "We got Robbie's phone number, courtesy of Flo. Do you want me to call or do you want to?"

$\mathcal{R}$obbie Randall fixed Paul Merriweather a glass of apple cider at her home of Naples. "You should tell your nephew you're here, safe and sound and that he hasn't lost you for good." She hadn't even decorated at all for Christmas and said it was a waste of time.

Paul loved to decorate. It made him feel the joy of Christmas. "No. I have to wait until I know if he and Jessie are mated. Otherwise, my nephew could just up and leave, returning to his dangerous missions, angry with me for this whole ruse and figure I could take care of the resort again." Paul was vehement about that. He'd already lost his brother and sister-in-law in the boating accident during a sudden squall on Lake Superior. He'd lost his own mate to breast cancer. He didn't want to lose his nephew too. Paul wanted to bounce grand-nephews and grand-nieces on his lap, though he wanted to be called their grandfather.

He'd thought Robbie and he might really hit it off when she said he could live with her in the meantime in Naples, Florida. They had agreed it to when he'd corresponded with her through emails and texts and phone calls. He'd had fun showing her around the North Shore while she stayed at his resort. But she'd been staying with her two girlfriends at one of the cabins. His living with Robbie at her home in Naples wasn't the same.

He thought he would never miss the snow for Christmas, but here he was already missing that too! He wanted desperately to call Emerson—to tell him he was okay, that he was sorry he had concocted this whole situation. But Paul was so afraid his nephew would leave and get himself killed in some foreign country where he was doing his missions, that Paul just couldn't tell him what was going on. The last mission Emerson was on had given Paul such a scare, he'd finally become desperate to come up with this scheme to bring him home and keep him there.

"What if Jessie—and or Emerson—aren't suited to each other at all? You said they had never met. Which means they don't even know each other," Robbie said.

"That's how I met my wife. In a blizzard when I was running the old resort. I know Jessie and I know my nephew. He's like the son my wife and I never had. He's good-hearted, fights for what's right, and so does Jessie. She was always bringing to light situations that need public assistance. And I believe Emerson is doing what he believes in his heart is correct in righting wrongs. But he needs a mate and to settle down before he gets himself killed."

"Have you ever thought he might want that kind of lifestyle? That settling down *wouldn't* be a good choice for him? Some people need a constant adrenaline rush. Managing a resort like you did might not be for him. And what about Jessie? Maybe she wouldn't like to be stuck in the boonies with him all the time. You said she has family in Loveland and Yuma Town, Colorado. She would be far from home."

She did love her family. Paul knew that would be a transition for her. But he also knew she loved to get away from them so she could get some work done on her books. Then again, if she were married to Emerson, would he keep her from writing too? She had told Paul she was currently working on a new book and was super excited to see him at the resort. She was the bright spot in his life whenever she visited him. Paul had felt bad about not being there for her this time. He never knew when his nephew would return home, but he rarely made it home for the holidays. And Paul had so wanted that this year, but doing what he'd done would mean he still wouldn't get to see him. Still, the notion his nephew would be safe from harm was tantamount.

"I think once they were thrown together like they've been with an element of peril, that will give them a chance to get to know each other. That's all my wife and I had before I'd completely won her over. If it's not meant to be, it's not meant to be. But I want my nephew to take the chance at turning his life around, to settle down, to have a family and a more normal life. He deserves it after losing his parents like he did. I truly believe some part of him felt he should have been lost at 'sea' with his parents, no matter how much he loved us and treated us like we were his parents, though we never asked him to call us mom and dad. We didn't want to pretend to be replacing them."

"Okay, then there's you and me."

Paul knew this was coming.

"We had fun at the resort and all our crazy chats about what was going on in our lives—how annoyed we were with life in general, or the funny things that had happened, but living with you is a totally different thing." Robbie wasn't angry or frustrated, just tired of him. She wanted to have her house to herself again. He wasn't the right one for her.

He smiled. He felt the same way about her. Robbie was a retired teacher and she spent hours on the phone visiting with retired teacher friends. She didn't want to run at night with him as a cougar in the wildlife preserve. She just wasn't interested in running on the wild side like he loved to do in the woods back home.

Robbie read books at night and turned up her nose at playing board games. He knew he could beat her and that's why she didn't want to play. Here it was getting closer to Christmas and she was watching her weight, and that meant no baking Christmas cookies, which he loved to do at the resort to share with his guests. He didn't want to bake all that stuff just to eat it himself.

He didn't have any more guest-related stories to tell and she didn't have anything further to share with him that was funny or fun. She was totally against what he had done, telling him daily, two or three times a day that it was wrong. Though he thought keeping his nephew safe wasn't something to consider lightly. He'd thought of every angle he could come up with and the only thing he kept coming back to was that the one thing Emerson would quit his job and return home for was if he knew he had to run the resort because his uncle was gone.

So that was a bone of contention with Robbie. Paul was trying to mind his p's and q's while he was living with her at her home. He was staying in a spare bedroom and the longer he was here, the longer he wished he wasn't. Not that he was unhappy about no longer managing the resort. That had become a burden and he had been lonely for a very long time. Sure, he always had guests to say hi to, but they were there on vacation, not there to visit with him.

Jessie was the exception. She had made him treats and had run over to his place to share lunches with him when she wasn't working on her book. They even watched the sunsets together and shared s'mores. She would make the perfect daughter-in-law.

Robbie put the dirty dishes in the dishwasher. "I think putting your friends—your bear friends—in charge of this charade is a mistake."

Everything Paul had done had been a mistake, according to Robbie. She'd tried to talk him out of it, but he was determined to save his nephew.

Paul's friends, two bear shifter twin brothers, Luke—his fur a lighter brown, though it had a lot of black guard hairs also, and Nathan, his fur nearly black, were the Bier brothers. Black bears, both of whom lived in the area and had had a chance meeting with Paul in the woods one time, when they were all running in their fur coats last winter. That's when he had the idea of soliciting them to help him with this scheme of his.

The twins had been worried something could go wrong. Paul didn't know what his nephew actually did in his job, except that he came home practically dead at least three times over the years and the last time was the worst. Though his bear friends had told him they thought Emerson might be Black Ops. Emerson had to convalesce at the resort for a month, he'd been shot so many times—yet, thank God, had survived—until he was fit to return to duty. That's why Paul knew how dangerous Emerson's work was. Paul had to share that with his bear friends, who were worried Emerson was some kind of assassin and if he thought they had anything to do with Paul's disappearance, they could have a fight on their hands.

"They could have really badly injured Emerson. They're bears. He was human when they hit him," Robbie reminded Paul.

"I warned them to be careful when they tried to spook Emerson and Jessie. So far, the brothers say that everything has worked according to plan. When the electricity went off, they broke into the shed and left the door banging in the wind, making it seem like a break-in during the blizzard. But I hadn't planned on them knocking Emerson out. Still, it meant Jessie stayed with him overnight, and the bears learned he was okay. They'd been careful not to hit him too hard, they told me."

Robbie scoffed. "How often have they simulated hitting a man when they're in their bear coats? I imagine never. They wouldn't know how hard they could really hit."

Paul had to agree with her there, even if he hadn't wanted to. "He's all right and Jessie is staying with him."

"Because they scared the tar out of her by showing up at her place!" Robbie sat down at the dining table with him.

True, and he hadn't wanted Jessie scared like that, but he knew it had to happen or she was going to be Miss Independent and stay at her own cabin otherwise. Now with, Paul, she would come over and have meals, but he suspected since she didn't know Emerson, she wouldn't have. Paul needed her and his nephew to be together, if they were really going to get to know each other. If she could still work on her book and keep Emerson company, and he enjoyed her being there, wasn't that half the battle?

Here, Paul felt like a stranger in Robbie's home. Maybe Jessie would feel that way in Emerson's home. He sighed. He just hoped it all would work out between them.

Then Robbie got a call and he was going to leave and take a walk, figuring it would be another one of her longwinded conversations with her friends when her eyes widened and she glanced at Paul. He immediately suspected something had gone terribly wrong with all his plans!

* * *

WHEN JESSIE GOT the phone number for Robbie Randall from Flo, she was ecstatic. So was Emerson. She wanted to call Mr. Merriweather, or at least the woman she thought he might be staying with, but she figured Emerson might want to talk to him first. He motioned to her to go ahead, and he stood by to hear what was said. "Hi, I'm Jessie Whittington. I need to speak with Paul Merriweather. I'm his good friend."

"What makes you think I know him?" the woman asked, trying to be evasive.

Jessie was certain Mr. Merriweather was staying with her. "You stayed at his resort on Lake Superior. I need to talk to him. And tell him his nephew is home for good. He quit his job already. He wants his uncle to come home and spend Christmas with him. Tell him we know he's not dead and very much alive."

"Here, I'm out of this," Robbie said to someone else.

Then a man cleared his throat and said, "Hello?"

Jessie smiled. It was him! "Mr. Merriweather! Emerson quit his job before he even learned you were dead. Emerson's staying with my family for Christmas and we want you to come too." She'd been so ready to scold him, but she wanted him to come home first and didn't want to scare him off.

Mr. Merriweather was silent.

Jessie put it on speakerphone. "Talk to your nephew. He's been beside himself with grief, but when he believed you were alive—no body in the coffin—he was so thrilled. He just had to find you."

"Uncle Paul." Emerson was all choked up and that made her feel the same way. "Hell. We had to open up your casket and discover your body wasn't even there. It's like Jessie said. I'm done with the job. I'm not going back to it. I was done before I even learned you had a heart attack. Return home. You can retire. I'm running the resort now. You don't have to worry about a thing."

"You've got to come home," Jessie said.

"What about the two of *you*?" Paul asked.

"I knew it!" Jessie said. "I told Emerson you might have hoped for that."

"Well?"

She laughed.

"You'll have to return home to find out for yourself," Emerson said. "You know you could have just told me you really wanted me to come home and take over."

"No, I couldn't."

"Well, it's a done deal. And what's the business with those two bear shifters? Are they friends of yours?" Emerson asked.

"Yeah, I needed to have someone help to make sure you had come home and then stayed there to protect Jessie."

"Are you with someone you want to be with?" Emerson asked his uncle.

Jessie had forgotten to even talk about that. For all they knew, he was happy to be in Naples and had no intention of returning without a mate.

"Uh, no."

"Good," Jessie said, "because if you want to meet a whole bunch of fun-loving cougars—Yuma Town, Colorado is the place for you. I don't want to scare you off, but we have a few single she-cats that you might really be interested in."

His uncle laughed. "I'm on my way home."

"Good," Emerson said. "When?"

"I need to talk to Robbie about when I should leave."

"Now," Robbie said.

Paul chuckled.

"I can't wait to give you a hug. You gave us such a scare," Jessie said.

"I'm so sorry. I just thought the two of you might hit it off, well, and then Emerson would want to settle down and leave that dangerous job of his. Robbie already has found the earliest flight I can return on. I'm booking the next flight out on her computer as we speak. I'll see you tomorrow evening at six."

"Okay, we'll see you then," Emerson said. "Oh, and call off your bears, just in case they think they have to continue to harass us."

"Have they been?" Paul asked, sounding concerned.

"No, but we think they're hanging around, messing with our stacked rocks," Jessie said.

Paul chuckled. "I'll certainly let them know." Then he gave them his new phone number so they could call him anytime they needed to.

Jessie was thrilled that Paul was coming home. She just hoped she could convince him to actually go to Yuma Town to visit with the single she-cats there and might even find one he couldn't live without.

She hugged Emerson and he swung her around. "You are a treasure. We can tell the guys everything is cool. The bears are being called off and Uncle Paul is coming home. Then the others can go home to their families. They'll be eager to make those snowmen and snow angels back home."

Jessie laughed. "Right."

"I'll run over and tell Leyton what's going on."

"Sure. I'll get back to writing. Oh, but I wanted to tell you, if, uhm, things work out between us, I would be happy to run the resort if your uncle ends up in Yuma Town and the CSF agents need you to help them out up here."

"You know what you're saying without saying it."

"Hmm, we'll see."

"That gives me hope."

"Well?"

"I wouldn't want to leave you in charge of the resort by yourself."

"I would be fine with it, if this is something you would really want to do."

He smiled down at her and kissed her. "I'll let Leyton know it's up in the air. I wouldn't want to commit to anything if I was up here alone managing the resort."

She kissed him back, and then he went off to speak with Leyton, and she went back to working on her story, feeling light-hearted that the bears were mostly harmless, and his uncle wasn't under any kind of threat. She was glad he had a home to come back to since it sounded like being with Robbie hadn't worked out at all.

She sure hoped someone in Yuma Town would be right for him.

CHAPTER 16

*P*aul was ecstatic about going home. Everything had worked according to plan.

"So is everything all good?" Robbie asked him.

"Oh, yes, my plan worked perfectly. I couldn't be happier."

She raised a brow. "You got lucky."

"I'm intuitive."

Robbie laughed, sounding suspiciously like she didn't think he had any intuition.

But Paul knew it had worked and that's all that mattered, and his nephew and Jessie still loved him. "Are we still friends?" Paul asked, because he hadn't meant to create hard feelings between them.

Robbie fixed him a cup of coffee. "Yeah, sure, I'll be out next summer to stay at your resort with my friends and you're welcome to come visit me out here anytime you like."

He wasn't sure if she was being sincere or so glad he was going to be gone soon that she would say just about anything. "You've got a deal." About her staying at the resort, not about him visiting her in Naples, Florida.

He hurried to pack his stuff and couldn't believe his fortune that Emerson had decided to come home for good, and Paul suspected he was already hooked on little Miss Jessie Whittington.

Then Paul frowned. Why *had* Emerson quit his job before he'd even learned Paul had supposedly died of a heart attack?

* * *

WHEN EMERSON ARRIVED at cabin number five to tell Leyton and the others the good news about his uncle, he knocked on the door. Jack answered it. He and Chet had returned, and Leyton said, "You learned something. I can see it in your expression. You've learned your uncle is with that Robbie Randall."

"Yes. And the bears are friends of his. My uncle's coming home."

"Well, halleluiah. That's good news," Leyton said, slapping Emerson on the shoulder. "We love it when the case we're working on has a happy ending."

"So the bad news is you'll have to go home and make snowmen and snow angels," Emerson said.

The guys all laughed.

"But the other news is that I'll accept your offer to do contract work for you to handle rogue cougar cases if there are in my area, *if* I have a partner running the resort while I have to be away," Emerson said.

Leyton asked, "Partner?"

"Yes, if you all can help me convince Ms. Whittington of that —she said she would be willing, but we're not all the way there yet."

Smiling, Leyton shook his hand. "We'll welcome you to the team. Since our job is done here, we'll look into this business with Smith with Flo's help. She has resources we don't have. We also have a couple of retired FBI agents who might be able to come up with some ideas. So I guess the question is, are you and

Jessie safe here on your own, or do you want us to work from here?"

"Go home to be with your families. You're welcome to stay as long as you like, but I imagine you can work just as well from home," Emerson said. "Smith might never figure out where I am and there's no sense in you being here forever waiting on something that might never happen."

Leyton glanced at the other agents who inclined their heads in agreement. "All right. We'll leave first thing in the morning. But I want to say we've had fun with the two of you while we've been trying to track down your uncle, and I'm glad the outcome was good."

"I agree with Leyton on that," Jack said.

"Yeah. And having you on the team up here will really be an aid to us," Chet said "Otherwise we can get spread pretty thin."

Emerson nodded, glad to be of assistance. "We can have dinner tonight and breakfast in the morning together, before you all leave."

"Okay, that sounds good. We'll leave whatever we haven't eaten with you," Leyton said, "before we head out in the morning. There's no sense in us taking it with us."

"Sure, that sounds good. I'm headed over to the cabins to figure out what they might need to have updated."

"I think you're going to have to make some reservation time for cougars to come up here, once we tell them what you have up here," Jack said. "I know my family would love it. Some of the residents of Yuma Town could rent all the cabins out at the same time and just have a big cougar party."

"Hey, I like that idea. And, Chet, even you could join us," Leyton said.

Emerson smiled. "We can certainly arrange for that." He was thinking Jessie had been a real boon for business.

Emerson left their cabin, then checked over the outside of cabin four. Everything looked fine that he could see. He went inside and closed the door, then headed into the kitchen. The door to the cabin opened and he turned to see Jessie. "Hey, so now that your uncle is coming back, what are you going to do about living arrangements?"

Hell, he hadn't thought that far in advance. Emerson pulled her into his arms, liking that she was even thinking of that. "If my uncle still wants to have his hand in managing the resort still, I can understand that. If you decide you want to stick around long-term, we'll figure something out. We could find another home close by, maybe, build a home for you and me and my uncle could continue to live in his own home."

"Well, I had thought your uncle might find a woman in Yuma Town, but then I was thinking, what if—now that he's learned you've quit your other job for good—he's decided he still wants to help manage the resort, and even give you a break if you need it from time to time, just like you can give him a break. Maybe he really won't ever settle down with another woman because he's too set in his ways."

"Yeah, I don't know really. This is all new territory for me. But I don't want to lose you. We're going to make this work, if it's something you want to do, no matter what my uncle wants to do."

"I don't want to upset him," Jessie said.

"Are you kidding? He set this all up for you to meet me and fall head over heels for you. And he did that already. So he's probably thinking all this over too. And then your offer to have Christmas with your family and meet some eligible ladies? He might still end up meeting someone he needs in his life and want to live there with her in Yuma Town."

"Or move here with her."

"True."

Jessie began looking over the cabin. "This one is really differently decorated than mine. I have pictures of cougars in mine. What if we had pictures of bears in one, foxes in another, snow leopards in another, naming the cabins for animals, instead of numbered cabins. It could be more fun. We could even have a plaque on the outside of the cabin with a hand-carved animal to match."

"I like that idea."

She looked out the window. "It has a nice view of the lake."

"They all do. Yours is the most private, off in the corner like it is with woods between yours and the next four cabins."

"Yeah, I love it because they can't see what I do when I run as a cougar at night."

"Speaking of which, I wanted to go back to the lighthouse park and see which of us can reach the bottom as a cougar first. Why not do it with the guys too before they leave?" Emerson asked.

"Sure. It gets dark early and the park will be closed. We could do it and then return home for dinner if everyone wants to. I'll call them and see." Jessie got on her phone and said, "Leyton? We wanted to go to the Split Rock Lighthouse and see who could run down the 174 steps to the shore as cougars the fastest. Are you guys game?" She smiled. "We can go, then return to have dinner. All right. See you in a little bit." She turned to Emerson, while he was checking out drawers and cabinets in the kitchen to make sure everything was stocked well and didn't need any replacements. "Leyton said it was unanimous and he would win."

Emerson laughed. "Okay, sounds like fun. Kind of our last hurrah with them before they leave tomorrow."

"All right. I'm returning to work on my book then before we go."

"We'll work things out to everyone's satisfaction," Emerson said, wanting to make sure Jessie knew he wanted to make this work between them no matter what his uncle wanted to do.

"I just couldn't imagine what we were going to do. I don't want to live with your uncle in the same house. Not because I don't love him, I do. But because with writing I need some quiet time and your uncle tends to talk my ear off—which I knew was all because he was lonely and so I gave him the time. But I could always go back to my cabin when I needed to write. If we all lived together, it would never happen."

Emerson smiled and kissed her. "We won't be living with him."

* * *

WHEN IT GOT DARK, Jessie started some wassail in a slow cooker to go with the evening meal and then she and Emerson drove over to the lighthouse, the others following in another car. They parked as close as they could get to the park without arousing suspicion and then ditched their clothing in their respective vehicles. Leyton got out into the snow and left the SUV door open for the other guys to jump out as cougars, locked the door with the keypad and turned into his cougar. Emerson did the same for Jessie, then locked his door the same way and shifted.

They leaped over a fence and headed straight for the area of the park where they could reach the stairs. That was one nice thing about being a cougar. They could leap as high as sixteen feet in the air, and at a run, they could leap forty-five feet!

When they reached the stairs, they had to make a decision. It was wide enough for one or two people to walk abreast, and certainly two cougars could manage. All five of them would be a crowd. Next to the stairs was the old tramway, an elevated railway that had hauled supplies up on a flat car to the dock where the ships tenders were docked. A spur of the rail system was used so the lighthouse keepers could push a carload of supplies to the oil house and storage barns where the supplies were stored until they needed them since it was a 130-foot high cliff. The wooden part of the structure was gone, leaving the concrete bases as the foundation for the tramway for all time all the way down the hill. As springy big cats, they could leap and dive over the rocky terrain too. The three CSF agents indicated they would leap down the concrete bases, letting Jessie and Emerson take the stairs.

Jessie was thinking the agents might even have the advantage because the bases were so large and there were boulders or solid ground they could leap onto all the way down. She only wanted to beat Emerson down. The other guys were eager to best each other so this gave them all the same playing field.

Leyton snarled, telling them all it was time to test their agility and speed and they all sprang into action. Jessie was thinking what a beautiful shot that would have been if she'd had her camera on a tripod down below, capturing the picture of all five cougars leaping into the air at the same time. Better still, a video of the action in case someone won by only a nose would have been great.

Jessie was giving it her all to reach the bottom before Emerson, but she didn't think he was trying very hard to win—unless he was trying to win her favor! Which she thought was nice of him. She wasn't really all that much of a competitive sport, instead just enjoying the process. She had envisioned Emerson pulling away from her with a longer and more powerful leap than she could make because he was a male and he would reach the bottom a couple of minutes before she did—not to mention the other men were so gung-ho and would be down at the rocky shore before they would be—so this was an unexpected pleasure.

She glanced at the guys and saw Chet and Leyton were concentrating on beating each other, but Jack was the one in the lead by a nose. She wanted to laugh. Chet and Leyton, having worked together as a team previously with CSF seemed to be the best of friends, but, boy, were they competitive.

She made a huge leap from forty feet above, which Emerson hadn't accounted for and she hit the bottom and made a sharp turn, accidentally running into Chet who had reached the bottom too. Jack was already at the bottom, beating them all.

Emerson and Leyton landed next to them, and they all took off on the path through the woods. They could have run back up the stairs to the top to see who would be the winner climbing, but Jack had won the prize today.

Then they ran the long way around the path through the woods, racing each other. Even though she knew Emerson could keep up with the guys, he lagged back to run with her, which made him the perfect hero in her story. The others waited for them at the place where they needed to jump over the fence and return to their vehicles.

They all began jumping over the fence and then Leyton and Emerson shifted and unlocked their respective cars and opened doors. The other cougars jumped into their vehicles, shifting and dressing and then Leyton and Emerson climbed in and did the same. Then they drove back to the resort.

"That was so much fun," Jessie said. "You didn't even try to beat me."

He smiled. "I was enjoying running with you. But I hadn't expected you to make that last final jump or I would have done the same."

She laughed. "I was waiting until the end to make my move. I wanted to win. And I had fun with you too. Chet and Leyton were so intent on beating each other, they weren't paying any attention to Jack and he ended up winning."

"I thought the same."

"I think we'll miss them." Though she realized they had another problem. Emerson's uncle would return and then he would stay at the house. Having relations would be impossible in the same house. "When your uncle comes in tomorrow night—"

"I was thinking we need to move to your cabin so my uncle can live in his house and you and I can continue to enjoy our time together, if you're comfortable with that, and I'm hoping that you are."

She was glad Emerson was feeling the same way as she was. "What about doing research on the internet, if I need to?"

"I've got a technician coming in to hook it up at all the cabins in the morning."

"Oh, terrific. That will work, and yes, I want you to stay with me. What if I need protection still?"

He smiled. "I will be that for you."

And more. She was getting way too use to being with him at night and she didn't want to end a good thing. "Do you think Paul will really come home with us to see the family for Christmas?"

"Yeah, I do. He won't want to spend Christmas alone and there's no one at the resort which would require him to stay, but more than anything, he'll want to meet the rest of the family he's sure to hope will be part of his own extended family. Maybe he'll even attempt to convince you I'm good enough for you."

She laughed. "I can't tell you how much I've enjoyed being with you."

"That's good to hear. When I came home from that mission, all I wanted to do was have peace and quiet. If my uncle had been here when I arrived, I'd planned to spend Christmas with him, naturally. So when I learned he was dead, I just shifted gears. Instead of running around some other country, handling a mission, I would be chilling and catching up on movies I hadn't seen yet and trying to learn what I could about where Smith had gone to."

"You haven't watched the one Christmas movie I borrowed yet."

He smiled. "All right. We can watch it tonight, and if my uncle is in the mood for it, we can watch another with him tomorrow night."

"Yes! What are we going to have for dinner tonight?"

"If you want to brave the cold again, we could all have hamburgers over the fire pit on the shore."

"Okay, that sounds like fun. I'm sure the guys would like that since they won't have a chance to do that again, unless they come up here for a vacation with their families."

"Or a rogue ends up in my area, you're helping me out with managing the resort, and I have to chase the rogue down. I'm sure I'll have assistance from the other agents."

"True." She got on her phone and called the guys. "Hey, how does cooking hamburgers over the fire pit on the shore sound to you? We thought you might enjoy one last night on the shore before you leave tomorrow."

"Yeah," Leyton said on Bluetooth.

"Sounds good to me," Jack said.

"I'm all for it," Chet agreed.

"Okay, we'll grab the stuff and meet you down at the shore," Emerson said.

"We'll help you take the stuff down," Leyton said.

It wasn't long before they pulled into the resort and parked their vehicles. Then they gathered the supplies and went down to the shore with the hamburgers, bags of chips, and the hot wassail Jessie had made for dinner in thermoses to keep it hot.

"I wish I'd had a video of all of us racing down to the bottom of the hill today," Jessie said as Emerson and Leyton began grilling the hamburgers and she and the others set up the folding chairs.

"Not me," Chet said.

"Nor me," Leyton said.

"Yeah," Jack said, toasting them with his thermos of apple cider, "I wish you had too." Since he'd won!

Everyone laughed.

They heard someone drive into the parking lot above at the house and two car doors open and shut. Jessie hoped it didn't mean trouble, but at least they had several men here who could deal with a threat.

* * *

EMERSON SAID, "There shouldn't be anyone turning up, unless they think they can get a cabin for a night or something, which they can't."

"I'll go with you," Jack said and Chet took over Emerson's grilling job.

"Are you armed?" Emerson asked Jack as they headed for the stairs.

"Yeah. You?"

"No. I thought with my uncle telling the bears we're good now, we wouldn't have any more issues." Now Emerson wished he had brought a gun.

When they reached the top step, the two men who had been asking to see Jessie before she arrived greeted them. They were all smiles, as if they were trying to make up for hitting Emerson in the head as bears. This time they smelled of men and bears, no hunter concealment.

They extended their hands to shake his. "Sorry I hit you too hard. I'm Luke Bier."

"I'm his twin brother, Nathan, and I want to apologize also for my brother's mistake. We were both glad to hear that your uncle is returning here after his untimely death."

Emerson smiled and shook the men's hands. "Any friend of my uncle, is a friend of mine, though I don't expect friends of his, or mine, to knock me out."

"Yeah, it won't happen again. Your enemies are our enemies," Luke said.

"That's good to hear. This is Jack Barrington, a special agent with the Cougar Special Forces who take down rogue cougars. Bears too, if they have to."

The bears smiled.

"Would you like to join us in having some hamburgers? I'll grab some more meat from the house," Emerson said.

"Hell, yeah, we smell them. That sounds good. What can we do?" Nathan asked.

"Go on down to the shore where the others are and introduce yourselves."

"I'll go with them," Jack said, "so they know they're friends, not foes."

"Okay, thanks." Emerson was glad the men had come by to apologize. He really hadn't expected that. He grabbed more hamburger from the fridge, and then took it to the shore where everyone was visiting.

Luke said, "Yeah, we've been friends with Paul for a while. We never expected him to come up with this heart-attack scheme, but he was adamant about us helping him to ensure Emerson give up his life of dangerous work and settled down with the little lady." He smiled at Jessie.

"But when Jessie didn't stay with you like we thought she would, we figured we had to break into her cabin, well, use the cougar door to sneak in, let her catch us, and then skedaddle out of there before you came after us shooting. We didn't expect her to chase after us! And, Emerson, your uncle said you could be just as dangerous as the people who had hurt you the last time."

Jessie was frowning as Leyton and Emerson were cooking the bears' hamburgers last.

"His uncle didn't know about his very last mission. Paul was already supposedly dead." Jessie looked at Emerson, wanting confirmation, but he didn't want to mention the mission before this one to the bear shifters.

Luke said, "Well, Paul was telling us about the last time Emerson came home on a mission. He was shot so many times, Paul really thought he had lost him. And it was touch and go, he said, for the first couple of weeks."

Emerson was frowning at him. He didn't want Jessie to hear about that.

"Like you all, we have enhanced genetics for healing, but were not invincible. That's when Paul began to think of a way to get Emerson to come home permanently. He really didn't think his nephew would quit the job willingly, not after the last time—that Paul knew of—and Emerson still hadn't quit," Nathan said.

Jessie raised her brows at Emerson.

"The team was sent to help get some refugees to safety. Rebel forces overtook us. I just didn't run as fast as everyone else." Emerson hoped to bring a little levity to the topic.

Jessie rolled her eyes, but didn't smile. Everyone else chuckled.

"We got the refuges safely out, the team got me out of there, sure, shot up a bit, but I survived."

"And went back and got shot again!" she reminded him.

The bears raised their brows.

"Just a shot in the arm, no big deal." But Emerson figured he had to talk about it now. "That time I was ambushed by the man who sent us. That wasn't the same as the mission before, though I decided at that point, I'd had enough."

"Hell, no wonder your uncle wanted you to quit. What kind of work were you doing?" Nathan asked.

"Sensitive work." Emerson wasn't telling the whole world of shifters what he had been working at.

Luke nodded. "Black Ops. We told your uncle we figured that's what you were working at. Then he was even more determined to get you to quit your job."

"Well, you can untell him that the work I was doing was Black Ops." Emerson handed the burger in a bun to Nathan.

"It's too late now. He would never believe us. Besides, you quit and that's all that matters." Nathan took the freshly cooked burger and began to add honey mustard, mayonnaise, and a slice of cheese.

"But he'll do contract work for us, if we hear of a rogue cougar up in this area." Leyton passed off the burger in a bun to Luke. "So what do you guys do about rogue bears? We thought *you* were some rogue shifters, by the way, and that's why we came up to investigate."

"And you thought to take us on?" Luke laughed.

Leyton smiled. "We were this close"—he pinched his fingers together—"to catching you."

"We have a bear sleuth, a pack, so to speak, and our leader decides the punishment. We take care of our own. Like you do. So if you ever hear of bears causing trouble for you—other than us—just let us know. We can get you in touch with the leader in your area," Nathan said.

"You know about all the bear sleuths across the States?" Emerson asked. They didn't know about different cougar—for want of a better word—packs, unless they ran into some of their kind and met the rest of them in the area.

"Most of them. When we run into one, we check in and let them know which one we belong to. Not that all belong to a sleuth," Luke said. "There are a number of lone bear shifters in the States."

"Are you from around here then?" Leyton asked the brothers.

"Uh, yeah, about five miles down the road. Even so, it was a surprise to us to run into Paul. He was taking a night run in our direction and we were taking one in his direction. We met at about the halfway point, shocking us and him," Luke said.

"I bet. So what do you do for work?" Leyton asked, and Emerson thought he sounded like he was interrogating the brothers a bit, not just being social.

"Bear Relations," Nathan said, smiling.

"Bear Relations," Leyton said, then took another sip of his wassail. "This is great, by the way, Jessie."

"Thanks. It's perfect for the holidays and cold days and nights."

"Yeah, Bear Relations is kind of like your CSF, I imagine," Luke said. "We deal with unruly bears, investigate new bears in our territory and we'll be mentioning about our encounters with your kind too. We already informed our sleuth about Paul,

Emerson, and Jessie. Just as a heads-up. We stick together, you know."

"You know how to fight?" Leyton asked.

"Yeah. Just like you do, both in our fur coats and in our human skin," Nathan said.

Leyton looked at Emerson and it dawned on him that Leyton thought he should mention about Smith and how he might show up here. But the bears had a sleuth to protect. They weren't here to deal with a rogue cougar, if Smith learned where Emerson really lived. He hadn't planned to tell the bears about his last mission. He would have to tell his uncle, however. Which made him think that it really would be good if his uncle found someone to love and live with in Yuma Town. The cougars there would make sure he stayed safe.

"Why did you quit your job?" Luke asked. "Your uncle said you had before you returned home. He didn't know why but he knew something had to have gone down or you would never have left it. He asked if you were walking with a limp or anything. I didn't want to mention my hitting you again. Why *did* you quit your job?"

"We're not supposed to discuss our missions with anyone."

"Right, but you're going to tell us anyway. We'll learn about it sooner or later," Luke said.

Emerson raised a brow in question.

"Paul will tell us—if only to keep you safe."

Jessie sighed. "Just tell them."

Emerson told them what had happened, and Luke shook his head. "That sounds just like what happened to one of the guys in our sleuth. He was Black Ops too and quit for the same reason."

"Was the guy who contracted your team named Smith also?"

"Sharp. But he fits the description you gave us pertaining to Smith," Luke said. "Barrett Grison is still keeping an eye out for the guy. When we tell him what happened to you, he'll want to talk to you about it. Don't be surprised if he wants to team up with you to eliminate the traitor. We assume Sharp took money to have the team killed. Barrett and his team members were luckier than you and your team. It happened a year ago and only two of his men were wounded, but they made it out alive. They didn't see any sign of Sharp there, but they all vowed revenge."

"It sounds to me like he planned the operation better this time. And he wanted to be sure the mission was a success, so he came to observe this time. I wonder if he's done this to other teams in between my operation and Barrett's, perfecting his crime in the pursuit of money," Emerson said.

"That's entirely possible. We all thought it was a one-time occurrence, he had a grudge against someone on the team, just something, and when he was offered money, he was ready to sell out the group." Nathan exchanged his cell number with Emerson and then Luke did the same. "If you learn where he is, let us know. Even if he's not the same man, we'll all take him on. He'll most likely keep doing it if there's easy money in it for him."

"Was Barrett the only bear shifter on his team?" Emerson asked.

"Yeah. I guess like you were the only cougar shifter on yours," Luke said. "But he was a cougar, just like Smith was."

"Smith knew I was. He must have known about Barrett too, if Smith and Sharp are the same man."

"He did. He was really surprised about it at first, but then acted like it didn't change anything. No one else knew about their mission, according to Barrett, so the team members were certain Sharp had sold them out."

"Same with our team. It seems like too much of a coincidence that two different rogue cougars were facilitating hits on Black Ops teams. What does Barrett do now?" Emerson asked.

Luke and Nathan cast each other amused glances and Luke said, "Childcare Development."

"Oh, that's wonderful," Jessie said, jumping in right away to comment, as if she was afraid the guys would laugh about it.

Emerson smiled at her and rubbed her back. He couldn't imagine taking care of a bunch of kids after doing the kind of job he was doing. Managing the resort was more his style.

"With five kids of my own," Jack said, "I don't envy him."

"I'm putting off the inevitable," Chet said.

Leyton shrugged. "The kids make me feel young again. I think it's great."

"That's because they're not your full-time job," Chet said.

Jessie looked up at Emerson and smiled, appearing to be waiting for his take on this.

"I think it's great that Barrett's taken on another challenging job after his retirement from the kind of work he was doing," Emerson said.

Everyone laughed.

"I think you wormed your way out of that one nicely," Leyton said.

The way Jessie hugged him and laughed, Emerson thought so too.

CHAPTER 17

"*H*ey, we've got to get on our way," Luke said to the gathered cougars, as if he realized he and his brother needed to head out so that the cougar friends could enjoy their visit in private.

"The other agents and I are leaving tomorrow morning for home," Leyton said. "If you could watch out for Jessie and Emerson if you're in the area, we would appreciate it, just to give them some additional backup."

"Yeah, we had the same idea. That's why we wanted to know if the trouble with the last mission had followed Emerson home," Nathan said.

"Hopefully not. I would much rather fight Smith somewhere far away from Jessie," Emerson said as everyone rose to their feet to say good night.

"Well, if he does show up here, just let us know. Believe me, you'll have a whole bear-fighting force at your back," Luke said.

"The cougar wouldn't know what hit him," Nathan agreed.

"Thanks. I really appreciate it." Emerson gave Jessie a squeeze and she knew he was glad he would have some backup for her, more than anything.

And for his uncle, when he arrived.

The men shook hands, the bears gave Jessie a hug, and then the bear brothers took off.

"Not to break up the party or anything, but I'm getting cold." Jessie was ready to take a really hot shower and jump into bed with a really hot cougar to get even more warmed up.

"Yeah, we need to get packed up and call it a night," Leyton said.

"Yeah, I've got another mission calling to me," Chet said. "So I've got to get my mind back on business and not so much on party time, though I have to say I'm sure glad I came up here to join you all."

"We're glad too," Jack said as they gathered up their things and headed across the rocks to the stairs. "That way you all know just how easily I beat you at the lighthouse stairs to the shore."

Everyone laughed.

When they reached the top of the stairs, they all went their own way and Emerson unlocked the door to the house. "Did I dig a hole for myself when we were talking about the bear who works in child development?"

Jessie laughed as she entered the warm house. All the Christmas lights were so cheerful and made her think of when she first had arrived, and nothing was decorated. She should have realized right away things weren't as they usually were. But now it was and with Mr. Merriweather coming home tomorrow night, she thought he would be really appreciative and it would be even more like when she had visited in the past. Well, kind of. She had a new romance going on with his nephew she would never have envisioned.

"Oh, I need to make another German chocolate cake for your uncle. And we can't eat a bite of it until he has some—this time," Jessie said.

"Hey, if he hadn't run off, he could have had some of the first cake you made."

"True. I bet you don't have any ingredients for one."

"We can check and if not, we can go to the store in the morning and pick some up. I want to get some steaks to welcome Uncle Paul home."

"Okay, that sounds like a good idea. We won't want to have a lot of food that we need to eat up before we leave. We need to leave in three days to drive home, which will be a two-day drive. We need to make reservations also at a hotel on the way down. I found one about midway between Loveland and here that's really nice and has an indoor swimming pool also."

"That sounds good."

She went ahead and made reservations for two rooms at the hotel then, thinking how much more fun it would be having company all the way home—and back, because she already knew she was going to be returning with Emerson and maybe his uncle, so she could have more fun writing and spending the time with Emerson.

She took Emerson's hand and said, "Ready for bed?"

"Hell yeah."

* * *

THE NEXT MORNING after a wild night of passionate lovemaking —which was getting to be something Jessie was really looking forward to—they had breakfast with the agents and then saw them off. Jessie would miss them! Here, she thought she was fine being with just Emerson, but they'd all had so much fun, it had added to the experience.

After that, they drove to the grocery store to pick up everything they needed for the next couple of days. She hadn't realized how domesticated or fun it would be shopping for groceries with Emerson. She figured he would just go his way and she would go hers to pick up what they wanted, but while she was pushing the basket and pausing to look at groceries they might need, he was kissing her cheek, rubbing her back, telling her he enjoyed this as much as she did.

Once they were done, they returned home and unpacked the groceries. She helped him put them away and was about to set out the ingredients for the cake when Emerson said, "I'm going to run over and change sheets and clean the cabin while you're baking and writing."

"Wow." She wrapped her arms around his neck. "And you clean. Now that's a real change from the guys I normally date."

"I'm one of the good guys, remember?" He settled his hands on her hips. "I can't tell you how much good you've been for me. I'd been trying to figure out a way to discover where Smith was now—and eliminate him before you got here. Forget about Christmas and anything good. But you changed my focus entirely —on the positive things in life. I want you to know, if you decide to stay with me, I'll be keeping up the place, just like my uncle did before me. You can spend all your time writing your books."

"Just in case my books can help sell the resort?"

"Oh, you bet." He kissed her mouth. "I need to get to work. We can move our stuff over to the cabin in the meantime. I know my uncle would tell us to just stay here and he'll stay in the cabin, but this has been his home forever."

"I totally agree. And yeah, I want to stay with you. You've been the best inspiration for my book and that sure counts for something."

He smiled.

"And I don't mind helping with anything that needs to be done around the place. I need breaks from the writing too."

"I'm going to ask your dad for your hand in marriage, just as a courtesy, at Christmastime."

"No way."

Emerson laughed. "Do you think he'll say no?"

"I'm sure after he gets a special report on your behavior from the other guys, no, but we're not waiting that long."

"Is that a yes?"

She frowned. "Did you propose a question?"

He laughed. "Hot damn, yes, Jessie, I want you to be mine forever. I love you. You are the light in my darkness, and I don't want to lose you for any reason."

"You don't want to wait and ask your uncle first, or tell him what we're planning to do?"

"This will be the best Christmas present he could ask for. You're the best Christmas present I could ask for too."

"I'm ready to mate you and make it official. I finally found a cat that is just the one for me and you're not getting rid of me ever. I love you, Emerson."

"Hell, yes! I should have asked you sooner."

She chuckled. "Now, is the perfect time. Your uncle isn't here. The guys are gone. The resort is empty. We have the whole place to ourselves. You can clean up the cabin *after* we get some important business done and I can write some more in my book, once I've made the cake."

"Absolutely. Man, I'm glad I had decided to quit the job and came home to meet you."

"I'm glad I wasn't dating anyone when I arrived."

"With your family, the bad guys didn't stand a chance." He took her hand and walked her to the bedroom.

She was ready to race him there! She hurried him along until they were in the bedroom, and then there was no stopping them. They were kissing and then tugging off each other's clothes at a frantic pace as if they were afraid someone would show up and they'd have to quit what they were doing. She was so ready for this, the commitment, the connection, cherishing the love between them.

Even stripping each other of their clothes was pure pleasure, heightening the sensations of touching and kissing. Cold air swept over their skin as they continued to strip off their clothes.

He pressed kisses over her throat and down to her breast,

whisper-soft kisses that made her ache for him and desire him in the most intimate of ways. His hand caressed her other breast and she loved the way he made her feel, sexy, complete, desired.

She ran her hands up his abs and caressed his nipples with her thumbs. They pebbled and he moaned.

"I am so lucky to have you," he whispered against her ear, kissing it softly.

"Oh, I feel the same way about you." She licked his nipple and then the other, kissing them and then kissing his hard chest. He was a wonder to feel up, and she would never get tired of running her hands over his delicious abs.

Then they were in the bed, naked, her on top of him, rubbing against his full-blown erection, loving the feel of him beneath her. He was exhilarating and her heart was hammering it was beating so hard. She heard his beating just as hard.

He ran his hands over her thighs, smiling up at her, his eyes dark with desire, but then he moved her onto her back and spread her legs. "You. Are. Beautiful." His fingers found her sensitive center and he began to stroke her. "And mine."

She lifted her hips to feel the strength of his strokes, escalating the tingling sensation between her thighs. She so needed this, needed him in her life. She could haven't loved him any more than this. Nothing she'd done over the years was more important than taking this step in her life.

He trailed slow, heated kisses over her belly and she shivered with intense need, running her hands over his arms, feeling his biceps flex beneath her fingertips. His fingers created a heated rhythm deep inside her that intensified the passion until she was ready to freefall.

As she climaxed, she shouted his name, "Ohmigod, yes, Emerson!"

He smiled and was on top of her, kissing her, his hot mouth on hers, tongues tasting and teasing. He was divine.

And then he was easing into her like a hot male cougar who was ready to mate his she-cat all the way, no more waiting.

Pleasure enveloped her as he pushed into her deeply, and aggressively thrust and nearly pulled out and thrust again. She enjoyed the hard length of him imbedded deep inside her, his warm, appealing lips pressed against hers again.

He pumped into her and she tightened her inner muscles around him as she clung to him. He held himself still and peppered kisses all along her breastbone and then her jaw, moving to her lips and she kissed him hard. He began thrusting again. And he came with a guttural cry and kissed her long and hard, thrusting until the end.

He rolled off her and pulled her into his arms, hugging her naked body against his and she felt wonderful, the bond between them unique and exquisite.

"That was only the beginning," he promised her, stroking her arm. "Want to take a hot shower together?"

"You read my mind." She was definitely up for more! Christmas had come early—for the both of them. She couldn't believe she had agreed to be Emerson's mate so soon after meeting him, but nothing would have dissuaded her from making that decision either.

CHAPTER 18

"*B*efore your uncle gets on his flight, did you want to call him and tell him we're staying at cabin five?" Jessie said, kissing Emerson's shoulder, not wanting to leave the bed for anything. That was so not like her.

"I thought you were going to tell me you wanted to reveal to my uncle that we are mated." Emerson kissed her forehead.

She smiled. "I think it will be more meaningful if we do it in person. The same thing with my family."

"Okay, I'll call him and tell him we're moving to the cabin." He got on his phone and called his uncle. "Hey, Uncle Paul, before you get on the plane, I just wanted to tell you that we're going to stay in the cabin Jessie normally stays at."

"Are you sure? You must have already settled into the house. I'm fine with staying at the cabin."

"Yeah. We're sure. That's the way we want it."

"Okay, that's fine with me."

Emerson knew his uncle would be more comfortable in his own home and he was glad he didn't object. Emerson was damn glad he hadn't gotten rid of any of his uncle's clothes or personal items. "We're looking forward to seeing you tonight. We're so thrilled you're alive and well."

"Yeah, I'm sorry about that, but I'm so glad you've quit that job and you're home for good. I'm just about to board the plane. And, uh, thanks for saving me from my mistake in going to Florida to stay with Robbie. I was going to have to find other lodging before long."

Emerson laughed. "We would have been happy for you if it had worked out, but I'm glad you're coming home and we'll have fun having Christmas with Jessie's family."

"I look forward to it. I've really got to go now. I'll see you and Jessie soon."

Then they ended the call and Emerson said, "Okay, he's fine with it." He got out of bed and started to dress.

Now that Emerson was out of the bed, she didn't have any reason to stay there. She slipped off the mattress and pulled on a pair of panties. "Did he suspect anything? About us?"

"I think he figured I would tell him if we had mated or had agreed to it." He gave her an appreciative look as she fastened her bra and he finished dressing and sighed. "Okay, I'm finally off to clean out the cabin and get it ready for us to move now."

"Let me know if you need me to help you with anything." She pulled on her jeans and then her sweater and began stripping the bed. He quickly helped her.

Then she followed him out of the bedroom and into the kitchen where she began bringing out the ingredients to make the cake.

"I will. After I finish straightening up the place, I'll help you move over some of our stuff."

"If I had been talking to your uncle, I would have told him."

Emerson chuckled. "Can't keep a secret, eh?"

"Not one that's this good." She smiled, kissed him, and let him get to work while she began to make the cake.

Though she hadn't told her family yet either.

He found the cabin the CSF agents was neat as a pin, the beds stripped, and the bath towels set neatly next to the door. The kitchen was clean, and there was nothing that he had to do in there. He really appreciated the guys. He grabbed the dirty laundry and headed to the laundry room they used for the guests. He started the wash. He needed to get the sheets from the master bedroom and the guest room Jessie had slept in and their towels also to wash.

When all the laundry was done, he began hauling some of his bags over to the house while Jessie paused in writing her story to pack her bags, then bundled up and started carrying them outside, but Emerson hurried to help her on the way to the cabin.

"Hmm, so which bedroom are we taking over here?" she asked.

He'd already changed the sheets on the bed and brought over fresh towels and he was ready to try the new bed out with her, but he needed to get them moved over and they would take some food and drinks to snack on. He knew they would be having meals with his uncle at the house so no sense in moving it all over there.

"It's your choice," he said.

"Then the one I chose to begin with. I always stay in that room. It's got a prettier view of the woods."

"Okay, that sounds good to me."

Then they set things up and Emerson had to get the rest of the clean sheets and towels out of the dryer and change the bath towels and sheets out in the house.

She glanced at the clock.

"It's about that time. We have enough time to change out my uncle's sheets. Are you ready to pick up Uncle Paul?" Emerson asked.

She smiled. "I hope he's happy when he learns what we've done." She helped Emerson make up the beds in the house—Uncle Paul's and the guest room's.

"He's going to be thrilled we're mated when he learns of it. You'll have to call him Uncle Paul too."

"I will be happy to. And the fresh cake is ready for him, so we're all set."

When they finally arrived at the airport, Emerson could sense Jessie's excitement. He was glad she was thrilled to be with his small family. He hoped he would get as good a reception from her family, but he was glad he and Jessie hadn't waited.

They went to baggage claim and waited for Uncle Paul to arrive. As soon as she saw him, she waved, smiling. Emerson smiled broadly at his uncle and hurried to help him with his carryon luggage.

They hugged and Emerson said, "Here I thought you were a cougar. You're a fox instead, setting me and Jessie up."

"Did it work?"

Emerson just smiled and took him to see Jessie. "Yeah, it did."

"You are in so much trouble," Jessie said. "I'm not letting you off the hook for scaring us to pieces." She gave Paul a warm hug and he hugged her back.

"Just promise me you're going to stay with Emerson and give up all those rogues you've been mixing it up with," Paul said. "She's told me about every one of them when she's come to visit and I figure she needed my rescue as much as you did, Emerson."

"Oh, yeah, that's for sure," Jessie said. "Merry Christmas early. We're mated, if you hadn't already guessed."

"Halleluiah. It's about time. And the little ones, when they come, I'll be bouncing them on my knee, and they can call me Grandpa."

Jessie smiled. "That works for me."

"I totally agree," Emerson said.

"So how's the book coming?" Uncle Paul asked, while they waited to get his luggage off the baggage carousel.

"Good. That's why I decided to mate Emerson."

Emerson laughed, and he felt his ears burn a little. Paul was smiling.

Jessie's cheeks were flushed and she looked like a blushing bride. "I mean, he was great about giving me the quiet time I needed to write. I don't know what else you could be thinking about."

Emerson and his uncle shared smiles. He decided not to mention to his uncle that she was basing the hero in her story on Emerson.

"Okay, so now who all am I supposed to be meeting in Yuma Town?" Uncle Paul asked, sounding intrigued.

Emerson hadn't been sure if his uncle would really be interested in meeting any of the single, she-cats in Yuma Town, so he was glad his uncle would give them a chance.

Jessie told him about a couple of women that she knew fairly well. "There are others too."

"You want to run the resort, don't you, Emerson?" Paul asked as he pointed out a couple of black bags on the conveyer belt. "Those are mine."

Emerson grabbed them.

"Yeah, I do. I told you I would do it as soon as I quit the job and as soon as you wanted to retire. Do you still want to retire? I don't want you to feel like you have to give up the resort to me just to keep me from going back to the kind of work I was doing," Emerson said. "I'll help you run the resort in any event, I'm staying for good." He wrapped his arms around Jessie's shoulders and squeezed. "And Jessie is happy to stay with me, which makes me the happiest cougar alive."

"You're lucky to have her. And yeah, I want you to manage the resort. I'm looking forward to just goofing off."

"You deserve it, Uncle," Emerson said.

"You do and I made you another German chocolate cake," Jessie said.

"I should have known you would have made me a special

cake. I'm surprised Emerson hasn't eaten all of it by now. German chocolate cake is his favorite too."

"Well, we both did and then when the CSF agents came, that was the end of the cake."

"Well, thanks for making me another. So when are we going down to Yuma Town?" Paul asked.

"It'll take us two days to drive down there. We can all go in one car—"

"No. I'll drive my own car," Paul said. "Just in case I decide to stay a while." He winked at Jessie as they got into Emerson's car.

Emerson smiled at his uncle. He'd never seen this side of him and he truly got a kick out of it. He was hoping his uncle would find a woman who suited him and vice versa.

"We thought we would leave in a couple of days," Jessie said.

"Okay, that sounds good."

"Hey, Luke told me you could have a hitman after you though, Emerson. When you said you had decided you were no longer working for the business you were in, I asked Luke and Nathan if they knew why. So they told me, some Smith character had betrayed you. Maybe I should stay here and watch your back. He said he and Nathan would. And another of their sleuth members, Barrett," Paul said.

"They'll be good as backup. I'd rather you be somewhere safe."

"And Jessie?" Paul asked, sounding concerned about her as they drove back to the resort.

"I'm staying with Emerson to help him out in case he's attacked and I have to see to his wounds," Jessie said.

"Oh, you're referring to Luke hitting him. I hadn't told him to do that. They were just supposed to scare the two of you so that you would stay with Emerson for protection. Of course I had no idea some guy was after Emerson on his last mission and put you both at real risk, so that's what you might have believed was going on."

"Not when we thought they were bear shifters," Emerson said.

"Luke said this Smith character may be the same one who set up Barrett's team," Paul said.

"It looks that way, though we can't be sure. I need someone to sketch his picture to see if it's the same man."

"Jessie draws pictures," Paul said.

Emerson glanced at Jessie, surprised.

"Not like that. Not as a sketch artist. Sure, I draw from photos or people I see, but I don't think I could do anything from just a description," Jessie said.

"We can give it a shot," Emerson said. "It would be better than nothing."

"All right. While you make dinner, you can give me the guy's description, and I'll draw it."

Paul chuckled. "She's got you cooking the meals?"

"I often cook so she can write."

"I'm glad you are, Emerson," she said.

When they got home, they unloaded Paul's bags and he sighed to be home. Emerson was thinking that his uncle might not really want to relocate and that meant finding a she-cat who wanted to live up here. Emerson wanted his uncle to be happy, no matter what he did.

"Oh, you made a snowman. I love it. Now I know Jessie was right for you," Paul said. "I don't think you have made one since you were a teen."

"You're right. We had a bunch of Cougar Special Forces special agents helping us," Emerson said. "We had fun."

Jessie brought out her phone and showed Uncle Paul some of the pictures of the men making snow angels.

Paul laughed out loud. "This is great. I love it." He smiled to see all the Christmas decorations up. "Thanks for decorating the house and Jessie's cabin. I didn't think you would do that."

"Jessie had a big hand in it. If she hadn't wanted me to give her decorations for her cabin, we would never have gotten this far."

"It was one of the things that made me wonder what was

going on with you because you always decorated for Christmas before Thanksgiving," Jessie said. "It made me think something wasn't right."

"Yeah, that was one of the clues I left for you."

They laughed.

"You could have left your emails on your computer or your password to get into it even somewhere that I would have remembered to look. It took us forever to finally get it, thanks to one of the agents," Emerson said.

"I figured you might check to see if there was something important in there," Paul said.

She warmed up some wassail for them and then sat down at the dining room table to draw the picture of Smith while Emerson made them steaks, fried potatoes, and broccoli.

Even Uncle Paul came over to help him peel potatoes.

"Okay, so Smith has a cleft in his chin, narrow eyes, he's black-haired, kind of a long face, and—" Emerson said.

"His ears jut out," she said.

Emerson glanced over at her.

"You told me that when you first talked about him to me."

"Right. His ears stick out. He's got a prominent nose." Emerson came over to look at the picture she'd drawn so far. She was doing such a great job, he thought she ought to work for a police department. "That looks just like him." She was frowning at the picture so hard, he said, "Jessie?"

"I dated him." She looked up at Emerson. "Remember I told you in the beginning when you gave me his description that he sounded a lot like a guy I dated? The one I rarely saw. That's him. Samuel Cathines."

CHAPTER 19

*J*essie couldn't believe the guy she'd dated could be that rotten. She knew he wasn't the one for her. She'd had this sixth sense about him, that something wasn't quite right, but when the CSF agents had looked into him, and even Flo had, no one had found anything amiss. But he would see Jessie while passing through Loveland and disappear, see her and disappear.

He had always had good, plausible, work-related excuses about why he couldn't see her, so she'd told herself she was just being suspicious because he had to keep leaving.

She and Emerson sat down to have dinner with Uncle Paul and enjoy the tasty steaks he had prepared.

"We need to tell the bears the news that Smith is the same person that Jessie was seeing at one time," Uncle Paul said.

Here she thought they were going to have a nice quiet meal with Emerson's uncle, but now this business with Smith had reared its ugly head.

Emerson agreed. "I'll take a picture of the sketch and send it to Luke and his brother. They can share it with their sleuth and see if Barrett recognizes the man."

Though she wouldn't normally approve of people texting others while they had company and were enjoying a meal, she did in this case.

While they were waiting for confirmation one way or another with the bears, Jessie asked Paul, "So what is Robbie like?" Even though it seemed Robbie had wanted Paul to return home and not stay with her any longer, Jessie wanted to know what there was about her that must have intrigued Paul enough to go out there and stay with her.

"She was really funny and had a ton of humorous kids' stories to tell. She was a retired schoolteacher. I had a lot of hilarious stories to tell about guests at the resort too." Paul shrugged. "I guess I thought that was enough. At the resort, we had our own places to return to and she was with her girlfriends too. So we didn't spend a lot of time together alone. I joined them on the shore to cook hot dogs. They had a nightcap at my place. When I talked to Robbie about the dilemma I was in with Emerson and desperately wanting him to come home for good, she said to let things run their course, what would be would be. But I was afraid that meant Emerson wasn't going to make it back the States alive. She has no family of her own, has never been married, so her life is made up of her retired friends. She didn't understand what it felt like to lose a mate, a brother and sister-in-law, and only have one nephew left, whom I feared losing."

Jessie's eyes filled with tears. She couldn't help it. She always felt Paul was like her extended family and she felt she'd failed him by not having more to do with him when she wasn't at the resort visiting.

Paul patted her hand in a comforting way. "Not only did I want to ensure Emerson was still with me into my old age, I wanted a mate for companionship. Robbie wasn't really inter-ested. She was set in her ways and she didn't like me disturbing her routine. I wanted to go to the park. She wasn't interested. Too hot, too buggy. So I went by myself. I've been doing that for years. I wanted someone who would enjoy doing things like that with me again. The last straw for her was when I wanted to bake cookies for Christmas. I was going to do all the work, all the cleanup and then give them to her friends from us. I thought it would be a really nice gesture and would give me something to do while I did something that felt familiar and I enjoyed doing. But she was really mad at me. You don't know what a relief it was when you called."

Jessie laughed. "For both of you, it sounds like."

"Yeah, she couldn't wait to get me out of there. She didn't even drive me to the airport. She hired a taxi, just so I wouldn't change my mind—I think."

"Or she wouldn't change hers? Have a change of heart, realizing how good you really were for her?" Jessie asked.

Smiling, Paul shook his head. "No. She was ready to celebrate when I was leaving. I overheard her talking to one of her girlfriends."

"Well, there are sure to be some other she-cats who would delight in doing some of the things you love to do," Jessie said. "Even if you don't find a woman that you can't live without, you could have fun dating in any event."

"That's true."

Then Emerson got a text and he picked up his phone. "That's him, Barrett said of the picture you sketched. He wants to know exactly where you met him and when, and when and where he came to see you, Jessie, after that first meetup in case we can pinpoint an area he might be from. For certain, Sharp and Smith and Samuel are one and the same man."

Jessie felt her skin chill. She really hadn't wanted to go out with bad guys. They just seemed interesting. Of course all of them had been consummate liars and she'd only known they were rogues after the fact. Now she realized Smith had duped them all. Flo, the CSF agents, Emerson and his team, and Barrett and his. She still didn't feel any better about it. What if she had raised her concerns earlier on with her family? What if by not saying anything about her gut feelings—since she hadn't seen the guy in six months—someone with investigative skills might have discovered the truth and the men who had been attacked on Emerson's team wouldn't have been?

Emerson rubbed her back. "Hey, it's not your fault. I already know you well enough to see that you think it is. This guy fooled us all. But we're having your delightful cake next, unless Uncle Paul doesn't want to share any of it, and then we can sit down to figure out what you might know about Smith."

Paul smiled. "Of course everyone can have a slice, or two. It's all about sharing that makes it extra special good. And I agree with Emerson. What Smith did was despicable, and we'll catch him and put an end to his crimes. You had nothing to do with any of this. Now, let's have some of that cake."

Once Paul carved nice big slices for each of them, they sat down to eat it with glasses of milk. "So if I don't come home for a while because I'm visiting with some new lady friends down in Yuma Town, are you sure you won't miss me too terribly much?"

Jessie sighed. "You will be missed, but we'll feel much better about it if we know you're having a good time."

"I will be. Besides, I suspect you're going to need some newly-mated private time together." Paul cut off another slice of cake. "This cake is so good."

"You always love them," Jessie said. "I couldn't let you down after Emerson ate your other one."

Smiling, Emerson shook his head. "Somehow I seem to remember one pretty she-cat eating some of it and offering more to three male cats."

"Yeah. They could smell the cake and I couldn't let them think we weren't being gracious enough. As for me, I couldn't resist eating some myself."

"You should have seen me eyeing those pieces they were taking," Emerson said.

Paul laughed. "I was just lucky you weren't around when Jessie was here before, bringing double-chocolate fudge brownies and other treats."

"You didn't tell me that, or that you were keeping Jessie all to yourself," Emerson said.

Jessie was so glad Emerson and his uncle had reunited and would be together for Christmas. They really did sound like a father and his son.

Once they finished eating and cleaning up, though both Emerson and Paul insisted Jessie go off and work on her book, as if she could while the guys were talking to each other in the kitchen—and that cheered her, she finally left them in peace and let them clean up the kitchen. She opened her laptop and checked her emails first and got a big surprise.

Hey, Jessie, I know it's been some time, but I was going to be in Loveland around the first of the year and I thought we could get together if you think you'll have some time. I know you're probably working on another photo book so you might be off on jaunts of your own. Just checking in. Samuel.

"He wrote me an email!" Jessie hollered. "Samuel. Smith. Sharp. Whatever his name is!"

Emerson stalked into the living room to check out her email, his uncle moving in on the other side of her. Sitting beside Jessie on the couch, Emerson got on his phone right away. "Hey, Luke, I need Barrett's number so I can call him and keep him informed on what's happening with Smith...okay, thanks. Jessie just got an email from him. Yeah. Okay. I'll forward it to you."

Emerson gave Jessie the email addresses of both Barrett and Luke and she forwarded the email to both email addresses. "Okay, hold on." He looked over at Jessie. "Do you usually answer him right away?"

"If I'm not in the middle of something. What do you want me to say?"

Emerson put his phone on speaker and said to Luke, "He wants to meet with her after the first of the year. Of course, we want him to meet with her earlier, or at least he believes he will be, but we want to end this now before he does any more damage to people who trust him."

"Can you lure him up here? Not Loveland?" Luke asked.

"What about Yuma Town? They have their own cougar force there—sheriff, deputy sheriffs, the CSF agents? He wouldn't stand a chance of getting away if he was down there," Jessie said. "We could try and get him down there before Christmas."

"You don't think he'd shy away from coming to a place where your family will be and he might feel like it's a case of you wanting him to meet your family?" Barrett asked, and they realized he and Luke were on speakerphone also.

"Okay, after Christmas then? I could say that my family was returning to Loveland, but he and I could get together for a couple of days after and stay at the ranch."

"I don't know. I'm afraid it might scare him off, or he might just plain say he can only come the one time, sometime after the new year begins," Barrett said.

"Or it will sound like she's eager to see him early and that might boost his ego," Emerson said.

"She can ask," Luke said. "If it were me, I would give it a try."

"Yeah, I would too," Nathan said.

She should have known both brothers would be together.

"What exactly did you want me to say?" Jessie asked.

"You need to sound like it's you—the way you would say things," Barrett said. "Ask if he can come a little earlier than that. That you've missed him, or however you would put it."

"I wasn't happy with him the last time I saw him. He'd been seeing another she-cat and denied it, but he didn't have a good reason for why he smelled of one."

"Then he must have ditched her and wants to get together with you again," Barrett said.

"Okay. Here goes nothing." She typed up a response to Samuel. "I'm so glad to hear from you, Samuel. Merry Christmas! I won't be in Loveland, but I'll be in Yuma Town, Colorado. Have you ever been there? It's just lovely this time of year. Could you meet me there? Maybe right after Christmas? My family will have returned to Loveland so you won't get to meet them, but we could have fun there. Unless you could come before Christmas, that would be great. I mean, well, during Christmas, if you want to, but it gets kind of crazy with family being all together. I can't wait to see you. Just let me know when we can get together."

Emerson scoffed. She reached over and squeezed his hand and smiled. She was ready to take her hunky cougar to the cabin and make love to him, but she hadn't wanted to leave Paul alone so soon after he arrived tonight. Maybe they could go for a cougar run in the woods first.

Since she didn't get an immediate response from Samuel yet, she forwarded her email that she'd sent to him to Barrett.

Everyone remained quiet. *Come on, come on.* She didn't want to sit at her laptop all night waiting for a response, but she didn't want to miss his response either or she would be thinking about it all night.

No response still.

"Hey, let's go for a cougar run. Maybe by the time we return from that, Samuel will have answered my email." She was hoping like crazy she hadn't spooked him somehow, that she'd tipped him off that something wasn't right. Maybe appearing to eager to meet up with him when she'd been angry with him the last time. Or maybe he was just worried that she was looking to have him meet with her family, thinking they should tie the knot, or something. Some women could be so forgiving to rats. Not her, but he might not suspect that of her.

"Okay. We're going for a run. We'll get back with you when

we return, if we have an email from him," Emerson told the bears.

"Did you want to run on your own? Just the two of you? I could watch for an email from Smith and forward it to the bears, if he sends one," Paul said.

"No way. You need to come running with us," Jessie said. "We can run all over the place out at the ranch too in Yuma Town, but we want to run with you here also."

"Okay, Fine. I was hoping you would convince me. I need to stretch my legs after that flight," Paul said.

Before long, the three of them had stripped and shifted and were running together through the woods in the direction of the craft store, and she thought of the ornament he had ordered that Emerson had bought for her. She needed to thank Uncle Paul for it. She had never run with him as a cougar before. She didn't want to wear him out, and she was afraid he would feel the need to show off to keep up. So she did side trips, like when she was on a long human hike with her parents and they needed a rest. She would stop to photograph wildlife and nature. She couldn't do that as a cougar, but instead, she leapt into trees and back down, just playing.

She swore Emerson would have laughed his head off if he could have, he was so amused. Uncle Paul appeared to be also. She was glad she could entertain them. Though when she was on the ground again, she chased Emerson's tail and had him going in circles before he just tackled her. She growled at him in playful fun. She loved him for having a sense of humor and that he could be playful like she was. When he had been so dark and moody when she first met him, she had thought he wasn't the one for her, though she had thought it might have been due to his losing his uncle. She was so glad Uncle Paul was still here and they could enjoy this with him.

She licked at Emerson's muzzle and he licked hers back while Uncle Paul continued to walk, as if to give them some time together on their own. They quickly rejoined him and licked his face in greeting, cheering him. She was glad he was happy to be home, though she still wanted to find a mate for him that he loved. Would his deceased mate finally move on then? Jessie hoped so.

Then she wondered what they were going to do about everyone who believed he was dead. They had to tell the family doctor, at the very least. Who else had believed he was gone? The owner of the craft store.

She sighed. That was the trouble with telling fibs. When he tried to tell them why he was really still alive, he would have to make up a new lie, because telling everyone he had done it just to protect his nephew from the job he was doing and getting into the business of matchmaking probably wouldn't fly. She hoped he wouldn't lose any friends over it. Though probably most everyone would be thrilled to learn he was alive and well.

She and Emerson raced each other then, and he ran so far ahead of her, probably to show her that he could win, even if she beat him at the lighthouse park stairs run, just because she outmaneuvered him, which she thought was funny. But when she came to the end of his tracks, she immediately looked up at a tree and saw him sitting on one of its branches, waving his long tail back and forth.

She smiled. She loved him and jumped into the tree to lick his face. He licked hers too and nuzzled her face.

Then they hopped down and ran off to meet up with Uncle Paul somewhere on the trail behind them, but they couldn't find him. They found his paw prints had ended at...they glanced up at a pile of rocks and there he was, crouched to pounce. Before Emerson could jump up to stop him, Uncle Paul landed on Emerson, and they rolled around in the snow, playing.

She wanted to laugh, take a video and pictures, they were so cute. Then they got up out of the snow, their fur covered with it, and shook off. She was glad Paul had played the ambush game with Emerson too. Paul was still just a kid at heart, and she didn't want him to feel he couldn't play with them also.

Then she nuzzled Paul and though she wanted to race Emerson back to the resort, they walked back with him so he wouldn't feel left out.

CHAPTER 20

*W*hen they returned to the resort from the run, Paul headed to his house and Jessie and Emerson returned to the cabin to dress. If they had been alone, they would have skipped dressing and gone straight to bed. He hadn't had this much fun with his uncle in ages. He never had expected him to ambush him on the cougar run, which had made it all the more fun.

Jessie put on her hot pink pajamas and her robe and slippers, then checked her phone to see her emails. "Smith hasn't responded yet. I know you want to talk to your uncle and then you can join me later. You two need to talk. And I'm going to make a list of the times and places I met up with Smith."

"Yeah, we do. Thanks for understanding. And great on making the list." He frowned at her. "Did you see him a lot?" Emerson realized as soon as he asked the question, he sounded suspiciously jealous. He hadn't meant to, but he did wonder just how many times she went out with him if she couldn't just tell them already offhand how many times and where it had been. He regretted asking her right away as her lips parted, but then she smiled, a twinkle in her beautiful eyes.

She wrapped her arms around his neck and kissed him. "Just a few times. Maybe five and they were brief. He was always off on a job. He said he was an undercover agent, and he couldn't tell me what it was all about. I didn't ask him more than that because I knew it could be important to keep the secret if he was working in dangerous environments. I don't recall the exact days I saw him. I've seen him on and off for the last couple of years. I could guess, but it would be better for me to go through my text messages or emails and see when he contacted me, don't you think? Bad data can be worse than no data."

"Yeah, sorry, honey, I didn't mean that like it sounded."

"Sure you did. You were jealous and I appreciate that you cared." She kissed him again and he wrapped his arms around her —a bundle of softness and sweetness–and kissed her back and smiled.

He loved her.

"Take as long as you need with your uncle. I'll be waiting for you," she said. "Just remember, this time when I make an engagement with Samuel/Smith, I will be like a spider in a web."

"Somehow, I can't see you in that way, but we'll get him. Thanks, Jessie. I won't be too long. My uncle wouldn't allow it, knowing that we would want to be together tonight." He kissed her again, then pulled on his parka to see his uncle. "See you in a little bit."

She locked the door after him, and he trudged through the snow to the house. It was a lot easier running through the drifts as a cougar. When he reached the house, he unlocked the door and found his uncle in his PJs and robe and slippers, watching a movie in the living room. If Paul had wanted to, he could have gone to bed to watch the movie, but Emerson suspected his uncle had hoped he would come over and talk with him for a bit.

Uncle Paul rose from his seat and Emerson gave him a hug. "I can't tell you how much I'm glad that you're here. Thanks for everything you've done for me over the years."

"You too, Emerson. I couldn't have asked for a better son to raise. You turned out all right. I'm glad I set you up with Jessie. I was sure the two of you would hit it off. She needed someone decent in her life who deserved her. And I fully admit I wanted to keep her in the family too."

Emerson chuckled. He should have known! He joined his uncle on the couch. "I don't know if you would call me good, exactly."

"You have a moral compass that steers you in the right direction."

"I didn't expect you to ambush me on the run."

"I still have a few tricks up the old cougar sleeve. Now, I wanted to ask you if her family knows what you were working at?"

"Yeah. They investigated me to make sure I wasn't a rogue."

"Okay, good. I didn't want to make a mistake and say anything that I shouldn't with them if they should ask me any questions about you."

Emerson leaned back in his chair. "You can't tell anyone I was Black Ops. The family knows, sure, but the fewer people who know, the less likely Smith will learn of it and where I'm currently located. I don't want to put you and Jessie and her family at any more risk than I have to."

"I understand. Did she make the list of dates and locations where she met Smith?"

"She's doing that now and we'll send the list to the CSF and the bears to see if we can run Smith down. He hasn't responded to her email yet."

Uncle Paul frowned. "Do you think something she said spooked him?"

"I don't see that she would have. He might have been on his computer or cell phone and now he's off doing other business."

"I hated to learn she was dating the bastard."

"I know. Me too. I would never have wished him on anyone."

"Take good care of Jessie. I know she'll take good care of you."

"She's already proven that when she went out in the blizzard to rescue me. But she's so much more than that to me. She's the bright spot in my life that I needed. I just hadn't realized it."

"Well, go enjoy your time with your mate and don't worry about having breakfast with me in the morning."

"Are you sure?" Emerson was so glad that he had his uncle back in his life, he really had wanted to spend as much time with him as he could, and he was sure that Jessie would want to also. "You know Jessie and I both planned to have meals with you."

"Yes, I figured that. But I'm having the bears over to thank them for helping me get you two together. They want to talk to Jessie, but I told them they would have to wait until *after* breakfast because you're the equivalent of newlyweds."

Emerson laughed. "Okay, thanks, Uncle. We'll see you in the morning—after breakfast."

And making love.

After his uncle locked the door behind him, Emerson practically raced through the snow to reach the cabin and the object of his desire, even though the snow was deep and wet and cold.

He couldn't wait to make love to his mate. But he had to get warmed up first. He didn't want to chill her when he arrived at the cabin. Stomping his boots on the patio, he tried to shake off most of the snow collected on his boots and pants. He had expected her to be settled in bed, writing or something, but she was at the door in an instant when he opened it. He hurried to lock it and she hurried to pull off his hat and scarf as if she was just as eager to warm him up. He worked on his gloves, and then she was unzipping his parka.

The walk from the house through all the snow to the cabin was long enough that his face and outer garments were cold as she kissed his lips and shivered. He pulled off his parka and laid it on the chair next to him. Then he wrapped his arms around her and really got into the kiss, warming her and him up at the same time. She was sliding her warm hands underneath his sweater and feeling up his abs. He smiled down at her.

She was so eager, and he loved that she was that way with him. After everything that had happened before he'd met her, from the moment she'd come into his life, she had brought him out of the doldrums and he knew then she was a keeper.

His, for all time. She was a free spirit, caring, and loving, and just what he needed in his life. So did his Uncle Paul. He certainly could see why his uncle wanted to keep her for good too.

"My uncle was so right about you, you know," Emerson said, kissing her cheek before she reached down to untie his boots. He sat down and she pulled them the rest of the way off and left them on the rug next to the door alongside hers. He smiled at the sight, the notion really sinking in that they were truly a couple. He even envisioned having a twin pair of small Mukluks sitting next to theirs someday in the future. He was thrilled at the prospect, even though he hadn't thought he would be thinking of kids anytime soon. But Jessie made him think of just that.

She slid his sweater up and pressed warm caresses with her mouth against his abs that felt heavenly. Then she pulled his sweater up higher and kissed each nipple.

He couldn't wait any longer, his erection already growing with her touches. He swept her up in his arms and carried her into the bedroom and set her on the bed. He began untying her robe and pulled it off her shoulders. She was so cuddly in her bright pink pajamas. She pulled at his sweater again, lifting it until he tugged it the rest of the way over his head. She kissed his mouth, starting a slow burn of pleasure deep inside him. Then she was kissing him all over his bare chest.

"Hmm, honey, you sure know how to rev up a big cat's motor."

"You do the same to me," she said, licking his nipple, her blond hair floating about his skin, soft, shiny, scented with peaches, tickling him.

Then she was sliding off his pants and he yanked off his socks.

He ran his hand up her pajama top and cupped a breast. "Beautiful."

She purred with pleasure. "Hmm, so are you."

He hungered for her, her soft touches, hot kisses, her teasing tongue, wanting to slide into her and make her his all over again.

* * *

OHMIGOD, Emerson was such a hot bodied cougar, his movements deft, heat erupting inside Jessie, every bit of his touches making her tingle with eroticism and need. She was so aware of everything about him—the sexy smell of her big cat and virile man, testosterone and power, pheromones jumping with excitement.

He slid off her pajama top and pressed eager, solicitous kisses all over her breasts. She purred again, loving the feel of his hot mouth on her heated skin. Intense need filled her, preparing her for him as he continued to kiss her breasts and run his hand over hair.

She pulled off his boxer briefs, watching his erection spring free and smiled. Then he slipped off her pajama bottoms and they were naked together, their bodies sliding against each other's.

She was wet with craving and wanted him in her now, but he had other ideas and he began to move his hand over her belly, then lower. He began caressing her between her legs, but he was kissing her mouth in a way that said he wanted to touch her all over, tongue tasting hers, lips sucking on each other's. He cupped her lightly between her legs, then inserted his finger between her feminine lips.

She gave a start and smiled. Her body quivered with his delicious touch and she kissed his mouth. He licked her lips and then he began to stroke her between her legs. "Emerson," she said breathlessly. He was driving her crazy in a wonderful way.

He was kissing her breasts again and rubbing her clit, making her feel like a million bucks. He smiled and kissed her mouth again. The sweet ache between her legs intensified until he pushed her all the way to the top and she came apart in a million wonderful pieces.

"Yes!" She spread her legs further for him, and he moved in between them and eased into her. She reveled in his musky scent and arched her back, accepting him.

Then he was pumping into her with gusto, as if he couldn't get enough of her, that he needed the intimacy and connection as much as she did.

"Oh, more," she said, wanting him deeper, as deep as she could get him.

He smiled down at her, kissed her, and drew her legs up over his shoulders so he could penetrate her as deeply as he could. Their hearts were both pumping hard, as he continued to thrust into her.

The intense undeniable pleasure of their connection heated her blood to an inferno. Until he came with a final thrust, and a groan of release, but he didn't stop there. He released her legs from his shoulders and then began to stroke her between her legs again. She couldn't believe he would be trying to make her climax again and she loved him for it.

She was already so pumped up, it didn't take long for his fingers to work their magic on her. She arched to his touch, cried out, and collapsed against the mattress, pulling him down with her.

"I love you," she said, and he kissed her eyes, her nose, her mouth.

"I love you right back, honey. We make a team."

"Oh, yeah, we do."

And then they snuggled together, sleeping some until the next lovefest hit.

"Hmm, you are just perfect for me," she said, kissing his chest.

He kissed the top of her head and wrapped his arms snuggly around her. "You are perfect for me."

CHAPTER 21

a fter Jessie and Emerson made love and had breakfast the next morning, he got a text from his uncle. "That was Uncle Paul. He said he, Luke, Barrett, and Nathan are finished with breakfast if we're ready to come over and meet with them to talk about Smith."

"I'm ready," Jessie said, helping Emerson clean up after they ate.

Hoping the discussion wouldn't upset his mate, he pulled her into his arms and hugged and kissed her. "They'll ask a lot of questions about Smith."

"Absolutely, I'm ready for it. I'm an open book as far as helping you guys to nail the bastard."

"Okay, good. I don't want anyone to upset you."

She kissed him. "It's more upsetting to think Smith is someone I have dated. Not that it's a surprise, given the inclination I have had for dating the wrong guys. I'm just hoping something I tell you all will help you catch him."

"Okay." Emerson kissed her again, and then they got their warm clothes on and headed over to the main house.

When they arrived at the house, they met the new bear,

Barrett. He was a big man like the other bears, about six-four, and dark-haired, bearded, wearing olive-drab cargo pants, hiking boots, a heavy wool sweater, and he had olive green eyes that assessed them. He shook their hands, then they all sat down in the living room to talk. "You said you met him in Colorado City the first time," Barrett said to Jessie.

She nodded. "Yes. I stopped at a hotel on the way back to Loveland after getting some pictures for a photo book. He was staying at the same hotel. We literally ran into each other swimming in the pool. He said he'd gotten something in his eye—"

"You," Emerson said, sounding growly.

Barrett agreed. "He's a strategist. He doesn't accidentally do anything."

"You could very well be right. When we got out of the pool, his towel was on a chaise lounge next to mine. Of course I smelled he was a cougar—"

"And you know he smelled your cougar scent before he even got in the pool," Emerson said, figuring she hadn't realized the guy was that conniving. "You were alone in the pool first, right?"

"Uh, yes."

"He targeted you. Not as in the kind of mission we were doing," Barrett said, "but for playtime, nothing more."

"Hey, I know. All right. I always ended up with the rogues."

"Not this time." Emerson patted her leg.

She smiled at him, then grew serious again. "He took me out to dinner—to make up for running into me. We had a nice time. I'm sure he wanted more, but by then I'd had trouble with two different rogue cougars, and I wasn't racing into any new relationships, despite him seeming so nice. He got an important work call and once he was done with it, he quickly exchanged phone numbers with me and said the next time he was back in Colorado, he'd call on me and see if we could get together. I said good night to him and that was it. Nice letdown. No problem.

Free dinner, fun dinner conversation, and then he was gone. No complications."

"Then he called you again," Barrett said.

"That time, he said he was passing through Loveland and on the off chance I was in town, could he see me? I hadn't heard from him in six months, the rogue I'd been dating had been terminated, so I said, 'Sure, why not?' We met and had a nice dinner out. He had another call, had to quickly leave after the meal was done, and I figured then he was just always on the run and I wasn't interested in anyone like that."

"You didn't think it was suspicious that he found you back in Loveland when your photography commitments took you all over?" Emerson asked.

Uncle Paul brought them all cups of coffee. He'd always been the perfect host.

"Thanks, Uncle Paul," Jessie said and took a sip of her coffee. "No. You know, I might be naïve about the story guys are giving me, but they're damn good con-artists and they duped everyone."

Emerson nodded. "He got me and my team."

"And me and mine," Barrett agreed.

"But of course, now, knowing what he did to you both, I can look back at the incidents and question his sudden arrivals and departures. Another time was in Denver. He said he had a flight in there, could I drive down there to see him and spend some time with him? It was only about fifty miles from Loveland. But I was already in Denver. I just thought it was so cool that he was coming at the same time when I would be at the same location."

"Right," Emerson said.

"I know, I know, I'm not one of you guys no matter how many times I date the wrong men, but I still have faith in people, you know." She sighed.

"Well, these guys are definite cons. The rogues. You have to expect that of them." Emerson finished his coffee. He set his mug down on the coffee table and squeezed her hand.

"Okay, so you said he met you in Cheyenne, Wyoming once," Barrett said.

"Yeah. Now that time, he called me and asked me if I'd like to meet him there because it wasn't too far from Loveland if I was back home. It's an hour from there also."

"Were you?" Luke asked.

"Yeah, I was. I guess he knew that before he called me. I don't think he was using me for anything though."

"No, just someone he could trust who wouldn't stab him in the back when he wanted to date a cougar," Barrett said.

The guys all looked at each other.

"Wait, so Smith has always known just where I would be when he contacted me to get together with him? He knows I am here?" Jessie sounded horrified of the prospect.

"Yeah, honey, I think that's a good possibility. That when he asked if he could see you, he was fishing to see if you knew what was going on with him."

"He might have even known when you were going out with another cougar," Luke said, "and didn't want to get tangled up with that scene. For the most part, he likes covert operations."

"Oh, right. He never once wanted to see my family. I figured he was afraid it would signal some kind of commitment between us. It didn't bother me at all since I wasn't looking for any at the time."

"He didn't really want anyone to see him with you," Emerson said. "He probably knew all about your family terminating rogues that you had dated."

"Uh, yes, I'd told him about them. Just in case he turned out to be a rogue."

Emerson smiled. "Like you told me."

"Sure. There's nothing sneaky about me. But what if he didn't want anyone to see him with me because of the true nature of his business and he didn't want me to get hurt? The guy had to have some sense of decency, didn't he? Not that it would be enough to make me change my mind about him, but even villains have some side of them that isn't quite villainous, I have to believe."

"I doubt it," Barrett said. "He's all for himself. If you became an issue for him, you could easily have been eliminated."

That's just what Emerson would have said if Barrett hadn't.

There was a knocking at the door, and all the guys, including Paul pulled out guns.

Emerson headed for the door, checked the security peephole, and saw it was the UPS deliveryman. He hoped it was legitimate. He opened the door, and the carrier handed him the box.

"Thanks," Emerson said.

"Have a great day." The man got into his delivery truck and left.

Emerson put his ear to the box and listened for a ticking bomb but didn't hear anything. He locked the door and turned to see Barrett behind him, ready to take someone down.

Emerson set the box in the table and opened it with a pocketknife. Inside, he found his wildlife motion cameras and security cameras. "Okay, good. We'll have eyes on the property now."

"Hey, we'll help you set up the cameras," Nathan said, taking some of the equipment.

Emerson was glad he had help with this. They would get it done in half the time or less than him doing it himself.

"After we help put these up, we want to propose we stay here until you leave for Yuma Town," Luke told Emerson.

"Yeah, sure. You can take any cabin you want. We have one through four available," Emerson said.

"Okay. We just feel after seeing how Smith deals with Jessie, he always knows just where she's at. If he knows that," Nathan said, "he probably knows she's with you."

"Two of us will bunk together in cabin four since it's closest to both your place and the main house and Barrett will stay with your uncle to protect him. My brother and I will split forces between your cabin and the house if attacks occur at both places.

We were prepared and brought some things we might need with us to stay overnight, just in case. Since Smith will be out for your blood, all the force might be on your cabin," Luke said. "Particularly if he doesn't know that Barrett is one of the men here too. We'll park our vehicle at the cabin so it looks like you have some guests."

* * *

"Maybe Jessie should stay with my uncle," Emerson said. He wanted her with him so he could protect her, but he and Barrett would be the main targets, though Smith might not know he was in the picture also.

"No way. I'll be with you, Emerson," Jessie said.

"Jessie seems to be a fighter, not like us in our occupations, but nonetheless, she did chase after us in her cougar coat. That took some balls," Luke said, smiling at her. "Still, it might be in her best interest to keep her out of the crossfire."

"No, I'm sticking with Emerson," she reiterated.

He rubbed her back.

"Are you going to tell your teammates what we've learned?" Nathan asked.

Barrett said, "I would. If it was me who had been hit, I would want to know."

"The one guy's head wound was pretty serious. I would hate to see him come here to fight a battle that soon after the injury. It will take longer for him to heal completely, even though he's a wolf shifter," Emerson said. "The others, I haven't been in touch with. I don't have any idea where they're located. Condor's been keeping up with them. I'll tell him as soon as Smith is history. He'll be glad to know he doesn't have to keep looking over his shoulder and that we got rid of the man who set us up and he can tell the others."

Barrett agreed. "Okay, yeah. Depending on where they live,

they might not be able to get here soon enough to help us deal with Smith."

"Right," Emerson said. Just like Condor and the others didn't know where Emerson lived.

"We may have to escort you down to Yuma Town when you leave here to go there for Christmas," Luke said. "If he doesn't show up here, or send goons to take you out, he could be waiting for you to drive out of here, if he knows anything about your plans."

"I told him I would be going to Yuma Town, so he knows my plans," Jessie said, sounding regretful.

"It sounds to me like he's just learning from you what's going on," Nathan said.

"Or what about social network sites?" Luke asked. "Because of Emerson and Barrett's jobs, I'm sure they're not on social media sites."

"Yeah, I'm on all the social media sites, showing the places I've been, the photos I'm taking. I could see where he would be following me on that."

"Did you mention Emerson at all? Show pictures of him?" Luke asked.

"Ohmigod, no, but I can see what you mean. Smith is a friend on my Facebook page. He never posts, but he did ask me to friend him when I first met him." Jessie patted Emerson's thigh. "Sorry, you'll have to remain anonymous for the moment. But once he's no longer a threat? We're in a relationship. I can use another photo of you though, in case you think anyone else is gunning for you."

"Yeah, well, we can work around that," Emerson said, not wanting her to feel she'd made a mistake in mating him. He was glad that must be the way Smith was keeping track of her and not that he'd put tracking devices on her personal items or had someone keeping an eye on her. That's what he'd been really worried about.

"Do you think he would wait until we were on the road to Yuma Town?" Jessie asked.

"I believe he'll hit us here, not wanting to get your family involved." Emerson was sure of it. Smith would want this to go in his favor and he might feel there was an unknown amount of firepower where Jessies' family was concerned. Unless he'd met everyone in Yuma Town, he might not realize about all the cougars there who would be after his head.

"Not because he's concerned for their safety, but because he would be afraid of what they could do to him," Jessie said.

"Exactly." Emerson rose from his seat. "Let's put up the video cameras and start monitoring for Smith's arrival, should he come here."

"I'm staying here to protect Jessie," Uncle Paul said, which was just what Emerson had planned on.

"I'm going to write." Jessie got off the couch and gave Emerson a hug and a kiss. "Stay safe out there."

"We will. No telling when Smith might hit us. He knows you and I and Uncle Paul can see at night so he won't have the advantage. But he still might believe we won't think he'll hit us during the day." Emerson began pulling on his parka.

"You let Uncle Paul and me know if you need our help."

"We will." Then Emerson kissed her, and he and the other guys finished dressing warmly before they headed outside with the equipment into the snowy cold.

"You're one lucky cat," Luke said to Emerson.

"Yeah, and I have my uncle to thank for that." Emerson shut the door and heard the lock click on the inside. "I just hope to keep them both safe through all this."

Then the men began to set up the first of the security cameras. They were going to split up into pairs, but they figured they should have two watch for trouble instead. All of them were armed, so if they came under fire, they would be prepared.

* * *

"I'm taking some cocoa out to the guys," Uncle Paul said to Jessie after the guys had been outside for about an hour and a half as she was busily typing away on a scene and he was busy in the kitchen. He was so sweet and set a hot cup of cocoa on the coffee table for her too.

"Okay, sure. And thanks for the cocoa!" She figured he felt cooped up and wanted to go out and talk with the guys for a bit. Maybe so he wouldn't disturb her, and she knew they would appreciate some cocoa to warm them up. "Make sure they're setting everything up right."

Paul was zipping up his jacket. "How did you know I planned to do just that?"

She chuckled and took a sip of her cocoa and he finished pulling on his hat and scarf. She quickly got up from the couch and got the door for him so he could carry the armful of thermoses of cocoa outside. She noted he had enough for even himself. She shut the door and went back to working on her story, hearing the men thanking Paul for the cocoa and she smiled, so glad he was here with Emerson and her. At least he wouldn't be alone any longer, but she still had it in mind to do some serious matchmaking.

She'd been working on the story for some time when she realized Paul had been gone for a while. Then she heard someone approaching the house and she peered outside. Paul was trudging through the snow, returning with the empty thermoses, smiling. She didn't think she'd ever seen him happier than now. He was totally in his element, his nephew home and mated, and his bear friends all here.

Jessie heard something in the master bedroom, not sure what. Just something. She got up to check it out before she had to open the door for Paul. To her horror, she hadn't made it to the hall when she saw Samuel, or Smith, or whatever his name was, coming out of the master bedroom, his gun pointed at her.

"You tried to set me up by having me meet with you in Yuma Town. And to my amazement, you're with Thor," Smith said to her. "Don't you realize what happens to people who betray me?"

Thor? "And the men you set up, had they betrayed you?" Jessie knew they hadn't. That Smith was just a bastard who did it for monetary gain, at least she figured.

Smith shrugged. "All's fair in the game of assassinations. They should have known I wasn't to be trusted."

"So it was their fault you had them ambushed first?" She couldn't believe anyone could be that twisted. "Just for money." She guessed, but she wanted him to admit it for sure.

"Money talks."

That was exactly what she thought, and she shook her head. "And me?"

"You can't imagine how amused I was that you were telling me about all these rogues you had dated, and your family had taken it upon themselves to eliminate them. I can't believe you were naïve enough to believe I wouldn't figure out your game when you wanted to get together with me in Yuma Town. And your family would have been ready to eliminate me. What kind of fool do you take me for?"

"One that would come here and be right where we wanted you."

"What, here? With Barrett and a couple of other bear shifters to fight for Thor? Losers. The whole lot of them. My men will take care of them." Smith forced her to go to the master bedroom. She realized he hadn't planned to just shoot her there. What was he planning to do? Take her with him? It would never happen.

Uncle Paul opened the front door, his hands holding the tray of empty cocoa mugs and Smith raised his gun to shoot him. No!

"Watch out!" she shouted to Paul in warning, shoving Smith's arm up. He still got a shot off and Paul crumpled. "No!" she screamed.

Gunfire erupted in the woods around the resort and she figured that was Smith's plan. To wait for Uncle Paul to return to the house, kill him, and then the gunshot would signal to Smith's men to open fire on Emerson and the bears before they could come to Uncle Paul's and her aid.

Smith dragged her to the master bedroom where she saw the window was already open, and she realized that's how Smith had gotten in. And that must have been the noise she had heard when she was in the living room and went to investigate. Uncle Paul must have had it open sometime during good weather and never locked it. Smith let go of her and told her to climb out through the window, but she wasn't about to. She ducked behind the bed for cover, hoping he would flee. He fired a shot at the bed, but missed her. She waited a moment, heard Emerson ask if Paul was going to be okay, and was on his phone with 911, calling for an ambulance.

"Jessie, bedroom, Smith..." Paul managed to get out.

Smith was climbing out the window while she was hurrying to strip off her clothes and shift. She couldn't let him get away no matter what or they would continue to have to watch their backs until he was dead. She knew Emerson would take care of his uncle. Shots were being fired outside still as she leaped out of the window as a cougar, landed in the snow, and raced after Smith. Shots sounded farther away, down below at the water's edge, not in her direction and she assumed the guys had been putting a wildlife camera up down below.

Smith couldn't outrun her as a human. He wouldn't have heard her silent pursuit, but he glanced back just the same to make sure no one was following him, saw her, and stopped to fire a shot. She dodged out of his line of sight, hoping she wouldn't be hit, but she wasn't letting him go.

Before long, she didn't hear any more shots fired near the

resort. The sound of a siren way off in the distance was headed in the direction of the resort. And more sirens wailing indicated police cars were on their way. She prayed Uncle Paul would be all right. And that none of the others had been injured. She was still in hot pursuit of Smith. She was relentless when she had to finish something and, in this case, it was to make sure Smith wouldn't hurt anyone ever again.

She assumed Smith was running to where he had a vehicle parked, but before he could turn and get another shot off at her, she saw a big cat, her mate, running deeper in the woods parallel to her. Man, was she glad to see Emerson. She could have gone back to be with Paul at this point, but she knew the ambulance would be coming for him, and probably the bears would be there with him and telling the police what had gone down. Which meant she and Emerson couldn't be found as cougars.

Suddenly, a bear stood up in Smith's path. She thought it was probably Barrett, since she'd seen Nathan and Luke as bears, but this bear had more light brown fur on his chest. Holy, cow, the bear was huge, ferocious, imposing. Smith had turned back to shoot at her, not realizing Emerson was on his trail and the bear was ahead of him. She'd dropped back a bit so Smith couldn't shoot her as easily, knowing Emerson was going to get the bastard and Smith hadn't seen her mate. He certainly hadn't seen the bear drop to all fours and charge him. He was concentrating on her instead. *Concentrate on me, Smith,* she wanted to tell him, *while the men you betrayed catch up to you.*

Then Barrett roared. His growly voice was quite impressive, just as her mate turned and knocked into Smith. The two of them tumbled toward the cliffs and Jessie's heart nearly gave out. Smith could fall to his death and make it easier on everybody, but she couldn't lose Emerson.

Smith had a hold of Emerson's forelegs as they tumbled toward the cliff, not letting go, telling him if he were to die, so would Emerson.

She was so close to them, running her heart out, leaping as far as she could go, Barrett pounding the ground in their direction when Smith and Emerson went off the cliff.

She screamed as a big cat, horrified, her heart beating out of bounds, her blood running cold. She and Barrett peered over the cliff and down at the rocks.

Smith was holding onto Emerson's front legs and dangling off a narrow ledge. Emerson was holding onto the ledge, not about to be pulled off the cliff. Before she could leap down to join her mate and bite Smith, Emerson snarled and bit Smith's hand. Smith cried out in anguish. He released Emerson's legs and fell to the rocks and water below.

Emerson glanced up to see Jessie and Barrett watching him and he leaped up the rocks to the top. A human couldn't have done it that easily.

Jessie and Emerson licked each other's faces, nuzzled, and then raced each other back to the resort to see to Paul. She realized Barrett had disappeared and she assumed he had gone to wherever he had ditched his clothes to shift and dress. She wondered if Emerson had shifted at the house like she had done, and if the police were still there, how they could explain all this.

Emerson suddenly veered off, calling to her to come with him. She obliged and he shifted near where he had left his clothes, then quickly dressed. He gave her a hug. "Hell, I thought I'd lost you."

She felt the same way about him, but she couldn't say so as a cougar.

"I'm going to the house. I'll climb in through the window and grab your clothes, if I can. If the police aren't all over the place, I'll bring your clothes to you here."

She realized she should have done the same thing as he had done. She wasn't as good at this covert stuff as he was. She licked him and then leapt into a tree to wait and hope he was successful, and they didn't have a real mess to deal with once they had to speak with the police.

Thinking of that, what was she supposed to say?

* * *

EMERSON SMILED at Jessie sitting in the tree to reassure her since she looked so worried, then he raced through the snowy woods to the main house, hoping to God his uncle was going to pull through all right. He was just damn glad Smith was dead and Jessie was okay. Now they just had to work out the details of what had happened to share with the police.

He finally reached the back of the house and peered into the open window of the master bedroom. He didn't hear anyone inside, and he hurried to climb in through the window, then grabbed Jessie's clothes and climbed out the window again. He ran back to where she was sitting in the tree still. Once he reached her, she leaped down and wound herself around him in greeting. Then she shifted and he helped her to dress. He suspected that she'd never had someone help her to dress as a cougar in the woods like this after shifting since she was grown.

It was bitterly cold out and she was shivering. "What's our story?" she whispered.

"The men will say we all live here, since we do, and no one knows who most of the shooters are, since we don't know all of them. We can't tell them about the Black Ops missions. There's no way to verify what we do."

"You knew some of the shooters?" Jessie asked, sounding shocked.

"Reginald, the bastard. I'd served time with him as an army ranger."

"And Smith?"

"We'll tell them he took you hostage, which he did in the beginning, and then I caught up with him and we fought. He fell to his death off the cliff. The others were undoubtedly hitmen, mercenaries. The police might not be able to learn who they are, but we're all local and they're not. Not to mention Uncle Paul hasn't ever harmed anyone."

"But what do I say about Smith?"

"He was a man who had dated you and shot at you and you escaped through the same window he came in. I take it that's how Smith got in?"

"Yeah, the window wasn't locked. I suspect that Paul had opened it sometime earlier in the year and when he shut the window, he never had locked. It."

"Okay, so we go with that story. Smith was chasing you and as soon as I had help coming for my uncle, and Nathan was looking after him, I hurried off to rescue you. I knocked Smith off the ledge, only he grabbed hold of me and pulled me off with him."

Jessie looked worried. He didn't blame her. He was used to making up cover stories.

"He fired shots at me."

"We'll add that to the story."

Once she had finished dressing, they headed to resort, but walked around the back, his hand on hers, squeezing tight, trying to give her comfort.

As soon as they saw the police, they explained who they were and how Smith had taken Jessie hostage.

"We dated before," she said. "He was angry I was dating Emerson now."

"Smith orchestrated the hit on us. When he took Jessie hostage, I took after him."

Barrett said, "I did too. Emerson and Smith got into a scuffle as Emerson was trying to free his fiancée. Then while they were fighting, they both fell off the cliff. Jessie and I feared they had both died. But when we looked over the cliff's edge, we found Emerson on a small ledge and he was making the climb up. Smith had fallen to the rocks below."

"My Uncle Paul was serving us hot cocoa when we were putting up video cameras. The storage unit had been broken into a few days earlier, but nothing seemed to be missing and I replaced the doorknob, so I didn't report it," Emerson said. "But still, I wanted to get some security cameras up. That's when all hell broke loose. Also, you'll find bullet casings where Smith was trying to shoot me as I ran after him to free Jessie."

"We wounded the three other men," Luke said. "They appeared to be well-trained, whoever Smith had hired."

"Why were they after you?" the officer asked, taking notes, acting as though they hadn't explained to him about the relationship Jessie and Smith had had.

"Jessie was the reason. Some men just go off the deep end when they can't have a woman they want. How he knew the other men, I have no clue," Emerson said. "Oh, except for Reginald Bates. We served in the army together—a fellow ranger. I couldn't believe he would stoop so low."

The officer shook his head. "You'll have to identify him for us. None of the men had any IDs on them and they won't talk."

"I will."

"I'll take you to where Smith fell," Barrett said.

Emerson cleared his throat. "If we're free to go, Officer, Jessie and I need to get to the hospital to see my Uncle Paul."

The wounded men had already been taken away by ambulances, or Emerson would have just identified his ass right there.

"Yeah, sure, you'll be staying here then?" the officer asked.

"Yes, we will," Emerson said.

"And we live nearby here also," Luke said. "Wish Paul the best from us, Emerson, Jessie."

"We will."

"I'll meet up with you at the hospital," the officer said. "The men are being treated for wounds they received in the shootout and you can ID Bates. I need to get Paul Merriweather's statement also when he comes out of surgery."

Then Emerson and Jessie took off in his car and headed to the hospital. "I can't believe Smith got into the house while Uncle Paul came out to bring us hot chocolate."

"He was waiting for the right moment to begin the shootout. I imagine he would have sneaked in anyway and shot Paul, just to alert the hired mercenaries to take you all out." She explained what Smith had said to her. "I think he really didn't want to shoot me, but he knew he had to. Leave no witnesses behind."

"I thought you would have stayed with my uncle when he was shot."

"I would have but I heard you calling an ambulance for your uncle and I had to go after Smith. I couldn't let him get away and continue to send men after us."

"I knew I'd met the right she-cat when I'd met you." Emerson had to let her know with all his heart that she'd made all the right choices.

a s soon as Paul was out of surgery and had finally been moved from the ICU to the recovery room, Jessie said to Emerson, "Thank God, he's fine."

"Yeah, a Christmas miracle." Emerson hugged and kissed her as they stood over his uncle, waiting for him to wake from the anesthesia, then got some chairs and sat down next to him.

"I need to call my family again and tell them we won't make it for Christmas. I'm sure they assumed that when we took him to the emergency room for surgery, but I just need to confirm we're not coming," Jessie said.

"You could—"

"No way. I want to be with my mate and Uncle Paul needs me too."

Emerson smiled and reached over and squeezed her hand.

She squeezed his back and then called her sister. "Hey, Tracey, Uncle Paul is out of surgery and in recovery. He's going to do fine the doctor says. But we won't be able to come down there for Christmas."

"We all discussed it—Mom and Dad and the rest of us. We're

coming up there if you have enough room for us. You said you have several cabins and they're not rented out right now."

"Oh, yeah, we would love that." Jessie said to Emerson, "Tracey and the family want to come up here and stay in the cabins."

"Absolutely. Would they make it in time for Christmas though?"

"We could have Christmas late," Jessie said.

"Nothing doing. We're flying up there in a private jet that another cougar owns, and we'll be up there before you know it," Tracey said. "The kids can't wait. They were so excited when they saw the pictures of you with the snowman and making snow angels and stacking rocks, roasting hot dogs and marshmallows on the firepit, they're ready for the adventure. Not to mention they're thrilled about flying in a private jet."

Tears filled Jessie's eyes and she sniffled. She hadn't wanted to miss Christmas with her family when she was finally mated, and she'd wanted them to meet Emerson and Uncle Paul too. She knew that Paul would be thrilled to meet them. "That would be wonderful."

"Yeah, Sis, you know we got your back. Besides, you finally found the right man for you and no way are we going to miss seeing him for your first mated Christmas together."

"We'll be all set for you." That meant she and Emerson needed to decorate the other cabins for Christmas too. So much for Uncle Paul and Emerson not decorating the cabins before that, feeling there was no need.

* * *

"WE OUGHT TO GET TOGETHER, you and me, if you're not mated," Paul said to the nurse before Emerson and Jessie left the room.

Marjorie checked his heart rate and pulse. "I'm not mated, but I like my freedom."

"Going out for a bite to eat doesn't mean I'm mating you," Uncle Paul said, sounding a little growly.

Emerson thought his uncle needed to work on his dating social skills a bit.

"My momma used to always say at this age in life, men are only looking for a nurse or a purse, or both." Marjorie wrote on his chart.

"Well, you're the nurse, and I've got the purse." Paul winked at her.

Jessie was smiling. Emerson couldn't help but smile. Even Marjorie wore a hint of one, thankfully.

"The doctor wasn't happy you faked your death." She raised her brows at Paul.

"It's all my nephew's doing. You see what happened when I returned to see him after he quit that dangerous job? *I* get shot."

"What if it happens again? If someone else comes for Emerson? I'm only interested in doing fun things after I'm done with my duty," Marjorie said.

"Well, that's my plan too."

"We're going to get out of your hair," Emerson said to his uncle before Jessie yanked him out of the hospital room.

"You're getting me out of here before Christmas, aren't you?" Uncle Paul was frowning, looking worried he might be stuck at the hospital.

"As long as the doc says you're good to go, yes," Emerson said. "We're having the bears over also for Christmas dinner, a buffet probably."

"Oh, you've got to see them Marjorie," Paul said.

"Bears?"

"Shifters. Right. They came to help take Smith down."

"Now that sounds interesting," Marjorie said.

Then Emerson and Jessie gave him a hug and kiss and they left the room.

"I've got to make my patient rounds," Marjorie said to Paul.

"You could come to the Christmas dinner," Paul said to her.

"Hmm, I have other plans, but thanks for the offer."

Emerson shook his head at Jessie as they were unable to hear any more of the conversation before they met up with the officer in the lobby so Emerson could identify Reginald. "I think my uncle needs some guidance in dating."

"Are you kidding? Marjorie was definitely interested in him. Why do you think she hung out in his room for so long? She doesn't want to give him the idea she's too eager to go out with him though."

"Are you sure? I was thinking she was like Robbie."

"No. She wasn't brief and to the point and hightailing it out of there as if she hadn't been interested in him. She genuinely wanted to be there with him. Not that it's a sure thing as far as dating him and mating him—but hey, maybe, given a few months of dates, if they're that interested in each other, it will work out."

"You think it will take that long?" Emerson asked, seeing the officer in the lobby and he waved to him. "Look at us."

She smiled. "When I make up my mind about something, there's no sense in putting off the inevitable."

He kissed her. "That just the way I feel."

"I know. That's why we're mated."

Then Emerson went with Jessie and the officer to the room where Reginald was manacled to a bed, his arm and leg bandaged, though Jessie waited outside for him.

"Hey, Reginald, looks like you should have gone with the good guys this time. That's him, Officer. Reginald Bates," Emerson said.

"It wasn't personal. The pay was just too good," Reginald said, shrugging.

"Yeah, prison time is the best kind of pay for a guy like you, I guess." That was all Emerson had to say to him and then he left with the officer.

The officer walked with Emerson and Jessie down to the lobby. "Did you ever have a falling out with Bates?"

"No, sir. He was on my team in the army. We did our job. End of mission. Like he said, it was nothing personal. He did it for money. Unfortunately, there are a lot of men in the world who would do the same for monetary gain."

"But with the man you knew as Smith?"

"It definitely was personal for him."

"It seems odd," the officer said.

Emerson figured the officer had some bit of information on Smith that Emerson wasn't privy to.

"While you were visiting with your uncle, we had a team retrieve Smith's body from the rocks below. I was checking over his phone and he had a Facebook account."

"Did he have another girlfriend on there? He friended me right away, but the last time I saw him, I knew he'd been with another woman," Jessie jumped in to say.

"Over a dozen in all parts of the world. But you're the only one he seemed interested in taking hostage," the officer said.

"You'll have to check with the other women he dated. I have no idea why he suddenly went after me."

"Had you been dating other men?" the officer asked.

Her heart skipped a beat, Emerson swore. He knew why she would be worried if they investigated *her* background. The men she had dated were all dead. Even this one now. But they'd been rogue cougars and the cougar law enforcement would have hidden the fact any of that had happened. Still, Emerson didn't know if Jessie had posted anything about the men she'd dated, anything that showed she had a connection with them. And then they had all vanished over the years.

"Oh, I travel a lot, with the kind of work I do. Photographic books? So when I happened to be in some new area, I might have dated a guy, but just once. Nothing that was long-term. I don't even remember the guys' names. Certainly, we didn't share last names, just our first names. And Smith knew that. I always told him about the guys I had dated when I was seeing him. He didn't go by Smith, but Samuel, no last name."

"So you had an open relationship," the officer said.

"Right. I mean, I saw him five times in two years. We certainly weren't a couple."

"But for some reason, he felt differently this time. Why?" the officer asked.

"I don't know."

"On his phone, he had a text from you in response to a text he'd sent, planning to see you after the new year. You wanted to see him before. But I thought you were dating Mr. Merriweather. That he was your fiancé."

"Sure. I wanted to see Samuel before the new year to tell him that I was seriously dating Emerson. I didn't want to do it in a text. Samuel had always been really nice to me, so I felt I owed it to him to speak with him in person, as long as he was going to be in the area. I had no idea he was monitoring where I was and knew I was here, or that he was already close by. I suspect he felt I was being dishonest with him because this time when he got a hold of me, I didn't tell him I was seeing someone else, and I guess he knew it."

"He lived in Minnesota," the officer said, looking at both their reactions.

Since neither of them had known that, they both looked sufficiently surprised.

"Hell," Emerson said, "I wonder just how long he had known she was up here."

"Did you often tell him where you would be?" the officer asked Jessie.

"I didn't. But I did mention it on Facebook. All he would have to do was check out my page, and see I was at the resort, taking pictures of the sunset and stacking rocks on the shore."

"And he must have realized you were close to where he lived

then. But why not ask to see you here? Why would he want to wait until you returned to Colorado?"

"Maybe because I didn't mention I was seeing Emerson and he already knew it."

"Right," the officer said. "That's what I figured. One other thing, one of the men your friends shot said you were Black Ops, that Smith knew it because he'd hired you for a mission, and he was looking to take you down, Mr. Merriweather. Can you shed any light on his statement?"

"It's possible that's what Smith told his henchman. I haven't a clue," Emerson said.

The officer nodded. "So if perchance you all were Black Ops assassins, I should just stop asking questions. Am I right?" the officer asked Emerson.

Emerson bit back the inclination to smile. "You're law enforcement and it's your job to keep asking questions."

"Good answer. Here's one last one for you then. When we brought Smith's body up, he had teeth marks on his right wrist."

Correct. The bastard was going to break Emerson's cougar forelegs if he hadn't reacted quickly enough and bit him. He didn't believe this was the officer's last question either.

"I didn't bite him, if that's what you're asking," Emerson said.

"Of course not. It didn't fit with your statement that he had hold of your legs and he was trying to pull you off the cliff. The bite mark was fresh, so he'd gotten it recently. An autopsy will reveal if he got it before or after he died. We know you couldn't have bitten him unless he had a hold of your wrist and you bit him to force him to let go before he pulled you off the cliff."

DNA results would prove the bite mark was made by a cougar so Emerson was off the hook on that one.

"It was as I said. He had a death grip on my legs"—forelegs in actuality—"and I didn't bite him."

"You're right. We think a wild animal bit him. DNA will show us what, but...did you see any cougars about?"

"Not while I was trying desperately to rescue Jessie."

"Okay, well, that's it for now. We'll be in touch."

Emerson suspected the officer would be too. He and Jessie thanked the officer for their quick response to a deadly situation and coming to their aid and then they left the hospital.

Emerson said, "I've got to call Condor and let him know Smith is no longer a problem. He'll tell the others."

"Yes. I'm sure they'll be glad."

"I know he will be, though he might give me grief for not letting him take part in eliminating him." When Emerson reached Condor, he said, "Smith is history." And then he explained what had happened.

"Hell, man, and you didn't let me help out? The other guys will be pissed too, though Kline's off on a mission right now. Bears, huh. Barrett? Don't remember ever working with the guy, but I'm glad it's done. And thanks for letting me know."

"Yeah, just a little Christmas gift for you."

"That's the best ever. Peace of mind. Thanks, Thor. We all owe you."

"No. You don't owe me a thing. Just get better."

"I will. Knowing it's over, I will. Merry Christmas. I'll let the others know you got him."

"Thanks, and Merry Christmas." Emerson ended the call and smiled at Jessie as they climbed into the car. "I think that's the best news I've ever had to give my team."

"I'm so glad for the both of you and for Barrett and his team members too." She patted Emerson's thigh as he was driving back to the resort. "You know what we have to do next, don't you?"

Emerson smiled.

She chuckled. "That too, but we need to hang Christmas lights up and decorate the cabins now that the family is coming to stay at the resort."

Emerson sighed. She smiled. "Here you hadn't planned to do any decorating at all for Christmas."

"Yeah, but you made it all worthwhile."

* * *

THREE DAYS LATER, with the whole resort decorated like it was Disney World—they'd had to get extra lights for that—Uncle Paul was coming home after Jessie and Emerson picked up Jessie's family from the airport. Tracey had insisted they just rent a car, which they had to do because of all the kids, but they had to bring Jessie's parents home too and Emerson wanted to meet them all.

Emerson hadn't known what to expect, but the kids called him Uncle Emerson—and he loved it—and the adults and children gave him heartfelt hugs as if he was just one of the family and had been all along.

"My daughter Jessie has always been a handful," her father said to Emerson. "I'm glad she has someone to watch out for her now."

She gave her dad a hug. "I just had to find the right cougar for me."

"Well, I know she's the only one for me," Emerson said, hugging Jessie afterwards.

It was wonderful being part of an extended family again, to hear the children's laughter, to have Jessie's sister smiling at him, not trying to figure out if he was one of the good guys or bad. To have hugs from their mother as if he was the son they hadn't had. He noted they treated Tracey's husband Hal the same way—as a son.

Then Jessie and Emerson had to run to the hospital and pick up Uncle Paul while the family unpacked their luggage and presents and set up housekeeping at the cabins.

Every time Emerson and Jessie had gone to visit with Uncle Paul at the hospital, they had found Marjorie catering to Uncle Paul's every need. Some of that probably had to do with them being fellow cougars. Emerson didn't know if anything would come of it, but he was hoping Uncle Paul would find someone to settle down with who lived in the area.

He and Jessie smiled at each other before they entered Uncle Paul's hospital room as they heard Marjorie say to him, "Now, just because you're leaving the hospital tonight, doesn't mean you can just go and do anything you want. No running as a big cat. A man of your age and after the bullet you took needs to take it easy for a couple of more weeks."

"Yes, dear," Paul said, amusing Emerson.

Then they entered the room and found Paul sitting in his wheelchair already, eager to leave the hospital. "The offer still stands for you to come and have dinner with us tonight," Paul said to Marjorie.

"Thanks. I appreciate the offer."

Then they said their goodbyes and Jessie and Emerson drove Uncle Paul home.

"So how has it been?" Paul asked.

"The family? They couldn't be more welcoming. I hadn't realized how much I missed having a family while I was away. And now it has increased like ten-fold all in one fell swoop. I couldn't be happier."

"They can't wait to welcome you into the fold too, Uncle Paul," Jessie said. "Tracey told the kids to be careful with their new granddad because of your injury. I hope that's all right with you if they call you granddad."

"Yeah, I'm ready for that. I have been for a good, long while."

When they returned to the resort, the adults all came out to welcome Uncle Paul home and the kids stood by, minding their manners until he opened his arms to them. They looked at Tracey and Hal and they smiled and nodded. Then they all ran to hug him.

"Gently," Tracey warned.

But Uncle Paul was in seventh heaven and he couldn't have been any happier this Christmas Eve.

That night, they had a big feast in celebration of family, of Jessie and Emerson's mating, that Smith was no longer a threat, and Christmas. Even the bears arrived, glad to take part in the big celebration. The kids were in awe and wanted to see the bears shift.

"If they want to, it'll have to be after dinner," Tracey said, Hal agreeing with her.

The bears made the special dinner even more festive.

A knock at the door had everyone glancing in that direction. Emerson and Barrett went to check it out since no one else was supposed to be coming to the party.

Dressed warmly in a parka and hat and gloves, Marjorie was standing on the patio with a bottle of red wine. She had showed up to the Christmas Eve dinner to everyone's surprise, but delight. Especially, it appeared, Paul's. He was all smiles when he greeted her and invited her in.

"I thought you had plans," Paul said.

"I had a shift to work, but when one of the other nurses heard I could have had dinner plans, she switched with me since she didn't have any plans and I never go out. There are no cougars around my age who are available in the area. Besides, I figured I would check on you and make sure you're all right."

"Oh, the minute you showed up, I was better than all right."

Marjorie smiled at him. "So I heard you went to Florida to stay with a cougar and she wasn't your cup of tea."

Paul's cheeks flushed a bit.

"The woman I was staying with said no to baking Christmas cookies," Paul said to Marjorie as he helped her out of her coat. "She was watching her weight but baking cookies to me is just a fun tradition. Of course, I would make them so I could share with those who were staying at the resort."

"Hmm," Jessie said, coming by to give Uncle Paul a hug. "If

you didn't know, that's why I always visited you when you were baking cookies for the season."

"That's why I always made them with extra chocolate chips because I knew you liked them that way."

"A little sweet in life makes it a whole lot better," Marjorie said.

"I couldn't agree with you more," Paul said.

"Well, I am all for baking Christmas cookies, New Year's cookies. They're good any time of year. I love the decorations you have up at the resort," Marjorie said.

Paul smiled. "Jessie and Emerson outdid themselves to welcome me home. Do you want to celebrate New Year's with us? If you don't have any commitments, that is?" Paul quickly asked.

"Yeah, I would. Thanks. I was just planning to watch the ball drop in New York City on the television. So what's the story about how your family discovered you were alive?" Marjorie asked as she and he began filling up their plates with food from the buffet.

"Emerson and Jessie were the true detectives. They discovered my body wasn't in the coffin and the connection between me and Robbie. She was a prior resort guest. They just needed her phone number. I have to say I left the clues on purpose, hoping to ease their minds that I wasn't truly dead, but I had to make it difficult enough that they wouldn't find me right away."

"Not until Emerson fell for Jessie," Marjorie guessed.

"That was easy to do," Emerson said, joining them, as he began filling up a plate for himself.

"Same for me. But without the phone number for Robbie, we might have missed finding you," Jessie said, in front of Emerson, eyeing the roast beef on his platter and she reached over and forked up some for herself. "And no Christmas for you."

Paul smiled. "I wouldn't have stayed at Robbie's house much longer and conceded it was a failed mission if Emerson hadn't become your mate. I have to tell you my bear friends said if you had been a bear, Emerson would have lost out."

They all laughed.

Paul was aglow with happiness. He was the nicest man and he so deserved that. His nephew was home for good. Jessie was now part of their family, and even Marjorie might be a keeper. Only time would tell.

Emerson wrapped his arm around Jessie's shoulder. All she knew for sure was Emerson and Uncle Paul were family now too and she couldn't be any happier this holiday season. And for once, she didn't care a bit about making word count. Making real memories with her family and his, and with new friends, was all that mattered.

ACKNOWLEDGMENTS

Thanks so much to Donna Fournier and making sure my names aren't the same as they are in other cougar books and all the silly corrections that need to be made. You know, Word should have caught some of them! She and I have this ongoing discussion about cold weather in Minnesota and cold weather in Texas, so I have to make sure my characters dress warmer when they are in her part of the country! And thanks to Darla Taylor in her dedication to finding mistakes too!! You ladies are the greatest! Merry Christmas!

AUTHOR BIO

USA Today bestselling author Terry Spear has written over sixty paranormal and medieval Highland romances. In 2008, Heart of the Wolf was named a Publishers Weekly Best Book of the Year. She has received a PNR Top Pick, a Best Book of the Month nomination by Long and Short Reviews, numerous Night Owl Romance Top Picks, and 2 Paranormal Excellence Awards for Romantic Literature (Finalist & Honorable Mention). In 2016, Billionaire in Wolf's Clothing was an RT Book Reviews Top Pick. A retired officer of the U.S. Army Reserves, Terry also creates award-winning teddy bears that have found homes all over the world, helps out with her granddaughter, and she is raising two Havanese puppies. She lives in Spring, Texas.

For more information, please visit www.terryspear.com, or follow her on Twitter, @TerrySpear. She is also on Facebook at http://www.facebook.com/terry.spear. And on Wordpress at:

Terry Spear's Shifters

http://terryspear.wordpress.com/

* * *

Heart of the Wolf Series: Heart of the Wolf, Destiny of the Wolf, To Tempt the Wolf, Legend of the White Wolf, Seduced by the Wolf, Wolf Fever, Heart of the Highland Wolf, Dreaming of the Wolf, A SEAL in Wolf's Clothing, A Howl for a Highlander, A Highland Werewolf Wedding, A SEAL Wolf Christmas, Silence of the Wolf, Hero of a Highland Wolf, A Highland Wolf Christmas, A SEAL Wolf Hunting; A Silver Wolf Christmas, A SEAL Wolf in Too Deep, Alpha Wolf Need Not Apply, Billionaire in Wolf's Clothing, Between a Rock and a Hard Place, SEAL Wolf Undercover, Dreaming of a White Wolf Christmas, Flight of the White Wolf, All's Fair in Love and Wolf, A Billionaire Wolf for Christmas, SEAL Wolf Surrender (2019), Silver Town Wolf: Home for the Holidays (2019), Wolff Brothers: You Had Me at Wolf, Night of the Billionaire Wolf, Joy to the Wolves (Red Wolf), The Wolf Wore Plaid, Best of Both Wolves

SEAL Wolves: To Tempt the Wolf, A SEAL in Wolf's Clothing, A SEAL Wolf Christmas, A SEAL Wolf Hunting, A SEAL Wolf in Too Deep, SEAL Wolf Undercover, SEAL Wolf Surrender (2019)

Silver Bros Wolves: Destiny of the Wolf, Wolf Fever, Dreaming of the Wolf, Silence of the Wolf, A Silver Wolf Christmas, Alpha Wolf Need Not Apply, Between a Rock and a Hard Place, All's Fair in Love and Wolf, Silver Town Wolf: Home for the Holidays (2019)

Wolff Brothers of Silver Town

Billionaire Wolves: Billionaire in Wolf's Clothing, A Billionaire Wolf for Christmas, Night of the Billionaire Wolf

Highland Wolves: Heart of the Highland Wolf, A Howl for a Highlander, A Highland Werewolf Wedding, Hero of a Highland Wolf, A Highland Wolf Christmas, Wolf Wore Plaid

Red Wolf Series: Seduced by the Wolf, Joy to the Wolves

* * *

Heart of the Jaguar Series: Savage Hunger, Jaguar Fever, Jaguar Hunt, Jaguar Pride, A Very Jaguar Christmas, You Had Me at Jaguar (2019)

Novella: The Witch and the Jaguar (2018)

* * *

Romantic Suspense: Deadly Fortunes, In the Dead of the Night, Relative Danger, Bound by Danger

* * *

Vampire romances: Killing the Bloodlust, Deadly Liaisons, Huntress for Hire, Forbidden Love

Vampire Novellas: Vampiric Calling, The Siren's Lure, Seducing the Huntress

* * *

Other Romance: Exchanging Grooms, Marriage, Las Vegas Style

* * *

Science Fiction Romance: Galaxy Warrior

Teen/Young Adult/Fantasy Books

The World of Fae:

The Dark Fae, Book 1

The Deadly Fae, Book 2

The Winged Fae, Book 3

The Ancient Fae, Book 4

Dragon Fae, Book 5

Hawk Fae, Book 6

Phantom Fae, Book 7

Golden Fae, Book 8

Falcon Fae, Book 9

Woodland Fae, Book 10

The World of Elf:

The Shadow Elf

Darkland Elf

Blood Moon Series:

Kiss of the Vampire

The Vampire…In My Dreams

Demon Guardian Series:

The Trouble with Demons

Demon Trouble, Too

Demon Hunter

Non-Series for Now:

Ghostly Liaisons

The Beast Within

Courtly Masquerade

Deidre's Secret

The Magic of Inherian:

The Scepter of Salvation

The Mage of Monrovia

Emerald Isle of Mists (TBA)